Jerusalem Blind

Alan Porter

Eyelevel Books

First published 2020
by Eyelevel Books, Worcester, England

ISBN 978 1902528 847

First edition

also available as an ebook

Typeset and Designed by Eyelevel Books

For more about Alan Porter and a list of other works, visit
www.alancporter.com

For AM

(1934-2014)
&
(1976-   )

1

There were seven empty seats on the plane; nine if the two in the cockpit were included. And they had to be. Leila could live with the fact that the cabin was empty, but she couldn't ignore those two up front. The altimeter read 22,500 feet and climbing, and there was no one flying the plane.

She had struggled up from sleep maybe two minutes earlier as the plane gave a violent shudder. They were passing through turbulence. She was familiar enough with that, the way the wings bent and everything inside – welded down or not – tried to rearrange itself. It took a moment longer, however, to understand why she was experiencing turbulence at all. She had no recollection of boarding this small, slightly shabby, but perfectly formed private jet. Right now, she had no recollection of anything at all before that shuddering rattle had brought her back to the real world.

She tried to stand, and fell back immediately into the deep leather seat. She shook her head and tried to focus, but there seemed to be nothing in her head to focus on. It was like looking at the world through a thick layer of dirty ice. None of it made any sense. She was not part of this scene. And yet, as the jet gave another lurch into a pocket of cold air, she knew she was very much part of it. Just not, yet, what 'it' was.

She made a second attempt to stand, this time more successfully. Her stomach rolled wetly and her head swam for a moment, but she remained upright, gripping the seat back as the plane rattled and shook around her. Satisfied that for now she was more or less stable, she made her way through the empty cabin, shuffling on legs that felt as remote and detached from her as the ground itself, thousands of feet below.

Up front the door to the cockpit was closed but not locked. She slid it open and found herself looking at the backs of two empty pilots' seats. She looked back along the cabin's length. She must have missed someone, hunkered down asleep in one of the seats, letting the plane take the strain for an hour. There was no one. She could see most of every seat all the way to the storage lockers and tiny galley tucked in beneath the tail, the toilet door that stood half-open, the whole magnificent emptiness of it all. There *was* no one else.

She half-clambered and half-fell into the pilot's seat for no better reason than that it was the closest. She could not trust her legs to carry her back to her own seat. Three display screens relayed information that even with a clear mind would have meant very little to her. The only thing she could easily identify was the altimeter behind the main throttle. 22,500 feet, and the little animated dial beside those figures was turning, ticking upwards. They were still climbing. The twin yokes twitched, making tiny synchronised adjustments under the sole control of the autopilot.

The plane gave a final half-hearted shudder then settled again. Her stomach did the same, but her mind was still a long way from settled. She tried to remember anything that might be useful, and there was nothing. Just that thick hazy ice, beyond which everything was distorted and meaningless. Not that it mattered much. The past was what it was, and it wasn't going anywhere. Her future, however, seemed to be heading skywards, and there was only so long it could continue to do that before everything went very bad indeed.

She looked down at the array of instruments. The artificial horizon screen in front of the pilot's seat showed mostly sky; the map screen showed mostly sea, with the only tiny sliver of land left sliding away off the bottom of the display. Out of the front window she could see nothing but blinding blue. On the starboard side she thought she could make out the irregular outline of mountains in the distance, but if they were real the digital display did not show them. The copilot's screens were a complete mystery and added nothing of any further use. She'd flown her brother's Cessna in level flight at two thousand feet many years earlier, but a complex jet, at altitude, and still climbing… she had no idea. But she didn't need to understand the details of the screens know one thing for certain. At some point she was going to have to make enough sense of the controls and switches spread out before her to get this beast on the ground.

Unless…

She stood again, staggered against the co-pilot's seat as her head swam and her vision blurred. She took a deep breath and willed her rising gorge to hold still for just a few seconds – a few seconds for her to get back some control.

A single white cloud floated just outside the cockpit's port window, still and calm in the dazzling blue. She turned away and made her way back into the main body of the plane.

Someone had been flying this thing when it took off, and he'd made his exit at some point. He must, therefore, have had some means of getting to the ground without hitting terminal velocity first. Maybe these executive jets carried parachutes. At fifty million for exclusive ownership, they should do.

There was nothing but the familiar life jackets under any of the seats and she found nothing in the main overhead lockers. Not a surprise there: it would be bad form to put a reminder of impending disaster so close to the passengers. In the rear baggage compartment she found a box containing medical equipment: a tray of instruments, masks, gas tanks and a portable high-intensity lighting system. Some of it appeared to have been used, and in another box she found a bundle of green hospital sheets that bore traces – in places large traces – of blood. She did a quick mental inventory of this thing that still didn't quite feel like her own body. No pain, no obvious injuries. The surgery had not been performed on her, but it had been performed on this plane…

Beneath the medical kit she saw something that rang a loud bell in her dull memory. A small red bag, the kind hikers use as day-packs. She pulled it out and unzipped it.

She'd had a pack like this… in London. A memory, a blurry, impressionist haze floated up beneath the ice. A small red backpack. Not the vintage Karrimor she had used for years, but another that came later… that played a significant role in a story that sank again into the darkness almost before she could grasp it was even there.

Inside the bag was a monocular, a rolled-up leather jacket, some lock picks and a roll of cash – twenties, sterling, maybe a couple of hundred pounds. It all seemed very familiar, but right now, and without the benefit of any identifying papers amongst the haul, she could not place it.

Leila's vision blurred again and she backed up to one of the deep seats at the rear of the plane. She sat for a minute with her head between her knees trying to stop the swirling sensation in her head. Her stomach did another wet rolling lurch, seeming to amplify the gentle vibration of the plane.

She sat back. She felt the chill of the cabin's air conditioning, and was very glad of it. Had the pilot turned it off, even the roller coaster of turbulence might not have been enough to wake her in time. Warm, she's have slept on. Cold, her body naturally came up to find out what was happening and what she might do about it. It was another survival thing…. She slipped the leather jacket on and more indistinct memories pushed at the edges of her consciousness. Not enough to be helpful yet, but they were there, lurking in the depths.

The jets hissed and whined outside and the horizon cut the wing at a slight angle. They were still climbing. The longer she left making a decision about how to get out of this mess, the less likely it would be that getting out of it would be an option.

She had to think, and she had to do it fast. The problem was, thinking was not her strong suit right now.

2

DCI Michael Lawrence knocked at the front door, more in case anyone was watching behind the ever-vigilant net curtains across the street than because he expected a reply. There was no sound from within the Victorian terrace house where he had been a welcome, if all-too-occasional, visitor once upon a time. He stepped back and looked up at the window above the door, a small spare bedroom still filled with unopened boxes and bits of furniture that didn't quite fit in anywhere, but were too meaningful to be consigned to the skip. The curtains were half drawn, as they always were. Having made the appropriate show of decorum by knocking on the door, he stepped awkwardly over the overgrown box topiary beside the path and peered into the sitting room window. He could see nothing but vague dark shapes through the net curtains.

He knocked again, certain beyond doubt now that there would be no reply.

He'd been calling Leila for four days. Many people at Counter-terrorism Command had been calling the missing Detective Sergeant, and they had all been getting the same result. Her landline went to the answering machine and her personal cell was dead – number out of service. The burner phone Leila had been using to talk to him on the night of the hostage rescue had been found, battery flat, on the apron of Epping Airport late the following day. It had been about the only evidence the police or forensics teams had found there, although Black Eagle had left plenty elsewhere. Their trail of destruction, starting with the massive bomb in Kensington and leading through the carnage at Mapleton House, ultimately led to that private airstrip. And there, as far as DS Reid was concerned, it went cold. Only the dead and discarded phone had been left behind. It seemed she had either dropped it or been relieved of it, then simply vanished off the face of the earth.

DCI Lawrence walked round the end of the street and into the narrow alley that ran between the back of Leila's road and the back of the next street along. Her house wasn't difficult to identify. The biggest – in some ways the only – feature of the garden was the vast brooding shadow cast by the London Plane tree that had been allowed free rein in her rear neighbour's garden. Find the tree, find the house. Neither was difficult. He looked up at the rear windows of her building. Bright sunlight reflected off the glass, making the deep shadows that filled the garden seem all the darker. He could see some shapes within the back dining room, and the straggly herb plants on the kitchen windowsill were, temporarily, fully illuminated, but he could not see enough from this distance to satisfy his increasingly uneasy curiosity.

He looked around. A tall black man with greying dread-locks almost to his waist crossed the end of the alley, glanced briefly in his direction and came to a stop. For a moment their eyes met. Probably just one of Leila's neighbours, but something passed between them in that fleeting instant. Not recognition, but a connection, something... something that said he was, in his own way, as out of place as Michael himself. Someone else come looking for his missing friend? Maybe....

Michael nodded; the man at the end of the alley returned the gesture and walked on. So far he had been the only living soul to be seen on her street this morning. The city had been quiet since the bombing and even out here in this quiet leafy corner of Tooting the dull shock of last week's events cast a shadow almost as oppressive as her neighbour's monstrous tree. The baking summer heatwave also meant most people were either in air conditioned offices or behind drawn curtains waiting it out. Waiting and watching...

Michael could see no one at any of the neighbouring windows but that didn't mean they weren't there. He was in uniform, and he could do without someone thinking it was a great laugh to watch – and probably film – a senior Met detective clamber over the wooden fence and fall into the garden. He wasn't here on official duty. The fewer people who knew about this the better – he was treading a fine line with his superiors already. If he found something, he could justify his actions. If not, he could do without his exploits headlining the Six O'Clock news. He'd told Commander Thorne he'd stop by DS Reid's place, take a look, maybe talk to the neighbours, not that he'd scramble over the back fence and break in. But he was powerless not to. He had to know what had happened to her. He had to silence the nagging suspicions.

He made it over the fence with more grace than he could have hoped for. At fifty-two and largely desk-bound he was not a fat man, but he was a man well past the prime of condition. The garden was mainly patchy lawn, now tinder dry and yellow from the long hot summer. Along the fence were some shrubs in need of taming. A tool shed to his right looked disused and in a sad state of disrepair, its windows obscured by cob-web curtains and its roof sagging so badly a heavy summer rainstorm would probably see it on the floor. Other than a patch of broken and trampled nettles behind the shed, it looked as if no one had been in the garden for months. Or years.

He walked to the back door quickly but calmly, still wondering exactly why he was here. Did he expect to find Leila dead – murdered by the group she had got so close to bringing down, or by her own hand – or did he expect to find her unconscious, sleeping off a massive binge of booze, or worse? Although he doubted both scenarios, he would not have been entirely surprised by either.

He looked in through the dining room window. The curtains were half-closed and the room was so dark that even up close he could not make out much detail. The place looked untidy. Leila was no domestic goddess, but she liked order – things had to make sense, be efficient, controlled. But things change, he knew that. She had changed. She'd slipped away from him and had, for a while at least, teetered on the brink of self-destruction. Had she taken a stroll down that treacherous road again?

He tried the back door, not expecting anything, and was surprised when the mechanism clicked and the door opened. Before opening it fully he crouched and examined it. There were tiny tell-tale marks around the lock – marks left by someone picking it. His heart beat a little harder and he drew his gun before gently pushing the door open and peering into the gloom of the utility room.

He stepped in, silently, sweeping his service-issue Glock 17 left and right before him. No point calling: if she hadn't answered the door or the phone, she wasn't going to answer him now. He crossed the kitchen, briefly taking in the scene but neither finding, nor expecting to find, much of any interest. He pushed the dining room door open and stopped, checking the details before stepping in and disturbing anything. The room had been ransacked. The chairs had been overturned, the dining table littered with the contents of the sideboard's drawers. Every picture had been taken down and stacked against the walls, but there was no sign of his missing DS.

Leila had told him someone had been at the house when she arrived back on the second day of the bomb investigation. He believed her. What was harder to believe was that in the intervening six days she'd done nothing about the mess. Yes, people can change. Yes, people do sometimes just give up – he'd seem burn-out often enough in his line of work – but not like this. Not Leila. He knew her, and he knew that if she was undergoing a disintegration as total as this she couldn't have hidden it. Not from him.

He walked along the short hall. The elderly answering machine display showed fifteen new messages waiting. He pressed play. The first was his own voice, sounding casual and more curious than worried, the morning after the siege. His was the second too, a few hours later, an edge in his voice that spoke of his growing concern. He stopped the recordings. He couldn't remember exactly, but he figured at least six of the remaining messages were his own and he didn't need to relive that journey into real fear and bewilderment again now. The point – the *only* salient point as far as the investigation was concerned – was that these messages had not been picked up by their intended recipient.

The front sitting room was in the same state of disarray as the dining room. Nothing appeared to have been taken: easily pawnable items like the hi-fi and TV were still there and he caught a glimpse of Leila's favourite, and by far most valuable, possession next to the sofa. She'd have lost the house before she lost that funny little drawing of the owl by Picasso.

With the gun still loosely in his hand he mounted the stairs. The upper rooms were tidier, Leila's bedroom overlooking the garden the only obvious exception. The curtains were half-drawn and bright sunlight burned across the carpet. The duvet was half off the bed, the wardrobe stood open and several items of clothing had fallen onto the floor at the foot of the bed. Leila was not amongst the mess.

Uselessly, foolishly, he crossed the room and laid his hand flat on the exposed bedsheet. That touch wouldn't tell him anything – the bed would feel the same whether she had left it half an hour ago or days ago. But he did it anyway.

He had the strangest feeling that it *had* been days ago that she was last here, maybe when his call had woken her up just minutes after Black Eagle's bomb had destroyed the west side of the Park Hotel in Kensington and this whole nightmare had begun. With that call he'd brought her into this and pushed her into the front line against the advice of every one of his peers. She'd done well; she'd probably saved the lives of all but one of the delegates at the Mapleton House siege, but she had always been a reluctant recruit, doing it more for him than for love of Queen and Country. And it had all stared here, his phone call while she was sleeping, the duvet tossed aside in the growing heat of another morning. It all started here.

So where the hell was she now?

* * *

Fifteen minutes after DCI Lawrence left Leila's house, a second figure slipped unnoticed along the alley behind the row of terraced houses. Six-foot three, thin as a rail and with long, greying dreadlocks, it had not been easy to stay inconspicuous while the bumbling detective did what he had to do. People see a man in police uniform loitering in a nice white-dominated neighbourhood, they assume the best. They see a black man, not so much, especially if said black man is wearing a long beard, life-long dreadlocks and an orange Rasta T-shirt with a giant spliff on the front. On the other hand, at least the latter mitigated against him being a Muslim fundamentalist, and after the events of the previous week – or decade – white people feared and suspected Muslims even more than out-of-context blacks. But he didn't think anyone had been paying much attention anyway. The streets were quiet, people hunkered down against the heat and lingering fear.

Now back in the alley, he checked sight lines and windows, just as Michael had, then vaulted the fence with a catlike grace the old police detective could only dream of. He was looking for the same things as his predecessor, and he would see the same things, but what he would do with the information he gathered was destined to change the course of events two thousand miles away in ways none of them could have imagined.

3

Leila checked her pockets. They were empty: no wallet, no ID, no more cash. She had no idea how she had got on this plane, who with or why. The 'when' was a little clearer – these small jets could not stay airborne for more than a few hours at a time – but even that didn't help much. She had no idea what day it was and her head swam and buzzed even trying to work it out. Not that it mattered right now. She could deal with all that once she was back on the ground, and given her one known fact – that these small jets could not stay airborne for more than a few hours – there was a certain pressing urgency to get there.

Looking at an oblique angle from a starboard window she could just make out a solid horizon behind her. And the mountains she had seen from the cockpit were real. They were indistinct and distant, and getting more so with every passing second, but they were there. The question remained quite where 'there' was. The blueness of the sea below suggested somewhere tropical but she could not see enough land to narrow the options any further.

She returned to the pilot's seat and tapped the screen in front of her. To her surprise an array of instruments appeared. Less surprisingly she had no idea what any of them were. The only familiar thing was the altimeter in the corner of the co-pilot's screen which now read 28,000 feet and still climbing. The jet would climb to its maximum cruising altitude – she guessed around 40,000 feet – cruise until it ran out of fuel, then glide down, dumping her in a watery and unfindable grave. No one had ever found MH370, and they knew what they were looking for. Compared to a Boeing triple-seven with a working black box, this private jet was a silent speck of dust. Someone might care that his Gulfstream had been lost, but no one would come looking for her. (And given that this plane looked as if it had seen better days anyway, they might not want anyone to find any trace of the wreckage at all until the insurance had been paid out, banked and spent.)

She looked up. The instruments from the screen were also projected onto a moveable HUD window in front of her. From where she sat the dials and gauges were backed by a pure, clear blue.

Above her head were switches. She ran her fingers over them, counting off the ones she could identify (landing gear, lights, cabin air) and dismissing the others. The tally of unknown switches amounted to all but five of them.

The pilot's yoke in front of her juddered and turned slightly to the right. The plane tilted then levelled out again. A few seconds later turbulence rattled the jet and she braced herself against the seat. The hazy mountains on the starboard side had now completely disappeared. They were heading further out into the wilderness of water below.

She took a deep breath and examined the main screen.

In the centre of the slowly moving dials was a virtual switch marked 'Autopilot'. Not expecting much, she tapped it and a subscreen grew, marked 'Resume Manual Control?' Below this simple question were two buttons and she tapped the one marked 'Yes'.

Immediately the control stick slid back towards her and she took it, surprised at the resistance she felt in it. Just as her brother had instructed her all those years ago in a plane far simpler than this, she tentatively turned it a little to the left. The plane rolled left, and as she turned back the yoke, so the plane (and the virtual horizon on the head-up display) came level. She pushed the control forwards slightly and the horizon – both inside on the screen and outside in the real world – came into view.

And so did the scar of land to starboard.

She turned the yoke again and feathered a little pressure onto the left rudder pedal. It was clumsy, rough and certainly not anywhere near getting her a pilot's licence, but after a few minutes she had turned the plane so that those mountains were now on the port side and clearly visible. If she had been flying away from land before, heading out to a watery grave, at least she'd managed to reverse that particular problem.

Altitude was also an issue. Her only guide to finding a place to land was going to be visual, so she had to get to a height where she could see more detail than just 'land' or 'water'. She levelled the jet out again and pushed the controls forwards. The nose dipped and the engines whined, sending judders through the stick. On her right was a handle consisting of a pair of levers, pushed three quarters forwards. She'd seen enough movies to guess that this was the engine speed control, so she tentatively pulled it a little further towards her to decrease the power. The engines settled and Leila breathed again. At a shallow angle and on reduced power she watched the altimeter tick down. Maybe the button just in front of her that deployed the landing gear might yet come in handy.

Reluctant to re-engage the autopilot and risk having it put the jet back on its original course, she had no choice but to trust that without external forces acting on the plane, it would remain steady for a minute or two on its own, gradually losing height. She still had a lot of it to lose, so a couple of minutes were not likely to throw up any catastrophic surprises. She hauled herself out of the pilot's seat and staggered back along the cabin. Each seat had a cubby-hole locker beside it, and in the third one she opened she found her goal. Three bottles of mineral water. She downed one in two long drafts, regretted it for a moment as her stomach threatened to bounce the whole lot right back out, then carried the remaining two back to the cockpit.

Not only had the plane been fine on its own, she could now see land ahead as well as to the side. What had appeared to be mountains from twenty-eight thousand feet were not really worthy of the name when viewed from closer quarters. Rough hills and scarred barren valleys with no more than a narrow strip of green here and there where they met the coast, this was desert she was looking at. Beyond the hills there was very little of anything.

She was beginning to get an idea of where she was, and

it was not good. After fifteen minutes and another bottle of water – taken at a more respectful pace – she was flying over land rather than sea and the view through the dusty haze was clear enough that her suspicions had grown to certainty. She could not be country-specific, but she recognised the general region.

There were no buildings anywhere in sight. A few faint lines cut across the barren ground and here and there were dark patches that might have been villages or might just be shadows from natural landforms.

Now over the relative safety of solid ground and with the plane under some basic control, she had a choice. Should she try to make it to an airport, or ditch in the desert?

An airport had a reassuring ring to it, but she quickly dismissed it. Even if someone could talk her safely down (and that was far from certain), she would have to be in contact with the tower for a long time, and whoever had dumped her on this flying coffin would be waiting for her as soon as she touched down.

Which left the prospect of setting down in whatever desert she was over. Find a run of a few thousand feet of flat, straight ground without too many obstacles and improvise some kind of survivable landing. Without an opportunity to practise first. Not ideal, but if she could do it, it might buy her enough time to figure out what the hell was going on. And she needed to figure it out.

Someone had gone to a lot of trouble to get her on this plane, and they were not going to just let her walk away from it.

4

DCI Lawrence had locked Leila's house up and gone straight back to Scotland Yard, arriving around the time that Leila's second visitor was himself locking up and leaving her Tooting residence. Lawrence had found nothing, and the longer his Detective Sergeant was missing the more willing CTC would be to fill the information vacuum with the kinds of theories Lawrence was keen to avoid. He knew there had to be an explanation for her disappearance, and yet... He'd talked to her as she drove away from Mapleton House and the carnage of the hostage situation there; he'd heard snatches of the conversation she'd had with the man who seemed to be behind at least some of that carnage. And in that conversation had been a question. He had never heard the answer – if Leila had answered it at all – but it was the question itself that was so telling. That Donald Aquila had even considered it worth asking spoke volumes. The phone had gone dead, leaving an empty, disconnected silence, and a small window of doubt. Had she answered Black Eagle's driver as they turned into Epping airport that night? And what had her answer been?

He knocked on Commander Thorne's door and waited,

watching through the tinted glass while his superior finished his phone call. Thorne beckoned him in.

'Did you find anything?' The CTC Commander said.

'Nothing,' Lawrence said. 'She told me the house had been searched the day after we brought her in. Ransacked might be a better word, but my guess is nothing was taken, and there are no obvious breakages. It appears that it was, as she suggested, a warning.'

'And there's no evidence she's been back?'

'No. All our messages are on the answering machine and the place is a mess.'

'You went in?'

'Back door was unlocked.'

'So…' Thorne said. 'We're left with the same scenario. The last contact any of us had with her was at Epping Airstrip. She told you she'd shot and killed Raha Golzar and we have to assume that the car we found burned out on Saturday was the vehicle Donald Aquila was using to transport her. Forensics have found nothing further and Reid has vanished.'

'But the full clips'-worth of bullet holes suggests she was telling the truth about Golzar, at least as she saw it. She also told me she was finished with CTC. She wanted a break.'

'Reid was already on a break until you brought her back in. Just to take a look around, I think was how you put it.'

'And I think my decision was vindicated under the circumstances. Things might have gone very differently if it hadn't been for Reid. But she was always reluctant. She made it very clear at the end that this would be the last time. As I said, she wanted a break, a permanent one this time.'

'And yet she hasn't been home in the last four days.'

DCI Lawrence shrugged. There wasn't much he could say to that.

'And therein hangs to problem,' Thorne went on. 'Her passport and credit cards have not been used. So if she has gone somewhere, she's not gone far – almost certainly not out of the country – and she didn't go alone. Five confirmed that no plane had taken off from the airport that night, and Aquila's car – or what we assume right now to be Aquila's car, burned out thought it is – was found ten miles away.'

'You're thinking she went with him.' It was a statement, not a question. Sooner or later it was always going to come to this.

'You're not?' Thorne said.

'I just don't believe it.'

'So you have considered it.'

'I didn't say that.'

'To believe it, or not, you must have considered it.'

'OK, maybe it crossed my mind. But if she did leave Epping with Aquila, surely it wasn't voluntary.'

'That's a very curious answer,' Thorne said. 'It suggests that at some point you've also at least considered the possibility that it may have been voluntary.'

'With respect, Sir, you're putting words in my mouth.'

'Because I don't get the feeling that all the words that are in there are coming out of their own volition. Is there something you're not telling me? You've admitted you met her on the South Bank on the morning of the Peace Conference, and you two have got history. Did she tell you anything else at all, either then or later?'

Lawrence sat for a moment in silence. There was one more thing that he had not put in his official report. That final question in the car that night. The last words he heard Donald Aquila say to her before the connection was cut. The question he never heard her answer, the invitation he hoped had been answered in the right way. 'Join us,' Aquila had said.

'No, Commander,' he said, 'there's nothing else.'

'And yet you went into the house this morning.' It wasn't a question, but it did demand an answer.

'I'm not investigating her,' Michael said. 'At least not in a criminal sense. I consider – considered – DS Reid a friend. I had to know she wasn't in trouble.'

'I don't think your investigation so far rules that out, DCI. It's more a question of what kind of trouble and how deep, don't you think?'

'I've ruled out what was, personally, my first concern. I'm satisfied that she's not cooling in a pool of drug-induced vomit. I'm sorry if that's not part of official procedure, but it mattered to me.'

'Then draw that line and move on. Or do I need to sideline you from this one?'

'No. I'm quite capable of being objective. And at least now we know where she *isn't*. She's not dead by her own hand.'

'We just don't know whether she's dead by someone else's,' Thorne said. 'Or if she's somewhere else entirely.'

Michael nodded.

'Then I have no choice but to escalate this to a missing persons enquiry,' Thorne said. 'And not one we can handle in-house. I'm sorry to say this, but we can't ignore the facts. DS Reid's most likely exit from Epping was in Aquila's car, and we know she never returned home. He's managed to get Golzar's body – if indeed she really is dead – out of sight. Maybe he's done the same with Reid.'

'Body? You think she is dead then?'

'Maybe.' He held eye contact with his detective across the desk for several seconds. 'Although I hope not,' he said eventually. 'Unfortunately, we cannot ignore the fact that the alternative might be even worse. If she's alive and with Black Eagle – whether by choice or by force – she knows enough about our operations to be extremely dangerous. I drafted a report for Thames House last night. The only thing standing in the way of it being implemented was you coming back here with news you'd found her. You didn't, so we need to bring in people who can.'

'Give me one more day. I'll talk to Phillip Shaw again.'

'No. Five will handle this now.'

'Handle?'

'Do whatever proves necessary,. If she contacts you, let me know immediately. You bent the line this morning, and I understand that. But this isn't personal any more. She's the loose end from Mapleton, and Five hate loose ends, especially ours. The longer this goes on, the worse it looks for all of us.'

'Not least Reid.'

Thorne regarded him for a moment. 'That will be all,' he said.

Lawrence stared across the desk at his boss then stood and walked out into the command centre. Phillip Shaw had been debriefed at a safe house in South London over the weekend but was now most likely back with his friends at Broadwater Farm, back to hacking governmental and corporate computer systems for kicks and eating from the profits of the Waterboys' drug operations. Leila had asked – told – Michael to look after the boy when the operation was over, and he intended to do exactly that. Phillip had been instrumental in getting Reid in and out of Mapleton House that night, and the country owed him that much. But first, that weird misfit kid was going to have to do one more job.

He was going to have to save Reid all over again, and this time he would not be saving her from the shadowy agents of Black Eagle. This time it was her own people who had her in their sights.

5

One thing was clear. Even dropping the plane to 10,000 feet allowed her to see nothing below her but desert.

She'd experimented with the controls for half an hour and could make the beast rise and fall, and perform basic turns. If she ignored all the data on the screens in front of her, it was a fairly simple machine. But the fuel gauge was showing low, and on the far distant horizon now was a smudge of black that was most likely a town. Useful in the long-term, but a liability right now. She had to set the plane down, and soon.

She dropped to 3,000 feet, an altitude that gave her plenty of margin for error and which allowed her to see enough detail on the ground to start looking for somewhere to land. This was not a sand desert: it was strewn with huge canyons and long, broken hill ranges. Between the hills were meandering strips of lighter earth which she guessed were dried river beds.

An alarm sounded and a light flashed on the screen. Low Fuel. She tapped it and the dial changed to remaining distance. Less than a hundred – miles, kilometres, whatever – at the current rate of burn. At four hundred miles an hour (or kilometres an hour, or knots, or whatever that four hundred referred to), she had less than fifteen minutes to put the plane down voluntarily or fate would take over and dump her wherever she happened to be.

She dropped another 1,000 feet and began to scan the ground. Below her was a wide dry wadi with shallow banks. She flew on for another five minutes, but the terrain didn't get any better. The hills crowded in on the old river and the ground was littered with boulders, patches of yellow grass, shrubs and scree. She had already passed what was going to be her best option. She put the plane into a steep turn and headed back south along the wadi. In the distance, sunlight flashed. A tiny shape moved in the sky, a trail of pale grey behind it. Leila maintained her course, eyes fixed on the slowly growing shape. Sunlight glinted off it, blinding flashes in a blinding sky. Head-on it was impossible to see what it was that was approaching, but it could only be one thing. And there could only be one reason why it was here.

In seconds the fully armed F-35 buzzed past her, clearing her starboard wing by no more than a few hundred feet. She heard the engines scream as the pilot put it into a sharp turn and flew back. He passed, pulled into a steep climb and was gone in a deafening roar of jet engine and a violent shimmering of smoke and heat. This was a show, first and foremost, or power, of macho intimidation, and it worked. Cocooned in her luxurious little cruiser she felt like a penguin bobbing along on a serene sea… until a killer whale breaks the surface to wink malevolently at her.

Over the sound of her own engines Leila didn't hear it come up behind her twenty seconds or so later. It levelled out a little ahead of her port wing and maintained a course parallel to her own. She saw the blacked-out visor of the fighter's single occupant turn towards her, watching, tracking her for ten long seconds as she stared back at him. Then suddenly it was gone. She watched it climb vertically once more until again it was little more than a smudge in the sky.

Leila put her plane into a steep right turn away from the range of hills that were beginning to fill her horizon, and pushed the nose down. She had to get this thing on the ground before the F-35 did it for her. There would be no negotiation. She'd had her warning – *get down, get out or get dead*. Whoever's airspace she'd strayed into, they would not ask again. For a moment the wadi was lost from sight and she frantically searched the ground for it. All she could see was cliffs and hills. She banked left and dropped to 1,000 feet and suddenly the snaking gash of pale sand filled her view.

She pulled the seat belt on and slowed the engines. Another alarm sounded and more lights flashed on the screen. They were a distraction on the head-up display, so she flipped it out of the way and tried to level the plane. She had no idea how to land, but she knew the first task was to go slow and low, so she adjusted the twin throttle levers and raised the nose slightly. The altimeter span quicker. Although she couldn't see much of it with the nose raised, the ground was coming up fast.

At four hundred feet she initiated the landing gear and three green lights came on on the console. The vibrations of the wheels coming down reverberated through the plane.

She levelled out and cut the engines further. Ahead was

a straight run of river bed for maybe a mile. Beyond that the river turned sharply past a dark rocky outcrop. There was going to be no second chance.

She needed to lose the last of her height and as much speed as possible. She slowed the engines to minimum thrust – forcing them through the automatic lock that tried to prevent anyone doing anything so stupid – and let the plane glide down. Against the insistent voice of the computer system and the increasing number of flashing lights she had brought to life, she felt the plane lurch and shudder as the lift from the wings was cut beyond any useful operational level. There would be no going back, no aborted landing now. Five hundred feet; four; three; two.

She tightened the seat belt, braced herself and gently pulled the yoke back. She was going to crash anyway, but she could do without going in nose-first. If she could drop the main wheels into the sand and hold the nose up for as long as possible, the cockpit might have a chance of surviving the impact.

At thirty feet she yanked back hard on the yoke. The nose reared upwards and the whole machine shook violently. She could not see the ground, only the steep cliffs some thousand feet away. For a moment the plane almost seemed to stop, to hang motionless in the air, but she knew this comforting illusion was just that: an illusion. The machine was still moving fast. And it was falling even faster.

She closed her eyes and trusted.

There was a sickening grinding from behind her as the tail scraped the ground. A moment later there was a huge bang and she was thrown forwards in the seat. The plane yawed sharply right as the starboard wheel was torn off, followed an instant later by the port wheel hitting the sand. She opened her eyes in time to see clouds of gravel being thrown up by the right wing as it skimmed the river bed. There was only one thing to do. She had to lose the last of the speed before she reached the end of the straight course of the river.

She pushed the stick forwards and slammed the nose wheel into the ground. Sand and rocks showered upwards, smashing the cockpit windows. The noise was deafening… briefly. A second or so after she had hit the ground the left wing dug into the ground. As it tore off it took the port engine with it. The cabin was briefly lit by a huge orange fireball and the entire plane was thrown sideways.

It probably took only seconds, but as Leila hung onto the stick and tried futilely but instinctively to rudder out of the crash, it felt like minutes. As soon as the fireball darkened to a thick cloud of smoke, the fuselage hit a rock in the riverbed, tearing the tail fins off and digging the tip of the starboard wing into the river bank.

It was violent, but it was the best thing that could have happened. As the body of the plane was torn apart on the sand, the wing disintegrated, taking the last of the momentum of the crash away. The remaining wreckage came to a sudden stop and for a moment the only sound was the whine of the engine on its stub of wing and the patter of debris raining down on the fuselage. Leila let go of the stick just as the engine took a gulp of gravel and exploded, the jet fins tearing through the cabin behind her.

Then there was only the falling stones. She looked out

through the shattered windscreen but the dust was too thick to see far.

In the sudden gloom of the cockpit the three display screens were all she could see, then something deep in the electronic brain of this beast exploded and she could see even less.

6

Leila struggled with the belt clip. Both her arms worked and her legs felt fine apart from the heat and shaking caused by a year's supply of adrenaline being dumped into her system in the last few seconds. No acute pain and as she glanced down, no blood blooming anywhere she could see. Her chest was badly bruised and her neck felt as if someone had tried to wrench her head off, but so far that seemed about the worst of it. The adrenaline shot had also cleared her mind a little, and although it had taken extreme measures to get there, a little clarity was going to be useful in what was coming next.

Through the clearing dust beyond the cockpit window she could just make out the hulking shape of the cliffs where the dry river bed turned sharply. The plane had come to rest at a forty-five degree angle to the river, and the starboard wing – or what remained of it – was dug in beneath a huge rock on the bank. Beyond that the ground rose steeply into a scree slope and beyond that a cliff rose some two hundred feet into the dusty sky. If she'd set the plane down five seconds later she would have ploughed right into it.

The belt released and she leaned forwards tentatively. The only sound was the distant crackle of the engine fire behind her. Fortunately there had been very little fuel left in the plane so the fire was not going to be a major problem. At least not compared to the problem she was now becoming aware of high above her. Out of the low random sound of the fire and the settling sand another grew: the rumble of the F-35. It was not too loud yet, but it was not going away. The pilot was watching, reporting, directing…

She stood, checking again that nothing was broken or so badly sprained it would need special consideration. There was nothing. She was fine. When she opened the cockpit door, she saw that 'fine' was a lot more than could be said for the fifty-million-pound jet she had just landed. Almost the entire port side was missing. The burning engine had taken most of the left wing and a big chunk of the fuselage with it. On the starboard side the main cabin was mostly intact apart from a peppering of holes where the engine fins had punctured the skin. The leather seats were shredded and wires and chunks of insulation hung from the wrecked body. Had she been flying with any passengers, she would not have many survivors.

She stepped into the cabin and ducked to scan the ground outside. The fighter jet screamed overhead at a couple of hundred feet, its roar deafening in the silence of the desert. She caught a glimpse of its ghostly shape in the dust cloud as it pulled up and flew out of sight over the hills. From where she stood, all she could see was the river bed stretching off into the distance behind her, and various plane parts coming into focus as the dust settled.

She had no more than a few minutes to consider her position before the F-35 – or whoever it was directing – came to investigate her sudden and explosive arrival, and right now she had almost no information with which to make a plan.

Her mind was fuzzy but clearing. This was not amnesia: it was not a haze, a bleary hangover. It was a block, a solidification of memory – probably the latent effect of whatever drugs had been used to get her on the plane. It was not, however, her most immediate concern. Right now her life existed only in the present.

The biggest problem was that she did not know where she was. Based on what she had seen from the air, her experience living in and flying around the middle east while she was with the Foreign Office – and a dim, hazy memory of some of the events of the last week or so – she could make a guess. A sea was to the south, and from what she had seen of it, it could have been the Gulf of Aqaba. Here was a fawn-coloured stony desert punctuated by dark hills and boulder fields, subtle washes of charcoal and orange and dry river beds of sand so pale it was almost white. She'd watched this land, or land very like it, slip by below her before as she'd flown in and out of Lebanon and Jordan. If pushed – and right now, she was very pushed to come up with something – she reckoned she could be somewhere in the Sinai peninsula.

So why had her kidnappers chosen here? As the Russians knew, things happened to planes in this region, and as the Malaysians knew even better, if the plane had made it out over open water then crashed, the chances of finding it would be slim-to-nil. With a combination of empty desert and sea, this was the perfect place to fly a plane into oblivion. There was also the fact that in the middle east it would be easier than in many parts of the world to take off from a minor airport with a falsified – or no – flight plan. Why she had been in this part of the world in the first place was still well out of her grasp, but she thought that for the first time since she woke up in this nightmare, she might have a handle on something useful.

She stepped out of the wrecked fuselage through a hole where the wing was one attached. Behind her were low cliffs. Left and right was the flat wadi; in front of her the desert stretched off into the distance, just rolling hills and scrub. There was no vegetation anywhere. As the dust continued to clear, the sun grew stronger. It must have been forty degrees, and bone dry.

She returned to the rear of the cabin and hunted through the shattered wreckage for what remained of the galley. The tail fins were a hundred yards back along the wadi, but much of the main structure of the fuselage was still present. She needed to find more water and at least a little portable food. In a refrigerated metal cabinet found dry crackers, a few tins of caviar, some cheese and another dozen or so bottles of spring water. There was also plenty of booze, but that would have reduced her chances of surviving in this heat to almost zero.

As she sat on one of the few remaining seat, eating crackers and taking on as much water as she could, she tried to figure a way out of this.

Sinai it might be, but she had absolutely no idea what

part, who claimed ownership of it, or just how much trouble she had caused by dumping her plane in this particular corner of Dante's Inferno. She needed to act, and fast. If the owners of that F-35 didn't kill her, the desert would if she didn't come up with a plan.

Waiting for rescue was a bad idea. Survival tip Number One was if your vehicle breaks down in the desert, stay with it and await rescue. Her vehicle had certainly broken down, and while it did offer a degree of protection from the burning sun – and a source of food and water far greater than she would be able to carry – it was also a target: a huge, ugly, impossible-to-miss beacon. Someone had gone to a lot of trouble to get her onto this plane and leave her here while setting a course for certain death. That someone would almost certainly be monitoring the flight, and would know that although she had crashed, she had not done so out of sight of prying eyes as planned. They would come to investigate. Sooner or later, they'd be here.

Then, of course, there was that F-35 still rumbling away in the background, watching. Anyone with humanitarian rescue in mind didn't send one of the most advanced combat weapons on earth to do the job.

So she would have to walk out of here, hope that she could disappear into the desert and get some kind of a lead while the authorities picked through the wreckage and discovered there was no dead pilot at the controls, or anywhere else in the vicinity. If she was in Sinai that gave her an unappealing list of options. She had not paid much attention to exactly which direction she had been flying in since leaving the sea behind her, nor for quite how long

she had been in the air. It was possible she could have
flown in a more or less straight line, or she could have
circled. Time, sun altitude, direction… things she should
have noticed. Things she hadn't paid enough attention to
while all her energy and what little clarity of thought she
had left had been taken up avoiding the one direction she
knew she didn't want to go in: down to an uncontrolled
meeting with the desert floor. And now, with the sun
almost directly overhead and no view stretching more than
a few miles, she had no way of working out her position.
Assuming of course she was even in the desert she
thought she was in.

If the strip of land she had seen from the air had indeed
indicated she was flying along the Gulf of Aqaba then she
was a long way east, technically maybe not in Sinai at all now.
Maybe southern Israel. West would take her into rebel
country in Egypt; east Jordan; south could be either, there
was no way to know. North, she would probably be heading
into urban Israel, but she could just as easily hit Gaza. She
could simply make her way to the dark smudge of a town
she had seen in the distance when she had first brought the
plane down, but again, without papers, and with the strong
possibility that someone there would know far more about
her than she knew about herself right now, she could be
walking right back into the lion's den.

Gaza was probably her best option. If she could skirt
its southern border with Egypt, she might have a chance
of persuading someone to get her in. And if she could
get in, she could pass herself off as a western aid worker
long enough to figure out how to get back into Europe.

Since entering Gaza was illegal anyway, her lack of passport was academic and her fluency in Arabic would serve her well.

She hunted through the debris at the back of the plane until she found the familiar red backpack. Her mind was clearer now than when she'd first searched the plane for a parachute. This was her bag – the one she'd taken on a job, packed with first aid kit, cash, monocular, lock picks. She'd driven into the countryside... looking for someone. She tried to force the image to mind, but it would not come. It was still trapped under the ice of whatever drug she had been pumped full of to get her into this flying deathtrap. The memory was there, looking up at her, but she couldn't see its face yet, couldn't put a name to it, fill in its back-story. Her brain buzzed and pulsed with the effort of trying. All she could see was that this story was a dangerous one – dangerous enough that it had already nearly cost her her life. If she stayed here too long, it would try again. She needed to move, now, even if walking out into the baking desert would, under any normal circumstances, be insane.

She stuffed as many bottles of water into the little red backpack as she could, then tore a square of light material from the hospital sheets to make a passable headscarf.

She stepped out of the shade of the plane into the searing midday heat. She would hide out in the hills until the sun was low enough to have lost some of its intensity and she could get an accurate bearing from it. By then that ice-bound memory might have revealed enough of itself to give her some idea what she was escaping from, and what safety – if any – might still exist.

She walked back past the cockpit and stopped dead.

In the distance, maybe five miles away, were three thin plumes of dust. There were vehicles heading her way, and they were moving fast.

7

Guy Roth had picked up the pilot's beacon an hour earlier. Reid slept peacefully on the ageing Gulfstream, while fifteen thousand feet below her, and fifty miles further north, the ex-RAF transport pilot had touched down in the desert and activated his TACBE for Roth to come and get him.

The plane had taken off from Amman in Jordan and flown south-west, then south over Israel, towards the gulf Aqaba as Leila had correctly deduced. At ten thousand feet and climbing steadily the pilot had set a course for the Red Sea and used the pre-prepared escape hatch in the service ducts beneath the main body to make his exit. According to the official paperwork the plane had been heading for Port Sudan in east Africa on a private pleasure trip. Unofficially, it had been fuelled and its autopilot programmed so that it would ditch, out of fuel, in the Red Sea off the coast of Egypt, far enough from civilisation that its demise should not be noticed. Even if it was spotted and anyone bothered to retrieve it from the sea bed, its only occupant had been furnished with enough personal items that it would be assumed she was piloting it solo on a routine excursion when it went down. The flight data recorder might show an unwise climb beyond the normal operating ceiling for this aircraft, but that would be insufficient to suggest foul play.

The steady pulse of the pilot's TACBE indicated that he was still in Israel. It would take Roth a couple of hours to reach him across the old Bedouin tracks and through the mountainous terrain of this hostile land, but it was a routine pick-up. He had been on his mini-odyssey for about forty-five minutes when he had spotted a small jet, flying where no small jet had any business to be flying.

It was at about two thousand feet when it first came into view. Roth glimpsed the out-of-place movement in the mirror of the Land Cruiser as he lit another cigarette and flicked through the MP3s on the entertainment system for more thumping rock anthems suitable for a desert drive. Anywhere else he would not have noticed it, but here low-flying planes were unusual. It was flying too fast to be military transport and too slow to be one of the F-35s that patrolled the skies looking for trouble. It was a civilian passenger jet, and he knew of only one of those that was likely to be cruising around this area.

Reid must somehow have taken control.

He swung the Land Cruiser into sharp turn, leaning forwards to watch the jet's progress across the sky. It was descending, which struck his as odd. There was no airport anywhere near here and no suitable place to land a fragile beast like this. Then he saw the military jet buzz it before climbing out of sight again. It circled and came back at Reid's plane from the rear. Someone else had spotted the private jet and was making an intercept. Bad; extremely bad.

Reid dipped below a mountain some five miles to the

north and Roth hit the accelerator. He headed in a direction that would take him across the tip of the low hill range from which he would hopefully be able to see where she was going. A few minutes later the little Gulfstream reappeared, this time much closer to the ground. It was nearly ten miles away now, but it would not be going much further.

He stopped and jumped out. Standing on the roof of the car he levelled his monocular on the plane. It was extremely low. The broken outline of its undercarriage suggested she had found a way to lower the landing gear, though Roth could not imagine what possible good she thought it would do her. For several seconds he could not see her, then a plume of dust erupted from the desert floor, followed by an orange flash and a wisp of black smoke. Reid had crashed, though from such a distance it was not possible to know how badly. She would be light on fuel, and judging by the pale streak of sand that seemed to follow the plane into the landscape, she appeared to have found a relatively soft place to put down. The crash was spectacular, but there was a good chance – or maybe a 'bad chance' would be more accurate – that it had not been fatal.

He drove on, fast, in the direction of the crash. In the event that Reid had survived, he had to get to her before anyone else did. The F-35 was still rumbling in the distance and it would have a good fix on her position. It was only a matter of time – and probably not much time – before Reid was found, and Roth's bosses had gone to a hell of a lot of trouble and expense to make sure that was not going to happen. They could not afford to risk her remembering too much when talking to the wrong people.

The one thing Roth had on his side was that she would be in need of someone to rescue her. She would not survive long out in the desert on her own, and she'd know it. If he could get to her before the local military did, she'd not be difficult to get back under control. Given what they had plied her with in the last couple of days, she would most likely not even know her own name yet, so he had a window of opportunity when she would be amenable to any helpful suggestion.

He got within three miles of the smoking wreckage before he realised he was not going to make it. He stopped again, mounted the car's roof and scanned the scene through the lens. Three vehicles were approaching from the north. He clicked the magnification to its maximum and sat down to steady the wildly shaking image. He recognised the sci-fi outlines of these vehicles: Plasan SandCats. One sported a rotating machine gun turret and they were moving fast.

He dropped back to the cab and took out the satellite phone, dialled and waited.

'We've got a problem,' he said as soon as the line was connected.

'Reid?'

'She turned around. She's crashed about sixty clicks south of Be'er Sheva.'

'Is she alive?'

'Don't know. I was on my way down when company showed up. They're approaching now.'

'Who?'

'SandCats,' Roth said. 'Three of them. My guess is

military, but who knows how official. I doubt if it's a bunch of rookie conscripts.'

'Get out of there, pick the pilot up. If Reid's stirred up something big down there, AWACS'll start paying more attention to his beacon, so you need to get to him first. Continue exactly as planned. We'll deal with other the situation from our end.'

'If Reid remembers...'

'She won't. Not in time. And they're not going to keep her in the Negev, so we'll intercept her when she's moved.'

'Hold the line.' Roth again levelled the monocular and tried to fix an image. He watched the soldiers fan out around the plane. He could not see much detail, but he could see enough.

'These aren't rookies,' he said. 'They're not even IDF regulars. Whatever she's just crashed into, it's important. They've sent Special Forces to deal with it.'

'Stand down. She's out of our hands for now, but she won't be for long. I'll activate agents to take her out.'

8

Leila made it into the foothills of the cliffs before the three vehicles were close enough to identify. Even then they were like nothing she had ever seen before. At first they had appeared to be standard military Land Rovers, painted in desert camouflage colours. The middle of the three had a gun turret on the roof; the rear one was a longer station-wagon configuration.

As they drew close to the plane she could see they were not Land Rovers – they were more like something out of a sci-fi movie, Arnie's Army sent back from the future. Each had tiny, trapezoidal windows, heavily tinted and barred. The buff-brown superstructure consisted of angled panels like those of a modern battleship, with curves below the windows designed to deflect incoming fire.

Two of the vehicles came to a stop fifty feet or so from the plane. The third – the one that sprouted a long-barrel machine gun and two grenade launchers from its roof – did a slow circuit of the wreckage before coming to a stop a little way from the tail section and pointing directly at it.

There was a long pause. Smoke from the burning jet engine drifted on the light breeze. Leila shrank back behind a rock a little way up what had once been the bank of this long-dead river. She had a narrow field of view that included only the two front vehicles and the main body of the plane. She had no line of sight to the gunner's vehicle and the rear of the plane.

The doors of the station wagon clicked open and six soldiers got out. They were dressed in desert battle fatigues with full-face black balaclavas. Each held a stubby machine gun across his chest and they fanned out to cover all points, working in pairs to maintain line-of-sight on the plane itself and the surrounding hills. A man got out of the other car, again holding a machine gun, and approached the plane. He shouted something in Hebrew and pointed at the unseen armoured car. Leila heard more doors open.

Again the leader shouted. He tried a third time, this time in Arabic. It was heavily accented, but Leila understood the words well enough: *come out, we have you surrounded.*

She was disinclined to comply. Hebrew confirmed her suspicion that she was in Israel, but these were not regular IDF soldiers. The high-tech, heavily armoured vehicles, the black balaclavas, the quiet confidence with which they moved, covering every inch of the terrain without a word, suggested Special Forces. And the sheer number of them who had come out to greet her downed plane suggested she had picked a seriously bad place to land. The Negev Desert was home to some of Israel's most closely-guarded secrets, and it seemed she might have just made a very visible incursion into one of them.

Two of the men from the station wagon moved towards the plane. They entered it, covering all points with quick sweeps of their weapons. The leader opened a pouch on his chest and took out what at first looked to be binoculars. As he put them to his face Leila recognised the distinctive shape of a FLIR portable thermal imager. CTC had tested them last winter, but while they were seriously impressive pieces of kit the cost had proved prohibitive. Obviously this particular branch of the Israeli military had no such budgetary restrictions. With a range of 2,000 yards, she was going to show up like a fly on a Christmas cake at barely two hundred feet.

She checked as best she could with such a limited view that none of the soldiers were pointing their weapon in her direction then called out.

'I'm here,' she shouted. The thermal imaging lenses swung around on her position. 'I'm a British agent, unarmed.'

'Come out, hands where we can see them,' a voice called in English.

Leila looked out through the gap in the rocks and saw that she had the attention of the whole troop now. Although only the thermal imaging binoculars could see her yet, every one of them had their machine gun sighted within a few feet of where she was hiding.

She raised her hands into plain view for a couple of seconds then slowly stood up.

'Where are the others?' the leader called. He scanned the cover either side of her. The other operatives adjusted their positions into cover behind the remains of the plane and their own vehicles.

'I'm alone,' she said.

Two of the soldiers approach the leader and talk to him. They pointed at her footprints in the dry river bed, hopefully indicating that they had found no others.

'Walk towards us slowly,' the leader said. 'Keep your hands where we can see them.'

She rounded the rock and walked half a dozen steps along the path that led down the cliff.

'Drop the bag! Drop the bag!' someone screamed. She could not see who it was, and for a moment had forgotten that she had the small red rucksack on her back. She moved to slip it off her arms but the pain in her neck made her wince and she shrugged forwards.

There was an explosion of bullets all around her. She dropped to the ground and tried to crawl back to the cover of the rock, but the hail of automatic fire had her pinned. They weren't trying to kill her or she would already be shredded and splattered over the riverbank, but they were not about to let her get to anywhere that they wouldn't be able to shoot her if it became necessary. She lay with her arms painfully raised over her head and her eyes shut against the storm of sand and pebbles until the shooting stopped. When she dared to look down, the leader had his hand raised.

'Remove the bag, slowly,' he said. 'If you try to detonate it, you will be dead before you reach the switch.'

'It's not a bomb! Let me take it off. I'm injured, please, let me take it off.'

'Move!'

She struggled to her knees and slipped the pack off her back against the furious protest of her injured ribs. She stood up slowly and kicked it away.

'Move towards us,' the leader called. Leila did, walking a wide detour around the bag and picking her way carefully down the loose scree of the cliff.

Two of the soldiers from the tail section of the wreck rushed her and forced her to the ground just short of the soft sand of the river bed. One covered her with his machine gun while the other hauled her arms behind her back and handcuffed her. He rested his knee between her should blades and pressed the muzzle of his gun into the back of her neck.

'Where are the others?' he said in heavily-accented English.

'No others,' Leila said. She struggled to breathe with her face in the dusty sand and the weight of the soldier pressing her badly bruised chest into the gravel.

'Parachute out?' he said.

'I don't know. Maybe.'

'When? Near here?'

'I don't know. I woke up, the plane was empty.'

'What was your mission?'

'Not to die.'

He pulled her to her feet and did a quick pat-down search. Finding nothing, he marched her to the largest of the three vehicles. He exchanged a few words with the commander in Hebrew and she was bundled into the back.

She sat on one of the bench seats that ran along each side of this weird space-age vehicle – a SandCat she now saw from the logo on the dash – and waited for their next move. The heat was unbearable, savage, in the enclosed darkness. Through the tinted trapezoidal window opposite she watched four of the soldiers head back into the hills while the commander searched the cockpit of the plane. Now and then he glanced in her direction but she could not see his face and she had no idea what those glances meant. Had he found something that she had been too doped and terrified to notice, something incriminating? Or was he wondering how the hell anyone could have survived the process of turning this luxury jet into the wreckage he now surveyed?

After ten minutes or so he returned to the SandCat and sat on the bench opposite her. The door was left open and the slight breeze did something to dispel the fetid cocktail of sweat and boots and gun oil.

'You are the pilot?' he said.

'No. I landed it, but I didn't fly it here.'

'Where is the crew?'

'I don't know.'

'You are not the pilot?'

'No.'

He waved over one of the soldiers who was standing point behind the second vehicle. They exchanged a few words. Leila could barely hear them, and knew no Hebrew anyway. She assumed they were not going to kill her, or they would have done so already, but beyond that the future was as hazy as much of the past. Given how unlikely her story of being alone on the plane was, they were at very least going to question her further.

The commander pulled a small black sack from his webbing. She shrank back along the seat.

'I need to put this over your head,' he said.

'Why?'

'I can put you in the cargo hold or I can knock you out. Or you let me put this over your head and you can stay here and upright. OK?'

Leila nodded and tried to lean forwards to receive the hood. The pain in her ribs was getting worse as the adrenaline wore off, and having her hands tightly cuffed behind her back meant she could not use her arms to take any of the strain of moving. The commander removed her improvised scarf and placed the sack over her head. He got out and slammed the door behind him. In her blindness she felt him – or someone – get into the driver's seat and the engine rumbled into life. A few seconds later another soldier got into the back of the Cat and sat opposite her. She could imagine the machine gun pointing at her.

They drove, fast, out of the crash site and across the rough desert. Neither the driver nor the guard spoke a word. After ten minutes of the Cat swinging around violently over rocks and ruts and around obstacles too large to take head on, the ride smoothed out. A steady rattle replaced the unpredictable movements of the vehicle. Leila guessed they were on what passed for a road out here, probably one of the ancient Bedouin tracks that criss-crossed this part of the world.

After another fifteen minutes or so the Cat slowed and the vibrations ceased. They came to stop and the driver spoke to someone outside the vehicle. A moment later the rear door opened and the hood was pulled up from her face. Through the window behind her guard she caught a momentary glimpse of a huge razor-wire-topped gate and a ten-foot fence running off into the distance before her head was turned roughly towards the open door. She blinked hard against the sudden light and the stab of pain from her strained neck muscles. A soldier, dressed in a grey shirt and dark trousers snapped a couple of photographs of her. For a couple of precious seconds she was forgotten as he checked the camera and – she assumed – sent the photographs to someone higher up in the ranks.

This new soldier had a pistol and taser on his belt and a device clipped to his webbing that looked like a radio, though it was the most sophisticated radio Leila had ever seen. More intriguingly, on the breast pocket of his shirt he had a device, about twice the height of a credit card and the same width, with a holographic image on the top half next to a service number. Beneath this personal identification was a black rectangle with a digital display on it. All very anonymous (though Leila had clocked his number), but there was one thing that had not been obscured. Beside the display was a three-armed yellow symbol. Whatever this facility was, they were using personal dosimeters to measure the inhabitants' radiation exposure.

Satisfied with his portrait, the photographer walked to the front of the vehicle and spoke to the driver. Leila glanced through the vehicle's front windscreen before her head was again violently turned away and the hood replaced. All-in, she'd had less than ten seconds to get enough information to dull the shocks she knew were coming.

She tried to replay the snapshot image she'd got of the compound, slowly bringing each element into focus and allowing her memory to fill in the surroundings. It was a trick she'd learned in the camps of Southern Lebanon when remembering faces and places could save your life. It had also been one of the tricks she'd used to stay one step ahead of her colleagues at CTC.

Apart from the gate and the formidable fence, there had been very little to see over her guard's shoulder. This area of the Negev looked as flat and featureless as the Sahara. There were a few hills in the far distance, and the snaking line of what might have been another dry river bed beyond another high fence some mile or so away, but there was not enough that she would ever be able to pick this place out on a map. Even within the compound, there was very little. Her brief view through the windscreen revealed a few concrete huts, on top of which were satellite dishes and long FM aerials. There were no people and curiously, considering this was probably where the three vehicles that came to the crash site had originated, no other cars.

The conversation with the driver ended and the door beside her slammed shut. The gate swung open and the Cat trundled forwards slowly.

They drove for a couple of minutes then came to another stop. Suddenly the ground shuddered and dropped with considerable speed. For fifteen or twenty seconds the light filtering through her hood changed from muted sunlight to the cold tones of fluorescent tubes, then they bumped to a stop and the last of the golden light from the sun went out completely. An alarm buzzed, the driver eased the vehicle forwards and the light level dropped further.

The Cat's engine sounded different now: louder, more defined, with a reverberation that suggested they were in a tunnel. The vehicle came to stop and the back door opened from the outside. Leila could smell diesel fumes and the cool dry air of air conditioning.

'We're getting out. Mind your head.'

Leila ducked out of the Cat and the guard steered her up a short passageway to a door. Gone was the roughness of her session with the photographer at the checkpoint – he had relaxed considerably now. Was it because they had her where they wanted her? Because they had her somewhere where she could not possibly do any damage… or from where she had no chance of escape? The driver walked ahead of them; she could hear his desert boots creaking. There was a hiss of air as a door seal broke and it slid open. The light in this room was brighter – daylight tubes judging by the bluish tinge she could see through the hood.

She heard voices: two men, three women, not in conversation with each other but speaking, listening, speaking. They were on comms systems. As she was guided across the room she heard the click of computer keys too.

'What is this place?' Leila said.

Her two companions did not reply. The driver took her by the elbow and led her into a corridor; she heard the change in the sounds of their footsteps as they passed doorways… one door, two doors. They stopped at the third and there was a pause. Again the door hissed open and Leila was led in.

'Someone will come to debrief you shortly,' the guard said. 'Is there anything you require?'

'I want to know what the hell's going on.'

'Someone will be with you shortly.'

He left the room and the door closed. Leila listened. She could hear nothing from the corridor outside. There was a faint hiss of air conditioning and a deep rumbling throb from somewhere in the distance, more felt than heard. With her hands still cuffed behind her back she leaned forwards and shook the hood off. She winced with pain and staggered back against the wall as her ribs and neck objected to the sudden movement. By plane-crash standards she was in pretty good shape, but she was going to have to remember that hitting the ground at four hundred miles an hour was likely to keep throwing up nasty surprises like this. She took a deep breath – or as deep a breath as she dared to – of the cool dry air.

She was in a small room, concrete walls, steel door with no internal handle in the wall opposite her, a window of one-way mirrored glass on her right. Mounted beside the door was an RFID card scanner and an all-seeing electronic eye. The room was brightly lit by daylight tubes in recesses near the ceiling. In the middle of the floor was a steel table with a steel chair on either side. Cameras in the corners of the ceiling covered every inch of the room.

She sat down. She could not adjust the chair because it, like the table, was bolted to the floor.

She tried to concentrate, to consider her position, in as much as she knew what it was. She still could not remember exactly what had led up to the moment she had awoken on the pilotless plane, but her mind was beginning to clear a little, fight its way back to something real. She remembered London, Mapleton House, the Kensington bomb. Mapleton most of all… she was working under cover for Counter-terrorism Command at the Israeli-Palestinian Peace Conference. June 19th. Friday. The date was a clear memory because it had been formed long before the event, while it was all being planned, dates arranged, delegates booked in. So she did know now where she had been on Friday June 19th, and that was a start... even if she had no idea whether June 19th had been a day, a week or a month ago.

And that was what the little red backpack she had retrieved from the plane had been about... kit for the operation. Lock-picks, monocular, medical kit, cash. She was sure of that much, but kit like this was not exactly standard issue police equipment, was it?

She shuddered in the cold dryness of her interrogation cell. Confused, fragmented images of the hostage crisis churned through her memory, but the harder she tried to put them into context the more clouded they became. They drifted in and out of focus, teasing, telling her something, but she could not yet hear their story. Just jumbled images, familiar but meaningless, a face she could see in the dark depths, but not clearly enough to recognise or even be sure whether it was of a living person or a corpse.

That face was her past; this concrete room was her present. Here, in Israel, in a facility that the government had gone to a lot of trouble to hide. There was almost nothing on the surface to suggest that this underground world existed, and whatever they were doing in this desolate patch of the Negev, it came with the danger of radiation.

She had a feeling she might have chosen to land in the worst place possible in what could otherwise have been a fairly good country in which to find herself kidnapped, drugged and left to die in a flying coffin. Somehow she had disturbed a very secret hornet's nest, and victim or not, without a good explanation she was not going to be allowed to just walk out of here.

The problem was, she had no explanation at all...

9

Fifteen minutes later, a quarter of an hour of trying and failing to make sense of her memories, the cell door opened and a female military officer stepped in. She was dressed in pale green uniform, white cap and belt, but without the webbing, the gun or any of the equipment that was standard military issue. Leila clocked the ID number on her badge (it, like the gate-keeper's, did not have a name), and the digital dosimeter.

The officer sat down opposite her and placed her hands on the table. She had no notes, no paper or pen, and an inscrutable look on her face. Neither of them spoke for almost a minute and Leila's lack of a blindfold hood was not mentioned. Whoever this first interrogator was, she was not important enough to require anonymity. Her puppet-master was somewhere on the other side of the all-seeing eyes of the cameras.

'Shall we begin?' the soldier said eventually.

'I'm waiting for you. I can't begin when I have no idea what you want or why I'm here.'

The female officer nodded. 'OK. Let's start with: who are you?'

'My name is Leila Reid, I'm a detective with the Counter-Terrorism Command in London.' She reeled off her force identification number. The soldier nodded again but did not write anything down. The whole conversation was probably being transcribed in another room anyway.

'Why are you in Israel, Miss Reid?'

'Am I under arrest here?'

'No. Again, why are you in Israel?'

'I can't tell you that. I woke up on the plane and I have no memory of what happened leading up to that moment.'

'Where are you?'

'You just told me I'm in Israel, and I'm inclined to think you'd know.'

'Where specifically?'

'I have no idea. The ground looked like the Negev, but I wouldn't know.'

'Have you ever been in Israel before?'

'No.'

'So a search of our records will not contain your name or any photographs of anyone looking like you?'

'I can't be sure of the latter. They say everyone has a double, but I can be certain that I have never officially entered Israel.'

'A curious answer.'

'I'm covering my bases. As I said, I don't know much about my recent past. That plane took off from somewhere, so who knows where I've been. Maybe you can tell me.'

Leila stared at her interrogator for a long moment. She was pretty, with refined features; too old for National Service and too young to be in a senior position. Small lines around her mouth and eyes gave her a pleasant, good-humoured look, but that would be an off-duty thing. Right now, in uniform, in this underground bunker, her dark eyes gave nothing away. There was no point playing games here.

'Do I need a lawyer?' Leila said.

'A lawyer would not do you any good, Miss Reid.'

'Then I want to speak to the British Embassy in Tel Aviv.'

'We will arrange something if you cooperate with our questioning.'

'*Before* I say any more.'

'We will make some calls. If your background checks out, we will see what we can do with the Embassy. Is there anything else you need?'

'Yes. What date is it?'

'Date?'

'Date. I need to know what *date* it is.'

The officer looked at her for a moment. 'It's Wednesday, June 24th.' A hint of that off-duty smile. 'You need the year too?' she said.

'No. I've not lost that much time. How long will I be kept here?' she said.

'If your claim to be with British counter-terrorism is true, you should be processed out in a matter of weeks.'

'Weeks?'

'If we don't get the answers we require, it is unlikely you will ever get out. So try to stay positive.' She stood up, brushed her ID against the sensor by the door and left.

In the silence that followed Leila closed her eyes and tried to take mental hold of one of the random images that swam beneath the surface of conscious memory. She could see Mapleton House, feel the crackling energy of the place, smell fire, death. Today was Wednesday, June 24th. The siege had been last Friday. So where had she been for the last five days? And what was the connection between Mapleton and this place? Somewhere in the ice was a hole, a place where the story of her past, that shrouded face, would come up to the surface and she would see it, understand it. For now all she had were images, sensations, random fleeting glimpses from the dark depths.

There had been a bombing in central London too – earlier, maybe a couple of days. One led directly to the other, though she could not yet remember how. At the moment it didn't seem very important. What mattered was why she had been so closely involved in the siege, why she had just been able to walk out of Mapleton House that night five days ago… and end up here. She knew she worked for CTC in London, there was no doubt about that part of her history, but there was a gap – a gap of logic as much as of time. Had she been part of CTC's legitimate investigation of the events last week? That… and only that…?

There was something else, someone else involved that she could not see right now. And it mattered, because the only concrete fact she had given her captors to verify her innocence was her CTC involvement. They were going to check it, were probably doing so right now, and what they found would determine what happened next. It would determine whether she would start the process of release, or whether crashing that plane in the desert would turn out to be the last free move she would make for a very long time.

10

Commander Thorne's phone rang at a little past ten o'clock. He answered it and the receptionist put through a call from Tim Albers-Jones, Vice Consul at the British Embassy in Tel Aviv.

The two men knew each other from university and pleasantries were exchanged. Thorne had the feeling the Vice Consul was circling around something and he wasn't quite sure how to land on it.

'A call from Tel Aviv to British Counter-terrorism is not a good sign I take it?' Thorne said when the preamble had run its short natural course. 'Do we have an incident at your end?'

'I don't know yet. Maybe. What can you tell me of an officer of yours by the name of Leila Reid?'

'She's in Israel?'

'So she is one of yours?'

'I can confirm she's Met police. You know I can't say any more than that.'

'What can you tell me about her?'

'Without knowing why you're asking, nothing.' There was a long pause.

'She's been found in the Negev,' the Vice Consul said eventually.

'Alive?'

'It would be much simpler if she was dead, but yes, she's very much alive. Your turn.'

'DS Reid worked for CTC until recently. She was put out on gardening leave while we investigated some impropriety with the press. She was brought in on a consultancy basis during the Kensington bomb investigation last week, but since the siege ended on Friday night we've had no word from her. Do you know why she's in the Negev?'

'Information's sketchy, as it usually is, if you get my meaning. She was found near a crashed plane somewhere the Israelis don't like people poking about. Currently being held in a desert facility – name and location unknown – while the military bods check out her story. So let's make sure we're telling the same story, shall we? I assume she wasn't there on any kind of official business for your people?'

'Not even close.'

'Come on, Thorne, you've got to give me more than that.'

'Absolutely nothing official. But I can tell you we need to get her back in Britain, and fast.'

'Interesting. She wasn't there on HM business, and you wish she wasn't there at all. Little deduction here… you're afraid that if she wasn't working for you, she was working for someone else?'

'It's possible.'

'Ergo, even if she *was* there harvesting information on

Israeli activities for an unknown third party, that's not necessarily your biggest concern. She might also be leaking information from a little closer to home.'

'She's got form for it, and she has a hell of a lot stored up. As I said, Reid was on suspension for being a little free with the facts on an investigation before.'

The Vice Consul laughed. 'And now you're pissed off that she's not free enough any more: she's started selling the dirty laundry instead to anyone with deep enough pockets!'

Thorne ignored the dig. 'I'm sorry to say this,' he said, 'but certain compelling evidence points to the fact that she may have gone rogue, yes. Switched allegiance.'

'Any idea to whom?'

'I'd rather not say at the moment. There are a lot of people who want to talk to DS Reid.'

'And the Israelis have just joined the queue.'

'Or jumped it,' Thorne said. 'Do you know if she was found with anyone else?'

'There are no reports of other British detainees, but that doesn't mean there wasn't anyone else on the plane. Could she have flown in there on her own?'

'I don't know. She never declared pilot on her induction, but the longer I've worked with Reid, the more of an enigma she's become. Let me make some enquiries and I'll get back to you.'

'I need to contact Colonel Yaniv within the hour, so make it quick.'

'You can expect my call.'

Thorne hung up and immediately called DCI Lawrence into his office.

'They've found Reid,' he said.

'Alive?'

Thorne nodded. 'Oh yes, very much alive.'

'Which you make sound like a bad thing.' He sat down without waiting to be invited. 'Where is she?'

'She's in the Negev. It seems she was on a plane that crashed in the desert… in a restricted military zone.'

'Restricted? As in…'

'It looks that way. And you still have nothing to add, no overlooked detail you think might now be worth telling me?'

'I know no more than I have told you. There has to be a logical explanation for her being there.'

'I'm sure there is, but your logic and mine are not quite the same when it comes to DS Reid. Tell me, do you know if she had a pilot's licence?'

'Not that she ever mentioned.'

'And would she have done? I mean, how well did you really know her?'

'I like to think we were friends, but I knew very little about her personal life, or her past beyond her time with the Foreign Office.'

'I doubt this goes back that far. You spent time with her outside of working hours?'

'Some.'

'Time that was nothing to do with work.'

'Some, yes.'

'If there's anything else I need to know on that front, DCI Lawrence, now would be the time to tell me. Reid is not a person who you would want to be too closely associated with in any future investigation. Make very sure you don't find yourself trapped in the bedroom when her house of cards comes tumbling down. Which I think it's going to do, very soon.'

'I don't really care for your implications, Sir. My relationship with Reid is first and foremost professional. Any social interaction we had in the past is of no concern to this department or this investigation.'

'Very well,' Thorne said. 'So I'll ask you again: in your… personal dealings with her, she never mentioned anything about having experience with piloting a plane?'

'No.'

'Which means she didn't fly the jet into the Negev on her own. She was with someone.'

'And you think it's…? She's defected to Black Eagle?'

'Don't you?'

'Why?' Lawrence said. 'Why would she?'

'Why does anyone defect? Because they come to hate their friends more than their enemies? They crave power, excitement, money?'

'I've never had reason to question Leila's loyalty to her country. She risked her life to bring the Mapleton siege to an end, and she had to go out on a limb to do so because this department gave her no credit or assistance whatever. Reid did more than anyone else to stop Black Eagle's ambitions in Britain: why would she be working with them now?'

'I don't know. That's what we've got to find out. If she's with them now, not only could she destroy seventy-five years of international relations with the Middle East and the Communist Bloc, she could bring down our entire intelligence infrastructure.'

11

Leila was left alone in the concrete interrogation cell beneath the desert. She dozed for half an hour, an hour maybe, she wasn't sure. Without a clock or natural light, and still battered by the combination of shock and whatever drug she had been knocked out with in the first place, time stretched and contracted in all kinds of unpredictable ways. She woke refreshed, so she figured it hadn't been more than an hour. More than that, during the day, sitting in a chair and she'd feel like death when she woke up, but she felt OK. The stabs of pain in her ribs had settled into a constant ache and her neck was suffering more from sleeping upright now than from the wrench it had suffered in the final seconds of her landing.

She looked up at the camera in the corner above the door. It didn't appear that anyone had been in to visit her during her siesta, but they had obviously been watching. Within minutes of coming back to consciousness the door opened and a man in military fatigues and a green beret entered. He was tall, about forty, broad-shouldered, straight backed, with hands that suggested long hard service before he had been appointed a desk job. He wore wire-rimmed glasses on a nose made crooked by repeated breaks.

'I am Colonel Yaniv, of the Military Intelligence Directorate. Can I get you anything?'

'No, I'm fine, thank you,' Leila said.

He placed a manilla file and a small portable digital recorder on the table. Light glinted off the gold fleur-de-lys badge on his cap as he took the seat across the table and switched on the recorder.

'This interview will be recorded in accordance with military law.'

He glanced at her and gave her a half-smile. His eyes were kind but too lively with cunning to be fully trusted. His trustworthiness was not enhanced by the charade of recording the interview. The lights were on on the surveillance cameras, so the whole thing was being recorded outside anyway. He was playing with her. She could play for a while too: she wasn't going anywhere after all.

'Did my story check out?' she said.

'It did.'

'So you know I am not here with any hostile intent.'

'We are not quite at that stage yet, Miss Reid. You are, at least partly, who you say you are, but your intent is still very far from clear. There is one troubling issue that has come to light.'

'Yes?'

'We have received a report stating that you assaulted one of our security men prior to coming here. A man by the name of Daniel Peretz, during the Mapleton House siege on Friday night.'

'Peretz, yes! I remember...'

'A compound fracture to the left knee, two broken ribs and concussion consistent with being kicked in the head. You *should* remember.'

'He tried to kill me. He was working for…'

'He tried to kill *you*? Medical evidence suggests it might have been the other way around, Miss Reid.'

'No.' She tried to get hold of an image that was floating on the edge of memory. It was there, and it was important. Peretz was only a bit-part player in the main story, but he had wandered into view now to introduce the play. Like the ghost of Hamlet's father, alone he was unimportant, but the whole story filled in around him, past, present and future… long after he had left the stage and been forgotten.

Peretz had tried to stop her doing something; he had tried to keep her from interfering with an operation, the thing she had gone to Mapleton House to stop. Peretz was…

'Peretz was…' she said, 'working for…'

'Us,' Yaniv said. 'As you must have known at the time.'

'No.' She looked the Colonel in the eye. 'He was really there with…an organisation called Black… Black…'

'Eagle?' he said.

'Yes, that's…'

'A name that has come up again for us recently too, but not with any connection to our man in London.'

'Black Eagle were behind the operation, the siege…' Leila said. She was close now. '… and it all led back to the release of a prisoner…'

'Do you know what happened to that prisoner?' The Colonel said.

'No. Not yet. Five seconds ago I didn't even remember there was one. But it's there...' She tapped her forehead. The ice was thinning. Swimming up from the dark depths a face was beginning to come into focus. She'd met a man in London (during the siege? ...after it?). Donald someone. They'd gone to the prison but the prisoner wasn't there... she'd already left...

Leila looked at her interrogator. Yaniv watched her in patient, fascinated silence for almost a minute.

'Shall we go back to Daniel Peretz?' he said eventually. 'That name seemed to trigger something.'

'Peretz,' she said, 'yes, he was part of it. Which I think should concern you greatly since you just informed me that he's officially one of yours. From which I deduce he's a lot more than just a regular security-for-hire, isn't he? And by the way, I didn't try to kill him. If I had, he'd be dead.'

'It must have been some confrontation, I'll grant you that,' the Colonel said with a wry smile. 'But Peretz works as a security guard at the Embassy in London, nothing more. What evidence did you have that he was working for someone other than Israeli security at the peace talks?'

'I'm fairly sure I remember he captured me and was about to shoot me before I managed to disable him.'

'Which in turn enabled you to escape from Mapleton House in an attempt to meet up with a prisoner at a jail in London.'

'The facts may be more or less accurate.'

'So you see how this is all starting to look very bad indeed for you.'

'You're putting your own interpretation on them, Colonel Yaniv, and it's not the only one. Anyway, if you know who I am, you probably know a lot more about what happened after the siege than I do. Your people were there – the delegates if not Peretz. It'll all be in the official record. I'll be in the official records.'

'We have confirmed that you are British CTC. Or should I say, you were. They too have been looking for you since you escorted said prisoner to a private airfield in the early hours of Saturday morning. You maintain your position that you have nothing else to say about that person's identity or why you were involved in the case?'

'Correct. Colonel, could I use the bathroom?'

'Of course. One moment.' He looked at the camera on the wall and nodded. Leila closed her eyes, desperate to pause the interview for a couple of minutes to try to grasp more of the story before she said something that she would not be able to unsay.

There *was* a prisoner, and there *was* a connection with Israel, with Black Eagle, with everything. She had to find that memory.

The door opened and a female soldier entered.

'So that we are clear,' Colonel Yaniv said, 'escape is impossible. Challenge or threaten any staff and you will be shot without warning. Even if you evaded them all, it would be impossible to exit the facility, and if, given some miracle, you did, outside your problems would be even worse.'

'I just need to use the bathroom,' Leila said. 'Without the cuffs, please.' She indicated her hands, still shackled behind her back.

Yaniv nodded to the female officer, who produced a set of keys and released Leila's wrists. She was then hooded again and led a few steps along the corridor and through another airlocked door.

'You can remove the hood,' her guard said. 'I'll be outside. You have three minutes.'

'Thank you,' Leila said, though the heavy sarcasm seemed to pass unnoticed.

She did need to use the bathroom, but mostly she needed a break, let her mind work at its own pace for a while, let the facts come to the surface in their own time. The more she pushed, the more they bobbed and sank beyond reach.

And she needed to flex and stretch her arms, which had been held in one position – and slept on – for far too long. Before knocking on the door to be released, she looked at her sorry reflection in the mirror. A dash of water did wonders for the caked-on dust and grime, and running her fingers through her hair helped a little, but she looked exactly as she would expect someone to look who had been kidnapped, drugged, dumped in the desert in a plane crash and stuffed in a concrete bunker. But at least she was still alive, and if she could continue to make sense of the fragments of memory that were slowly coalescing in her fogged-up mind, she might be able to stay that way a while longer.

Back in the interrogation cell, she addressed the Colonel before taking her seat. She hoped to distract him long enough that he forgot about the handcuffs.

'Look,' she said, 'we're going to get through this a lot quicker if you can give me something to get a handle on. A name, something.'

'That's not usually how interrogations go, Miss Reid. Not here anyway.'

'I know, but it's also not usual that the subject of your interrogation is as keen to get to the truth as you are. I know that I know all this stuff, I just can't find it. Listen: if I'm who I say I am, then I already know about the circumstances surrounding the prisoner release. Even if I'm not, the fact that you know I was there strongly suggests that I know what was going on. So give me a name, something. You sow the seed, you'll reap the harvest.'

'Samira Hussain,' the Colonel said.

Leila tried to hold the name, turn it over, but it would not stick. It was just a name. A puzzle piece from a different jigsaw. Two plastic cups of water had appeared on the table during her absence and she took a slow draft from hers. She shook her head. 'Sorry, I don't know the name.'

Colonel Yaniv glanced at his notes, flicked through a couple of pages without seeming to read a word, then looked up at her. 'How about Golzar?' he said quietly.

It was as if she had been hit by an invisible fist under the table, a fist that smashed through the ice and released a geyser of crystal clear water.

'Yes!' she said. 'Raha Golzar! *That's* who was at the centre of all of this...'

For a moment she couldn't grasp the full import of the name, but with it all the jumbled pieces of an entire story surged up at her from the black depths. This was the way in to everything she had lost. The first name Yaniv had given her had been a test. This one, the real one, was the prize for winning this game of truth or dare.

'Raha Golzar was who we went to meet,' she went on. 'Except she'd been in the boot of the car all along. I remember…'

'You admit you had contact with Raha Golzar last week?'

'If shooting her counts as contact, yes.' She had a sudden, crystal clear image of shooting as her driver tried to get away… of the car's boot springing open and blood dripping out onto the tarmac of the airport road.

'Your people are doubtful that Miss Golzar is dead,' the Colonel said. 'So are we. She faked her own death last year in Jerusalem. It seems she might have done the same thing again in London. And it seems that this time you were complicit in it.'

More memories came up from the cold depths. Golzar had been at the heart of this from the beginning. From long before the beginning in fact…

The Russian-trained bio-weapons expert had been in Israel fifteen months before Black Eagle launched their attacks on London, ostensibly to set up a meeting with the military. No one had illusion that the IDF would be stupid enough to acquire biological weapons, but Black Eagle knew that her very presence would get the right people nervous enough about that possibility that they would to start paying attention. And they did, but not in the way Black Eagle had hoped. Someone had discovered her plans and had put this valuable piece of information up for sale – first to Fatah in Ramallah, then to the CIA's man in Tel Aviv. The US government paid much better than the PLO.

The CIA had asked British secret intelligence to stage an assassination to clear the mud Golzar had stirred up in the carefully managed waters of Israeli politics. SIS had taken the job willingly – gratefully even – as Prime Minister Richard Morgan had seen his own opportunity for immortality hiding in the depths.

Rather than kill the Iranian weapons expert – or render to the US – the British smuggled her out of Israel and hid her in a lunatic asylum in England. Here she was used as bait by the government to bring the Palestine National Authority and Israelis to the negotiating table.

The plan had worked beautifully until Black Eagle realised their asset was still alive, and last week's storm had broken over the Home Counties to get her back. The Mapleton House siege had been to leverage Golzar's release, and on Friday night Leila had gone along with her handler as a human shield, to ensure a smooth conclusion to the operation. Except things hadn't quite worked out that way…

'I shot her at least eight times!' Leila said.

'And still no body has been found. Her escort, Donald Aquila, has not been found. You disappear from the airfield at the same time as they do. And then you turn up, flying a plane into a restricted military area, in Israel. Where the said Raha Golzar also has a somewhat interesting past. You see how this might be a problem, and how your apparent haziness in remembering how or why you got here makes that problem very much worse for you?'

'There's an explanation. I'm not there yet, but I'm not a traitor to my country. Or yours. Do CTC know I'm here?'

'We have told your Embassy we know where you are. The problem we now have is what to do with you.'

'Hand me over. They can sort all this out. And given the

extreme secrecy of this facility, and the fact that I guess you'd like to keep it that way, do you really want to risk the diplomatic fallout of keeping me prisoner here? Surely it would be better for all concerned if I was a prisoner of my own people rather than yours?'

'It may not be that simple, Miss Reid. It is a question of jurisdiction. Your own people are not entirely resistant to our theory that you were attempting an act of sabotage on an Israeli government facility.'

'Government?'

'Government, military, these are just labels. The pertinent fact is that whether you were attempting to start a war of bullets or diplomacy, sabotage is the correct term for your actions. Your people were very keen that we understood you were not working in any capacity as a British agent, and are therefore not strictly their problem.'

'I never said I was working for them in an official capacity, but my loyalty's surely not in question! I wasn't on that plane voluntarily.'

Colonel Yaniv took a sip of water and again read – or pretended to read – something in the file of notes on the table in front of him.

'OK,' he said. 'You've confirmed that you know about Raha Golzar, although I still fail to see how that works to your advantage as much as you thought it might. Still...'

'It's to the advantage of my sanity,' Leila said. 'One step at a time.' But he had a point. She had an uncomfortable feeling that rather than loosen the snare, this memory might just have pulled it tighter.

'Very well,' Yaniv said. 'Let's return to the plane for a

moment. You told my colleagues that you were alone. An F-35 pilot who intercepted you said you were at the controls.'

'I was trying to figure out where I was. I would hardly call what I was doing 'controlling' the plane. Someone had got us up there, but he was gone when I woke up.'

'Do you know who the pilot was?' he said.

'No.'

'Do you expect me to believe that this pilot simply vanished?'

'I believe he set the autopilot for a steady climb south over the sea then left.'

'And closed the door behind him?'

'I only know what I saw.'

'Let me put another scenario to you. You say you were heading south towards the sea, and yet when you spotted, you were on a path north through the Negev.'

'Because I didn't intend to put down in water.'

'So you admit that you deliberately turned into Israeli airspace.'

'I wasn't certain where I was, but it seemed like a reasonable guess. Wherever I was, turning back over land seemed the least worst option in the circumstances.'

'The point being that you made a conscious choice to alter course.'

'Yes.'

'Therefore you do know how to fly.'

'I had time to figure out the basics. You can see from the landing that I'm no expert.'

'And there we have the problem, Miss Reid.' He leaned

towards her. 'You know enough to be able to fly the plane left and right, up and down, but not how to land. Does any of that sound familiar?'

'Mohamed Atta. You think this was a suicide mission? That I intended to crash the plane?'

'You have no identifying papers.' He ticked off point one by holding up his index finger. 'The flight plan for that jet was registered in Amman heading for Port Sudan, and yet where you ended up is some way off an obvious flight-path between the two...' Second finger. 'You claim you are not a pilot, yet radar trace of your path shows considerable skill in manoeuvring a complex jet.' Third finger. 'You admit you knew you were over Israel but you still continued into a restricted military zone...' (Fourth) '...and crashed your plane in one of the most politically sensitive areas in the world.' He held his open hand up to her. 'How does that appear to you?'

'It appears that if I'm as good as you think I am, I'd have hit my target,' Leila said.

'And what was your target?'

'Oh, for God's sake! I was being sarcastic! There *was* no target. I had no aim but to get on the ground and try to figure out how the hell I'd got into this mess!'

'So tell me, Miss Reid: how did you get into this mess?'

'I still don't know. So far I'm up to shooting Golzar at the airport. After that... I woke up on the plane. The four and a half days between feel very blank indeed.'

'Maybe time will free up some more detail. You need time perhaps to consider your position. I will return in an hour to see what else, if anything, you are willing tell me.'

'I think I've said enough. If you had any real evidence against me, we wouldn't be wasting our time in this game, would we?'

'You need to understand, Miss Reid, that you are in a machine. I am merely a cog in that machine. A bigger one than your first interrogator, maybe, but still just a little piece of something much bigger. Each time you do not cooperate, you get moved further into the belly of the beast. We will find the truth. It is a process, not a game. You can not out-wit us, and you can not out-wait us.'

'Have you arranged a consular visit, Colonel?'

'That will be arranged for you when you are transferred to Camp Nathan. We do not have the facilities here for outside visitors.'

'Camp Nathan?'

'A military prison near Be'er Sheba. The next cog in the machine. You will be held as an enemy combatant until we can determine who you are working for. And if you stand by this fantasy of amnesia, my guess is that could be a very long time indeed.'

12

Much of CTC's official operational time was still taken up with the aftermath of last week's bombing and the ensuing Mapleton debacle. Prime Minister Richard Morgan had retreated to Chequers after the violent death of his daughter at Black Eagle's hands. Emma Whitehouse, Home Secretary for only six months following a meteoric rise from back bench obscurity in Morgan's last cabinet reshuffle, was more than happy to fill the void. If reports were to be believed, the 'Acting' in her title 'Acting Prime Minister' might soon be dropped in favour of a more permanent and satisfying epithet, and a very favourable house move. *If* she could clear up the mess her former boss had left the country in while he wallowed in misery, self-recrimination and single malt in his Buckinghamshire mansion. Most people on the international stage did not know – or much care – who she was, but she had every intention of changing that, and quickly.

Whitehouse was leaning on the Cabinet – and anyone else within range – for decisive action; the Foreign Secretary was leaning on SIS, and the new 'acting' Home Secretary was leaning on Five. CTC was mopping up the overspill and trying to make sense of intelligence flooding in from every direction. Within CTC a sense of unreality underpinned the sift through the data – senior officers conspired in whispers and the admin staff kept their heads down and their computer keyboards red hot.

The meeting was a closed one, barely even a meeting at all. Commander Thorne knew he was going to have to give COBRA something soon, something Emma Whitehouse could use, but he had nothing plausible yet. His main tech analyst, Mark Ross, had been arrested in a tip-off drugs raid three days ago and was unlikely to be trusted with state secrets again. CTC was now relying on a fresh upstart by the name of Fielding for the kind of intel SIS and Five should be sharing with their Met police counterparts, but very rarely did. He hoped his temporary tech analyst might give him a new angle that he could throw to the acting PM to chew on. Otherwise she was going to keep chewing on him.

With everyone focussed on outside events, Commander Thorne called DCI Lawrence into his office for a little domestic housekeeping. They dragged chairs to a side desk where Sam Fielding was tapping the password into his laptop.

'Have you found anything?' Thorne said.

'Satellite imaging came in from GCHQ,' Fielding said. He opened an image on the screen. 'This was taken by a reconnaissance satellite positioned over the area four hours ago.' He zoomed in on the image and pointed at an elongated dark smudge amongst a mess of grey and brown patches.

'And that's…?' Lawrence said.

'We think this is Reid's downed plane,' Fielding said. 'Compare it to the same image taken yesterday,' he switched to a new window, 'and the patch isn't there. We've run comparative analysis of the entire Negev area and this is the only significant change in the visual spectrum that's the right size and at the right time.'

'Do we know what's there?' Thorne said. 'The VC in Tel Aviv said it was sensitive.'

Fielding grinned. 'Look at this.' He switched to a third window which showed a dark, almost featureless image.

'This is an overlay of six months'-worth of non-visible-range imaging. Notice anything?'

Thorne looked impatient. Lawrence leaned in and examined the screen.

'There's a solid dark patch there,' he pointed to a faint circular disk among the random deep red noise.

'Star prize!' Fielding said. 'Look: there's three light ones here too.' He zoomed in to an area that showed the dark circle in one corner of the screen and three much brighter dots in a line in the opposite corner.

'Those are hidden satellite dishes,' he said. 'Ironically, get this… they can't been seen by satellites. Or not visually seen, if you know what I mean. These sensors pick up radiation outside the visible spectrum, high and low. The dishes might be disguised but they have a unique signature.'

'And the dark patch?' Thorne said impatiently.

'Gamma radiation black-spot.'

'Meaning?' Lawrence said.

'Tut, I thought you'd got it. Sad emoji, guys! Taking that prize away…' He grinned at Lawrence. No one was amused.

'OK, OK,' he went on. 'All this noise – the dark red stuff –
is natural background radiation. The earth is full of it. But
there,' he pointed at the blank circle, 'there isn't any.'

'It's not natural ground,' Lawrence said.

'Exactly. It looks like it on the photographs, but it isn't.
And this is six *months* of images. The only way a radiation
shadow that big and that long-lived could occur is if
whatever's there is deliberately masking radiation.'

'Lead shielding?' Thorne said.

'In the Negev? It'd be a puddle. No,' Fielding said, 'this
is military-grade Z Shielding. Tantalum to aluminium, maybe
boron carbide. Six months of background radiation, and
not a single spike in this patch. Not. One. This is seriously
impressive.'

'Nuclear power plant?'

'That well hidden?' Fielding said with a hint of a smirk.
'No, the Dimona reactor is well known and highly visible,
and probably not even currently on line. Not to mention
the fact that no plane could have got within ten miles of it.
This, gentlemen, has the signature of a weapons silo.'

He leaned back and allowed Lawrence and Thorne to
ponder the implications of his revelation.

'Does anyone else know about this?' Commander
Thorne said.

'You told me to report only to you,' Fielding said.

'But did you?'

'That hurts! GCHQ just sent over a bulk dump. You're
the only two people who've seen this, or – more importantly
– heard my interpretation of it.'

'Keep it that way. Everyone knows Israel is armed, but

no one "knows" it. It's outside the scope of this investigation to lay proof out for the world to see.'

'You don't think anyone else will have noticed? If we can see the signatures...' Lawrence said.

'Outside the scope of the investigation. With what Trump's done to the Iran nuclear deal, the last thing we want to do it furnish Tehran with evidence that they need to get their programme ramped up again. Thank you, Fielding. You can leave us now. And leave the computer.'

Sam stood up. He gave the two men a dejected look and left, without his laptop.

'Do we think Reid knew it was there?' Thorne said.

'How could she?' Lawrence said. 'If this is an Israeli weapons silo, even we didn't know about it. It has to be a coincidence.'

'Unless she had a source we don't,' Thorne said. 'Who's going to be most interested in Israeli nuclear ambitions? Iran, closely followed by Russia and China.'

'You're surely not suggesting...'

'It's a plausible connection. Raha Golzar is Iranian—'

'By birth—'

'Golzar is Iranian, trained in Russia, worked – or works – for Black Eagle, who she was representing in Israel fifteen months ago when SIS picked her up. And Reid went to a lot of trouble to get Golzar out of jail and, as far as we can tell, out of the country.'

'And killed her in the process,' Lawrence said.

'There's no proof of that. And anyway, it's not pertinent. Alive or dead, Golzar was Reid's way into Black Eagle.'

'It's all coincidence,' Lawrence said. 'Circumstantial,

based on one interpretation, but not the only interpretation…'

'Coincidence?' Thorne said. 'That Reid then flies a plane into the ground right next to what looks suspiciously like a nuclear arsenal? There's thousands of square miles of desert out there, and judging by the satellite images it's all pretty much the same. She could have landed anywhere. Or she could have gone on another hundred miles or so and made a controlled, guided landing at Be'er Sheva. I'm sorry to say it, but this looks very deliberate.'

'To what end?' Lawrence said.

'To what end did they bomb the Park Hotel? Murder Ruth Morgan? Diversion, antagonism, bravado? There's only one person who ever had a handle on Black Eagle.'

'No.'

'She was ahead of us at every turn. She outmanoeuvred us to get herself exactly where she needed to be on Friday night.'

'No!' Lawrence said. 'For one thing, there's a huge logical and operational gap between losing Reid after the siege and her turning up in the Negev. We have no idea how one leads to the other. But more importantly, we can be fairly certain she wasn't part of Black Eagle before any of this started.'

'Can we?' Thorne said. 'How so?'

'Because she wasn't part of CTC when this all started last Wednesday. How could she possibly have planned to get herself dropped right into the heart of our operation – the only place where she could have been of any use to Black Eagle?'

'Because you trust her. You *know* her, Commander. She

could have planned for *that*, don't you think? Huge counter-terrorism operation, who ya gonna call?'

'I do know her. And that means I know she wouldn't – couldn't – play me like that. She wasn't part of this when the bomb went off, I'm certain of it.'

And Michael Lawrence was certain of it because he'd heard Donald Aquila's attempt to recruit Reid while they were at Epping Airport, meaning she could not possibly have been with Black Eagle before that. The problem he had now created for himself – and Reid – was that he could not share the one piece of evidence that put her in the clear for the carnage of last week without also giving credence to Thorne's theory that she had subsequently become a double agent. He had, after all, never heard her reply to Aquila's invitation.

'No,' he said, 'I can not accept that all this was planned. Reid being in the Negev now can not have been an extension of Black Eagle's operation last week. It's impossible. So if you think she has defected, it would have to be recent: this whole series of events in Israel is new. But… how could she have put such a sophisticated plan together so quickly – leave the country undetected, vanish for days, only to pop up in Israel flying into a place even we didn't know about until five minutes ago? The intelligence gathering alone would be almost impossible without being traced!'

'Exactly.'

'So you agree?'

'No,' Thorne said. 'I think the sophistication of it may actually prove my point. You're forgetting Phillip Shaw. He was under the sole influence of Reid. Apart from your conversation with him during the siege, no one else ever had any contact with him. She couldn't have planned for that, or, as you say, what happened afterwards, but you know better than anyone that Reid is highly adaptable under pressure. She'd have seen Shaw as the perfect mole, and if we accept your assertion that she was not part of Black Eagle until a few days ago, she'd have needed that kind of help, and fast. There's no computer in the world that's completely immune to the attention of Shaw and his hacker pals.'

'You think that's how she knew about the Israeli missile silo?'

'Of course, and I think it's how she pulled off the whole disappearing act too. Who knows what other secrets she manipulated him into revealing along the way!'

'Shaw's debrief never uncovered the slightest hint of any impropriety.'

'Shaw's psychological report says he's emotionally retarded and immature, but highly intelligent,' Commander Thorne said. 'What it doesn't say is that he's got any kind of spectrum disorder. He's perfectly capable of lying.'

'But hasn't the boy been monitored since his debrief?'

'Of course he has, but he was never a high priority until this. His involvement seemed limited – deep, yes, but time-limited. We had no reason to hold him physically. We did, after all, have much more pressing issues to clear up. He was released, asked to keep himself available to us, and put under light observation. And we both know he could have found a way around even our most sophisticated electronic surveillance if he'd had reason to do so. He could have walked right through what we actually put on him and we'd probably never have known.'

'So what now?' Lawrence said.

'First we need to talk to Shaw again.'

'And Reid?'

'With what she knows about the events of the last week, and the operations of secret intelligence in general, she would be a valuable asset for Black Eagle. If she's gone rogue, finding her and stopping her has to be our priority. Shaw should be easy enough to break, then based on what he tells us, we deal with Reid.'

'*Deal* with?'

'Do whatever is necessary in the name if national security.'

'She'll be found zipped inside a suitcase?' Lawrence said, 'Or taking a cup of Lapsang polonium? You can't seriously...'

'Litvinenko was not one of ours, not our problem, not our doing. But yes, Gareth Williams was unfortunate. It should have been handled better.'

'So your suggestion this morning about making this a missing persons enquiry was never about trying to find her at all, it was about neutralising her, come what may?'

'Let's not get carried away,' Thorne said. 'My primary aim is to get Reid out of Israel for a controlled debrief here. I want to keep her safe as much as you do, if for slightly different reasons. If she's been turned in one direction, between us we might be able to turn her back and get a lot of valuable intel on Black Eagle. That would be the perfect outcome for all concerned, don't you agree?' Michael nodded. 'So, as I said before, keep me informed. Any contact, my door is open.'

Michael Lawrence left and Thorne picked up the phone. He dialled the PM's office over in Whitehall, still not knowing exactly what he was going to tell her. He just knew he had to tell her something.

13

Leila guessed it must be well past midnight when they took her from the concrete cell and walked her back past the incessant low-level chatter and tap of computer keyboards in this underground bunker. She was handcuffed again, having been allowed to remain unshackled after Colonel Yaniv had finished with her that afternoon. They had not forgotten: they were just confident that she knew as well as they did that fight and flight were both impractical dreams in her current situation, so restraint was not necessary. Her guard also blindfolded her again, this time with something more akin to an airline sleeping mask than a sack, although it had the same effect. She saw nothing of that short walk, or of the vehicle that awaited her at the end of it. She had little doubt it was the same one that had brought her in. Same driver and same guard, judging by their voices. These men were not part of this place, they were the efficient clean-up crew that kept the desert as pristine as in the days of Abraham. The platform shuddered and lifted them effortlessly back into that featureless desert.

They drove through the darkness over rough roads for half an hour before the ride smoothed out. The driver increased speed and the Cat purred over smooth roads, seemingly in a perfect straight line. No one spoke. Leila dozed, lulled by the two-part harmony of the desert tyres and the massive V8 engine running so lazily it was barely at more than an idle.

Neither the driver nor her guard spoke even when a whirring, hissing sound split the night. The missile screamed overhead and ended in a huge exclamation mark explosion just in front of them. Leila jerked awake, looking around pointlessly, trying to see something through the thick material of her blindfold. The driver swung the Cat hard left over rough ground, the massive engine at last springing to life and surging the six-tonne beast forward in a shower of rock and dust.

A couple of seconds later a second RPG exploded just behind them. The back wheels of the Cat were momentarily lifted clear of the ground as either by reflex or because the force of the explosion had thrown him off balance, the driver floored the accelerator. The engine revved and the back wheels hit the rocky desert with a bone-shuddering thump. There was a loud bang from somewhere under the cab and the engine stalled.

'What the…?' Leila shouted.

The blindfold was torn from her eyes and the guard hustled her to the floor. Behind them, through the barred rear window, she caught a glimpse of fire and a cloud of dust and smoke.

'Hamas rockets,' the guard said. The driver was trying to get the engine restarted, without success.

'They targeting us?'

'No. Lucky strike. They lob them over the border now and then to make sure we're still awake.'

'What do we do?'

'Nothing,' her guard said. 'We're safe in here from anything short of a direct hit.'

The engine had still not caught. Leila figured the bang was probably the drive-shaft giving up when the unstoppable force of a six litre V8 met the immovable rocky substrate of the Negev. Something was going to give up, and if it was only the driveshaft they had been lucky. They were stuck, but they were safe. Or so she thought for a few blissful seconds…

She looked out of the little window behind her guard's head. In the far distance the lights of Be'er Sheva were a soft orange glow in the deep purple sky, and against that dark backdrop lights had appeared – two pairs of halogen headlights approaching on a direct line. They rolled and flashed as each vehicle took a slightly different route over the sand and scree but there was no mistaking their intent. They were closing fast the disabled SandCat.

'Were we travelling with anyone else? Guards clearing the road?' Leila said.

'You're not that important.'

'Then that wasn't a Hamas rocket,' Leila said. 'Look.'

The guard turned and looked out through the window behind him. By now the vehicles were less than half a mile away. At their current rate of approach, they would be on them in under thirty seconds.

The driver was watching too. He gave the engine one last try. Nothing happened. He grabbed the radio and began speaking. It was in Hebrew, so Leila didn't understand the words, but the calm staccato of his voice was universal. They were under attack, and they needed help.

'Can you at least undo these cuffs?' Leila said. 'Give me a chance?'

'We're safe in here until rescue comes,' the guard said. 'The Cat's armoured. No way in. They'll send someone from Camp Nathan.'

'Undo the cuffs,' Leila said. 'I'm not going to make a run for it into incoming fire, and you've got all the guns in here.'

The guard looked at his driver. The driver unclipped a bunch of keys from his belt and threw them back. The cuffs were released just as the blazing headlights of the approaching cars came to a stop some twenty yards away. For a moment there was silence, then the Cat was rocked by rapid fire from at least two machine guns. Bullets ricocheted off the vehicle's curved ceramic panels. The two tyres on the right side were hit and the vehicle canted over. So far the two soldiers inside did not seem particularly concerned.

A man stepped into the light of the closer of the two cars. He stood in silhouette.

'Let the woman go,' he shouted.

'These are your people?' the guard said to Leila.

'I doubt it. Even I didn't know where I was. The only people who knew I was on that plane were the ones who left me on it to die.'

'You have thirty seconds to release the woman,' the man called.

'We can hold out long enough for reinforcements to come,' the driver said.

'Unless they hit us with another rocket,' Leila said. 'A direct hit's odd-on from that range, don't you think?'

'If they hit us with a rocket, they're not that interested in you being alive, are they?' the driver said.

'Fifteen,' the silhouetted man called.

'Can't you shoot back?' Leila said.

'Not without opening the door,' the driver said. 'This is an armoured carrier, not an assault vehicle.' Again he spoke into the radio in Hebrew. The response from base was short, precise.

'They're on their way,' he said. 'Ten minutes.'

Leila looked out into the night through the side window. The desert faded away in the light of the two vehicle headlights, the long shadow of the Cat haloed with random highlights as stones caught in the cold beams. Despite the glow of the city on the north side of the car, it felt as if they were in the middle of nowhere. They probably were.

'You have one more chance,' the man outside shouted. 'Open the door now, or we'll do it for you.'

There was a pause of no more than five seconds then a new sound split the night. A small petrol engine sprang to life and out of the blinding light of the vehicles' headlights a man in bomb-proof body armour appeared. In his hand he held an angle grinder, its blade spinning.

'They're going to cut us out?' Leila said.

The driver laughed. 'This'll be entertaining. We've got two-inch ceramic armour. He'll skate that toy around like a puppy on ice.'

Or so they thought.

The man climbed onto the bonnet of the Cat and leaned

down. He looked at the three faces inside and grinned, knowing that no one would be able to shoot at him. The glass was bullet-proof, which meant nothing was getting out any more than it was getting in.

He jabbed the angle grinder at the central bar of the windscreen. It bit, showering sparks into the darkness around him. In under a minute he was through the toughened steel. He kept the machine in place.

At first the diamond-studded blade just skidded off the glass, but with it wedged between the arms of the bar, it held firm enough to start to cut a groove in the thick glass. And once it had a groove, it had sufficient purchase to keep on cutting.

Still neither the driver nor the guard showed any real sign of concern.

The tip of the blade broke through the glass and the Cat filled with the smell of exhaust and burning. With a hole some three inches long and half an inch wide the blade withdrew and the engine was cut. Mr Angle-Grinder dropped to the ground and walked away. He high-fived his leader as he passed.

The man who had spoken earlier approached. He leaned in to the windscreen, keeping his head close and enough to one side that it would have been impossible to shoot him through the hole. He spoke, quietly and slowly.

'Open the door,' he said. 'We only want the woman. We have no quarrel with… the rest of you.'

'We were tasked to take her to Be'er Sheva,' the driver said. 'When we get there, she gets out. Not before.'

'Very well.'

He beckoned to one of his men. Another figure emerged from the light carrying a tank with a long hose attached.

'Shit,' the driver said, 'gas. Get the masks.'

Leila's guard reached under the seat and pulled out a long box. He opened it and threw a gas mask to the driver, then one to her. By the time she had it on, the nozzle of the tank had been pressed against the hole in the windscreen.

'Can't you shoot it out?' Leila shouted through the thick mask.

'Too much chance of ricochet,' the guard said. His voice was muffled and distant. 'Sit tight. Rescue's no more than three minutes out.'

And they might have been all right if all that came out of the nozzle was gas. But it wasn't. The driver, who had remained in his seat staring defiantly at their attackers was hit first. The jet of liquid shot from the nozzle and hit him in the chest. In seconds he was screaming, clawing at his bullet-proof vest where the acid had penetrated the seams. He turned in his seat. Already the mask was disintegrating and the flesh of his throat was red and blistering.

The guard pushed Leila aside and hauled the screaming driver over the seat and into the back of the Cat. He was followed by a jet of acid. The angle grinder had cut the perfect aperture in the windscreen: tall enough and wide enough to allow the nozzle to hit most of the front half of the vehicle.

Leila tried the shuffle under the seat, away from the line of acid that followed the driver up the cargo bay of the vehicle. She could not get far. Something had been wedged under the seat.

'We've got to get out!' she shouted.

'They'll mow us down the second we open the door,' the guard said. 'Rescue's coming. Just hold on. Stay low!'

The guard's gloves were blistering where he had touched the driver's vest. He looked up at the hole ahead and was caught by a splash of acid in the middle of his visor. He tried to wipe it away but already the toughened perspex was turning milky. A line of acid spray trickled along the floor and stopped just short of where the dying driver was lying. Outside the night had fallen silent.

Leila looked to the front of the cab. The nozzle had jammed in the slot and rather than just spray acid uselessly into the front of the Cat, it was being wrestled free in preparation for another attack.

She sat upright against the rear door, the final pool of acid just beyond her foot. Paint blistered and the stench was acrid and nauseating. Beneath the seat on her right she saw what had prevented her getting under cover: a familiar red rucksack had been tucked under there. Her strange and still inexplicable kit from the Mapleton operation, the bag that had followed her to the middle east, across the desert and now into this stinking metal and ceramic tomb was still at hand. Her partner in crime.

The guard turned the driver over. He was already dead, or as close to it as would make no difference however quickly rescue arrived. His throat had disintegrated and blood poured out of the gaping hole, dark and glistening against the smoking remains of his uniform. The guard removed the now-opaque mask and there was no life in the eyes that stared up at him.

Outside no one spoke. For another fifteen seconds or so the desert was silent. Then the angle grinder fired into life and the Cat rocked as its operator climbed back onto the bonnet. In his new-found confidence at his tactical superiority, the hot and bulky bomb-disposal uniform had been abandoned in favour of a black t-shirt. He jabbed the cutting wheel into the slot and began to improve the angle of fire.

If a rescue vehicle was on its way, there was no sight or sound of it yet. And there was no way they could hold out against this attack much longer.

14

'Give me your gun,' Leila shouted over the noise of the renewed assault.

'Stay down,' he guard shouted back. His visor was almost completely opaque and he was effectively blind. They both huddled in a small space at the back of the vehicle, getting what cover they could from the body of the dead driver. There was still no sign of the promised rescue.

'Don't be so stupid,' Leila said. 'If they open that slot another half inch, we're finished. But while that guy's cutting it, his mates won't be paying too much attention, so we've got a tiny window of opportunity. Now give me your gun!'

There was a moment's hesitation, then practicality won out over protocol. He handed the rifle to her. 'You know how to use one of these?' he said.

'Enough.'

'You've got thirty two rounds, automatic. The safety's off.' He checked his own pistol.

'I'm going to open the side door,' Leila said, her mouth an inch from her guard's ear. 'Open your side and give me covering fire. Sweep towards the lights, three seconds. OK?' The guard nodded. She shuffled forwards and clicked the manual lock on the Cat's door as her guard did the same. '*Three, two, one…*'

They both cracked their doors open and as her guard began firing blindly into the lights of the vehicles at their side, Leila pushed the muzzle of the rifle out of the top of her door and let off a burst of automatic fire. The man with the angle grinder stopped work and turned towards his own people; Leila could see his silhouette through the windscreen, a stationary target just feet away. She risked it.

She opened the door and angled the gun as best she could at the front of the Cat. She squeezed the trigger. A hail of bullets sprayed the dust around the front tyre. She raised the barrel and there was a dull thud and a cry. The front of the Cat shook as the man standing on it fell to the ground.

There was incoming fire now from beyond the blinding lights of their attackers' cars. They both retreated and relocked the armoured doors. For several seconds bullets continued to skid off the Cat's ceramic plates and thick glass, kicking up clouds of dust outside. It was pointless, but their attackers were well-enough equipped that there seemed to be no need to save ammunition. She had probably disabled one of them, but without outside rescue there was still only going to be one way it would end.

The gunfire outside fell silent and she saw two men rush forwards to rescue their fallen comrade. The angle grinder lay on the bonnet of the Cat, but it had failed to make much of an impression on the windscreen. The man wielding the acid tank had also withdrawn.

For ten or fifteen long seconds there was silence again.

And then the balance of power shifted.

The arriving team was as much a surprise to Leila and her guard as it was to the group outside the Cat. The assault came out of nowhere. More importantly, it came out of the darkness beyond the bright lights of the original attacker's vehicles. There had been no lights, no sound to warn of incoming forces, just a sudden roar of gunfire.

Leila tore off her gas mask and tried to see what was happening outside. Two of the original assault group lay dead in the pool of vehicle lights. Three others had taken cover beside the Cat and were firing towards the rescue team beneath the vehicle. Under a hail of covering fire, one ran across the open area to one of their own cars.

A moment later there was a huge burst of flame as a rocket propelled grenade roared into the IDF team's position. A lucky shot, it hit a vehicle and a ball of smoke and flame erupted into the darkness. The level of incoming fire dropped dramatically.

For almost a minute there was a stand-off. Each side was regrouping. The two men beside the Cat reloaded. One raised his head and looked directly at Leila through the side window.

'Come out now,' he shouted. 'These people are not here to rescue you. We can get you out of here, but you need to move now.'

'Don't,' her guard said. 'This is nearly over.'

'I wasn't going to,' Leila said.

There was a sudden movement from the IDF position. A soldier in desert uniform ran forwards and got a burst of fire off at the man with the grenade launcher before he even knew he was there. It was a brave move, but not a wise one. He had no idea there was another gunman hiding in the lea of the Cat, and he was instantly cut down like dry grass under the scythe. A second short burst of fire finished him off as he lay on the ground.

There was silence again.

'Are there more of them?' Leila said.

'I hope so,' the guard said. He had removed his acid-clouded mask and for the first time in this mission he looked rattled. Not scared yet, but not as confident as he had been.

There was another burst of automatic gunfire from the darkness. Boots ran across the sand, single rounds pinged off metal. No one shouted orders; everyone out there knew exactly what was going on and what they had to do.

Stray bullets ricocheted off the Cat, but all the fire appeared to be directed between the two groups. After the initial automatic fire, shots seemed to be directed; there was no wild covering fire and sometimes several seconds ticked by in silence.

Until the second grenade exploded.

The night turned orange in an enormous fireball as another of the rescue team's vehicles was hit. In the sudden light Leila saw several bodies on the ground – some in black uniform, others in desert cammo. Both groups had taken heavy casualties. A figure ran from behind the remaining headlights and into the darkness. He was momentarily illuminated by the fires from the RPG strikes, then was gone.

The radio in the Cat's cab crackled. Leila's guard looked at her and shrugged.

'We wait,' he said. 'No way I'm wading through that shit to answer the call.' By now the front seats had melted down to their metal frames and much of the dashboard was a shapeless mess. A voice spoke in Hebrew through the radio's speaker.

'There's no one left,' the guard said. 'That's base asking if there's anyone in here.'

The message was repeated over the radio, but again it went unanswered.

'And now they think there isn't,' Leila said.

'Then it's up to us. Their side has taken a lot of hits too. Apart from that guy who just ran south, my guess is they're all dead or out of action. If there was anyone else, they'd have mounted another attempt on you by now.'

'So if they're down to one, and we're down to us, the question becomes: who gets more people here first?'

'They do.'

'But you've got bases all over. If they're freelancers, they may not even have reinforcements in the country.'

'Reid, nor do we.'

'What?'

'This was a closed mission. Whoever you are, there are barely a dozen people who know about you. Most of them are tucked up in bed in Tel Aviv. By the time they assemble another rescue unit – assuming they even bother to now that they think we're both dead anyway – whoever wants you so much they're prepared to kill us all to get you will have sent in more forces of their own.'

From the orange glow of the vehicle fires south of their position there were four single shots in quick succession.

With the IDF team now eliminated the sniper had a perfect line on the remaining actors in this improvised battle. With each shot, one of the lights on the vehicles beside the Cat went out. They were plunged into almost total darkness. Only the smoky glow of the fires and the silvery light of the quarter moon low on the horizon gave any light at all. That was not going to be enough to see anyone who knew what they were doing approaching their position. And he would. With all competition eliminated, he was not going to just give up and let them walk away.

'We need to get out of here while we still can,' Leila said.

'You're staying here,' the guard said.

'Like hell I am. Look, they want me alive, right?' The guard nodded. 'That guy's got clear sight of us, so if we both get out it's you he's going to fire at.'

'Wow, you're really selling that one!'

'No, listen. You draw his fire, I'll get a direction on him. And the last thing he's going to expect is me being armed.'

'You'll never see him. Our night scopes are at the front of the vehicle. If they still exist at all.'

'I can aim at his muzzle flash. Putting out all the lights has actually given us as much of an advantage as it's given him.'

'You sure about this?' the guard said. 'I've been doing this a long time, and believe me, there's nothing in the manuals about deliberately stepping out in front of a hidden sniper.'

'I'm sure we don't have a choice. Unless you fancy trying your buddies on the radio. No? So let's get on with it while he still thinks he's got us pinned.'

The guard opened a metal cabinet beneath the seat and threw three bullet clips to her. He then opened the side door of the Cat and slid the body of his colleague out to act as a blocker preventing the sniper hitting him under the vehicle. As Leila replaced the almost empty clip on the rifle, he dropped out himself. There was no incoming fire.

The guard let off a single pistol round. Two single shots came back, ricocheting off the Cat's armour and whining off into the darkness. Leila opened the rear door and dropped to the ground, covering the angle to the shooter with the huge back tyre.

The guard fired again; again two shots returned. They were sizing each other up, and that gave Leila all the information she needed. The shooter was about thirty yards away. The muzzle flash seemed to spread out across the ground immediately in front of it, so it was not being fired from any height. He was in a blind where she would not be able to hit him until he raised his head to fire. She was only going to get one chance.

'Draw him out,' Leila whispered. She wasn't sure the guard had heard her for a moment, then she heard the click of a new magazine being rammed home and he let off a long stream of bullets.

Leila aimed the rifle as best she could in the dark. The ground was momentarily lit up by another shot from the blind. She squeezed the trigger and released a two-second burst of fire, sweeping the barrel a couple of degrees in each direction.

There was a moment's silence, then automatic fire lit up the night again, this time in her direction. Leila scrambled along the Cat and took cover beside her guard.

'Missed,' Leila hissed, slipping a second full clip into the rifle. 'He knows there's two of us now.'

'I'm going to make for their cars, widen his angle. As soon as he fires, stand up and empty the magazine at him. We're not going to get a third chance.'

'OK. Be careful.'

'I always am.' He slapped her on the shoulder, glanced in the direction of the sniper, then ran for the vehicles on their right, firing the pistol with every step. The sniper strafed the ground along a line where he was running. There was a dry click as Leila's guard ran out of ammunition, then a skidding thud as he dived for the cover of the car.

Leila stood, took aim over the rear wing of the Cat and squeezed the trigger. Her firing was wilder than it would have been on the police range, but it was effective. There was a dull cry and the muzzle flash turned in her direction. Bullets cracked over her head. She let off another burst then everything went silent.

She clicked over to manual fire and let off another half dozen shots. There was no return.

'You OK?' she called. No reply. She fired again at the blind and heard the bullet thump into the ground thirty yards away. When the echo of her shot had died away in the stillness of the night she ran over to the dark shape that was her guard.

He was dead. He'd taken a bullet in the head. The skidding thud at the end of his run was not him diving for cover. He was most likely dead well before he hit the ground.

Smoke drifted from the IDF vehicle that had taken the grenade, and all around were the shapes of fallen men, their blood picked out like jewels in the moonlight.

It was 4.17am and Leila was once again completely alone.

15

Leila slung the rifle over her shoulder and picked up the guard's pistol. With a new clip salvaged from his webbing, she let off a single test shot to make sure the dry click she'd heard was indeed him running out of ammunition and not a jam. She did a quick recce of the scene, and found only corpses. The combination of extreme aggression, skill, a need for speed and over-the-top firepower had ensured total mutual destruction. She was on her own, and she couldn't stay here in the hope that the next people to arrive would be coming to help.

The SandCat they had arrived in had two flat tyres and, most likely, a broken driveshaft. And that was just what was obvious in the dark; there could have been more. The acid also meant that even if it had been mechanically sound, it had no front seats, dashboard or steering wheel. The two IDF rescue vehicles – lightly armoured MDT personnel carriers – had been utterly destroyed by the grenades, and the two vehicles their attackers had arrived in were riddled with bullets. Among the wreckage she hoped there might still be something that could be made to serve her purposes.

Her first move had to be to get to a populated area and

contact Michael Lawrence. She had no idea what she had dropped into but she knew she was going to need a lot of help to get out of it. She was confident her old boss had already started pulling the right strings to make things happen. He might have understood her need to quit CTC after the siege last week, but he wouldn't have just sat back and watched as she vanished off the face of the earth. He'd probably have been to her house already when she failed to answer any calls or file a report on the operation. With the mess her house was in after the burglary-that-wasn't-a-burglary by Black Eagle he would have known something was wrong. She now needed to update him on how badly wrong it was.

Behind the Land Rovers the lights of a city twinkled in the distance, maybe ten miles away. Her guard had said his task had been to take her to Be'er Sheva, so those lights were, hopefully, shining from that ancient biblical settlement of seven wells. Or whatever sprawling industrial city had been built over it. Whatever it was, it was big and it was bright, and that was exactly what she needed right now.

She might be able to walk it in three hours, but she did not fancy the idea of being so exposed for so long. Even if this was a covert mission that only a handful of top brass in Tel Aviv knew about, the RPG blasts and lack of radio contact would send someone out to investigate eventually. There was no cover in which she could avoid the oncoming patrols, so walking for three hours was asking for trouble. She would have to use one of the remaining vehicles to get her closer the city and hope it was not spotted. A bullet-holed car out here would raise exactly the sorts of questions she was neither qualified nor willing to answer.

The Land Rover from which the RPG had been fired was relatively intact. It had been peppered with holes, but the vehicle in front of it had protected most of the important bits from stray fire. Fortunately the sniper shooting from his blind thirty yards away had been accurate enough to take the headlights out without hitting the radiator or anything else. The keys were still in the ignition and it started after just a few wheezing attempts. While it idled she returned to the Cat and dug her backpack out from beneath the rear seat. It had come this far with her, she wasn't going to leave it behind now. It was no longer an operational kit so much as a talisman.

With the rifle on the seat beside her and her guard's Jericho 941 in her lap, she turned the Land Rover round and headed back onto the main road. Without headlights and the moon now dipping below the horizon, she drove hunched over the wheel, peering into the night. It was not as difficult as it might have been.

It was a little before five in the morning when she came within sight of a vast industrial complex to the west of the road, a menacing sprawl of chimneys and metal buildings behind a high fence. Dawn was creeping over the horizon on her right and with every passing second the covering darkness was shrinking away. It would not be long before she would have to ditch the bullet-riddled car. A truck pulled out in front of her some quarter of a mile ahead and she fell in behind it as it lumbered towards the city, close enough that she could follow its hulking black shape in a kind of stupor and switch off for a few minutes.

A couple of miles later, with the first of Be'er Sheva's outer settlements strung out along the roadside, vehicle lights twinkled in the distance, coming towards her. She had seen vehicles now and then along the highway, though at this time of the morning very few that were heading out of the city towards the desert. What they all had in common was the one thing her own car lacked – a fine, matched pair of headlights. And that was why she noticed this new vehicle particularly. The lights were low to the ground, and there were at least four of them. Two more were mounted high on the roof. It was either a heavily customised civilian off-roader or it was military.

She pulled out from behind the tanker. They were too far away to see who it was, but there was a good chance it had come from the military compound on the edge of the city – the place General Yaniv had called Camp Nathan; the place where she should now be enjoying a snooze in a quiet cell followed by a fine middle eastern breakfast. The place they had been expecting her to arrive at hours ago.

She moved up closer to the back of the truck, keeping a little way out towards the middle of the road to watch the oncoming vehicle. Against the lightening sky she saw the silhouette of a gun turret on the roof: another SandCat. Strange that there was only one of them – stranger still that it had taken them so long to mobilise forces to get out to the scene of the battle. Surely no one could have missed the two RPG fireballs even from this distance. Maybe this approaching Cat was nothing to do with her, just a routine patrol, but she couldn't take that chance. It was barely a mile away, and there was nowhere to hide.

She dropped back slightly and moved into the blindspot behind the tanker. She was doing forty. If the SandCat was doing the same, a mile ahead, she had around forty-five seconds before it would pass her. With so few other vehicles on the road she was going to be impossible to miss. .

The right edge of the road dropped slightly into desert strewn with small stones and the occasional boulder. There was no cover whatever.

Twenty seconds. Assuming her estimate of the Cat's closing speed was right.

Ten. The tanker driver gave a long blast on his horn and Leila moved. She swung the Land Rover right into the desert and floored the accelerator. The car bumped and jerked over the stony ground and she could see almost nothing in the cloud of dust thrown up by the truck as it too pulled into the dust to give the approaching SandCat plenty of room. The tanker driver gave another short blast on the horn. Leila kept her foot down and cleared the length of the truck in seconds. She steered back onto the road, fighting to bring the Land Rover back into a straight line. There was no sign of the Cat. As the truck shrank in the rear-view mirror she moved out into the centre of the road. Way behind them the armoured car was continuing its journey. She'd got lucky this time, but if this little posse was heading out to the battle scene it wouldn't be long before they realised there was one very important body missing from the carnage. And from that discovery it would be a fair guess that she'd made her way towards the only town of any size in the area.

By the time they widened their search, she needed to be gone.

16

Donald Aquila's limo was making its way through the rain-soaked streets of Frankfurt when Guy Roth's final call came through. The ex-Royal Marines mercenary was pinned down in an improvised shooter's blind in the desert, thirty yards away from an armed Leila Reid and her last remaining guard. In the battle that would surely follow, Aquila would have backed Reid every time, whether it was a battle of skill, will, intelligence or simple luck. Although he couldn't know it, as his driver turned into Kennedyallee, his bet had paid off. Shortly after his final contact with Roth, his hired gun had taken the military escort out with a lucky shot to the head, but he himself was now dead too, and Reid had once again slipped through the net.

Fifteen hours earlier, in that critical window when Leila was still airborne, confident she could make the plane go up and down and left and right, but not yet sure how she was going to make it stop completely, he had paid a visit to the safe house south west of Jerusalem. Golzar was still alive, though the doctor had departed for his condo in Bet Shemesh saying her chances were slim unless she was taken to a proper hospital. That was not an option, but on balance

Aquila was happy enough with the outcome of the operation in London. As long as the world thought Golzar was alive Black Eagle had a negotiating position, and with Reid out of the way – her plane would run out of fuel very soon and dump her into the ocean – things could be moved along nicely at his Frankfurt meeting.

He had not been angry – or even particularly surprised – when Roth's call had come through informing him that Reid had managed to get the plane under control. The tranc dart he'd used to bring her down at Epping Airfield had, he realised too late, been designed for much bigger prey. She'd been easy to handle, but had been out of it for over twenty-four hours. When she did come round she barely knew her own name, but throughout their interrogation she retained enough of her wile and composure not to give them a single useful fact. And she never wavered from her position of loyalty to Queen and Country either. They might have more or less fried her mind for four days, but they had never broken the woman inside.

The dose of sedatives they'd given her to get her back on the plane had been more modest. Enough to keep her sleeping through the flight, but not to kill her. Apparently, it had not really even been enough to do either. Aquila had to give her full marks for initiative, especially when his driver out there in the Negev told him she had actually survived her improvised landing, albeit said landing had attracted a lot of the wrong kind of attention from the locals. She was resourceful.

He had hung up on Roth and smiled as he walked back to the kitchen and poured another mug of coffee from the jug. If this could be handled right, things might work out even better than he had thought. DS Reid was indeed resourceful, and he admired that – he'd admired Leila Reid since she first crossed his radar two years earlier. It was just a shame that when they had finally met last week it had been under such stressful circumstances. Circumstances that had meant decisions needed to be made quickly, and they needed to be final.

Or so he had thought. With CTC's most naturally talented detective, 'final' was not quite as terminal as it would be with most people.

He took his coffee up through the hatch smashed through the farmhouse roof and sat in one of the plastic chairs that looked out over the desert. He wouldn't be here long. He was a cold-climate man. The sun annoyed him, but he was sick of the stifling air of the safe house. Why his men all had such a taste for curry and pizza was beyond him. That he had to inhale the fumes from their disgusting food – and fumes from other disgusting places – was a source of deep irritation to a man of his sensibilities. A few minutes on the roof would give him time – and oxygen – to think. And with Reid back in the picture, he needed to think.

In front of him a sniper lay looking along the narrow road that led from the main highway to this house nestling in a hidden valley. Behind him the scrubby hills folded their arms around the property in a secret embrace. The place was well hidden, easily defended, secure. It was not entirely unknown, but fine for short operations where they could be in and out before too many leaks could spring and secrecy was compromised too badly. Black Eagle had few resources in Israel. This old farm was more or less the limit of their real estate, and the number or operatives they could call up at short notice struggled to make it into double figures. One was lying in front of him, two others were guarding the inside of the farm. Three in Tel Aviv; four in Jerusalem; Guy Roth out in the Negev somewhere and their pilot waiting for pickup.

He took a swig of coffee. If it could be called that.

As things stood, Reid had survived her improvised landing and had been picked up by Special Forces. Special Forces meant she had ended up somewhere very sensitive, which in turn meant they wouldn't keep her there for long. Sooner or later – probably after an emergency interrogation, a bit of back-and-forth among that secret interface between top military and government, and some hastily made arrangements – she would be moved. Probably under cover of darkness. Diplomacy, the Achilles Heel of all right-thinking democratic nations, meant she would not be made to disappear completely, at least not immediately. But they would take her to a military camp, not a civilian prison.

'Aston!' he called. The sniper turned, swept his cap back and looked up at Aquila from his prostrate position at the front of the roof. 'Is there a military prison in the Negev?'

Stu Aston through for a moment.

'Nothing big. Four and Six, the main two, are further north. There's a detention centre at Camp Nathan, just south of Be'er Sheva. About it, I think.'

Aquila nodded. It was a long shot, but it didn't feel too long. When an idea's right, it has a resonance to it. Some people call it instinct, gut, hunch-think. Whatever it was,

Aquila trusted his. If he could get people into the area between the crash site and Be'er Sheva in the next six hours, he was in with a shot of getting Reid back. And his gut, his hunch-think, told him that getting Leila Reid back under his control was even more important than regaining control of the prisoner who now lay in a cot hooked up to drip lines and painkillers in the room below. He fancied a second run at CTC's finest. There were things he still wanted to discuss with her.

He dialled the phone. It rang three, four, five time then Guy Roth picked up.

'Status?' he said without preamble.

'They've taken her, alive. Three SandCats. Just loaded her up, heading out north now. You want me to follow?'

'No. If they're Specials you won't intercept her. We've got an idea where she's going to end up though. I need you to assemble a team. Get Tel Aviv and Jerusalem together, whoever you can mobilise. Two vehicles.'

'Everyone?'

Aquila thought for a moment. 'No. Take military, leave one intelligence operative in each location. Just in case.'

'What's the op?'

'They'll move her. It's guesswork, but I want people on the road south of Be'er Sheva from sundown tonight. We'll try to monitor movements as best we can from here and tell you if we find anything.'

'You want her alive or dead?'

'Alive, at all costs. She's not going to remember much in the next six to twelve hours, so she won't know what the hell's going on. Persuade her your mission is a rescue, not an assault. But you'll have to go in hard. If they're using the SandCat to transport her, you'll have to get creative. Take RPGs for show, but use your wits to get her out. OK?'

'No problem. We'll be there. You tell us where the target is, we'll get her out.'

Aquila hung up. He took a final swig of coffee and poured the remaining half mug away. If he was right, Reid would be here at the safe house in a few hours, a day at most. And if he was wrong – if the transport didn't take place, or if Roth and his men had to retreat without her – they'd just try again. And again. And again. He'd keep one man in Tel Aviv to keep an eye on the Embassy, another in Jerusalem. They knew where she was now, and most importantly, they knew she was alive. Even if they failed to get her in the desert, her options would be very limited after that, and her movements predictable. She'd never get out of the country.

What he hated about this otherwise favourable turn of the cards was that he was not going to be around to supervise the operation himself. He was due in Frankfurt first thing the following morning and needed to be in Tel Aviv to get the jet at about the time Roth and his men would be assembling on the highway south of Be'er Sheva.

And so he was. He boarded the Learjet 75 (his replacement for the elderly and scruffy plane that had been destined for scrappage in the deepest part of the red Red Sea until Reid had flown it into the desert) at 9pm. He was in Frankfurt when Roth's final call came in from his sandy shooter's blind out in the desert. The ex-Royal Marine sounded desperate.

'They're all dead,' he whispered. Aquila didn't reply. He stared out of the window of the limo that was taking him on the thirty minute drive into the city. Frankfurt shone in the rain of the cool dark night. Just how Donald Aquila liked it.

'Reid is still alive,' Roth went on. 'All our men are gone. IDF rescue team ambushed us. They're dealt with, but Reid and her Specials guard are still out there.'

'Close?'

'I can see them. What do you want me to do?'

'Where are you?'

'Who knows. Pinned down, but there's two of them, and Reid's armed.'

'Then there's not much I can do for you, is there? You are paid to solve problems, not ask questions. Recapture Reid or we have no further use for you. Goodbye, Mr Roth.'

He hung up. The limo turned onto Kennedyallee heading for the hotel and the meeting at which Aquila had hoped to announce the recapture, and maybe even final recruitment, of his most enigmatic and elusive of prizes.

Leila Reid had escaped him again, but at least she was still alive. Their paths would cross again soon. He'd make sure of that.

17

Leila ditched the Land Rover a mile or so south of the city. She had floored the accelerator and put as much distance between herself and the military patrol as possible. She slowed a little when other vehicles approached, but there had been only a handful. When the city came too close to ignore, she knew she was going to have to get rid of the car and break the last link between herself and the carnage back down the highway. There was nowhere to hide it, so she didn't try. She pulled off the road and abandoned it in a patch of scrub that marked the start of what appeared to be a well-worn hiking trial. It would attract attention eventually, but from the road it was not immediately obvious that it was abandoned or, more importantly, that it had seen some seriously hostile action before it got there. It would be assumed to be a vehicle parked up by a fisherman, a hunter, someone who couldn't be bothered to walk all the way from the highway. With the shot-out headlights and bullet-pocked body her efforts to make it look legitimate would make no difference in the end, but every tiny advantage she could gain might make a big difference for a while.

Two things she had taken from the battle site would, unfortunately, no longer be able to offer her an advantage, tiny or otherwise. She pushed the rifle under the seat, then with great reluctance wedged the pistol in beside it. She would have preferred to keep at least the little Jericho hand gun, but it would be too dangerous. Sooner or later she would have to dump it, and doing so in the city would be risky. Being caught with it would be worse. And if she was ambushed again before she could get to the city, this little pistol was not really going to do her much good against a rocket propelled grenade anyway.

She slung her backpack onto her shoulder and began to walk. The tanker passed her a few minutes later as she cut an oblique line back across the scrubby desert towards the road. There were other vehicles on the road now too. Nothing military, just civilian cars heading into the city from the outlying settlements. No one paid any attention to the lone walker kicking up dust from the edges of the road.

After half a mile or so the rattle of a big engine approached from behind. She turned, momentarily panicked that the Cat was heading back from the battle site, probably having already reported the absence of the target of their operation. She turned and saw the unmistakable square form of a bus cresting a small rise half a mile back. Her progress was too slow: sooner or later the Cat *would* be back, and she needed to get off the road before it did. Flagging down the bus to take her the last mile or two into the anonymity of the city was better than being stuck out here now that the sun was about to break the line of hills to her east. The bus rumbled to a stop and the doors hissed open.

The driver spoke so little English that Leila could only demonstrate her lack of local money with the universal mime-show of turning her pockets out and shrugging sadly. She looked dirty and tired, but by no means disreputable, and the driver took pity on her. He did his own mime of magnanimity and waived payment. They both knew it would cost him more to change her British currency than the ride was worth. The bus picked up just a few more passengers as it threaded its way thorough the city's outer suburbs and after twenty minutes they pulled into a sprawling grey bus station downtown. The driver pointed her at a shopping centre that was beginning to open up. She saw from the his watch that it was 6.22am.

Leila sat in a bench beneath an elderly tamarisk tree. Already the morning was heating up and the sun cast long lazy shadows along the straight streets. This was a typical desert town – flat, dusty and deathly still in the dawn light. Even at six thirty there were people about: street cleaners, shopkeepers, businessmen in suits, getting to wherever they had to be before the heat became unbearable. While store owners raised the metal shutters and turned on the lights in cafés and takeaways catering to the commuter crowd, Leila sat taking in her surroundings.

She couldn't stay here. This would be the first place they'd look – whichever 'they' were coming first. Both the military and whoever had been behind the original ambush that brought them to a sudden stop in a hail of bullets and fire would quickly track her down. They would see she was no longer in the desert, they'd spot the Land Rover from air or from the road, and they'd pick up her trail. And that was only the two groups she had run into so far. By now the British authorities also knew she was here – but not why – and they too would be very keen to get her back under control as soon as possible. Depending on what theory they had settled on to explain her incarceration by Israeli Special Forces, it was far from certain that they were hunting her to give her a nice cup of tea and a first class flight home.

Most of the shop signs were in Hebrew, so she scouted the area around the shopping centre until she found a café-sandwich-bar that had its breakfast menu doubled-up on the board in English. She went inside and stood behind a middle-aged man buying pastries and coffee for what appeared to be his entire office building. When he was finished, she stepped up.

'Good morning', she said. The young woman behind the counter looked surprised for a moment, then smiled.

'Boker tov. How can I help you?'

'I've got a problem,' Leila said. The server nodded – *I can see that* – but said nothing. Leila dug into her backpack and pulled out the little roll of bank notes.

'I've only got Sterling,' she said. 'Any chance you could change some for me? I don't care about the exchange rate, just need enough Shekels to get me through the day.'

'Had a busy night?' the girl said.

'Something like that.'

'No problem. We get British tourists in here often enough. I'll be able to change it back. How much do you need?'

Leila peeled two twenty pound notes from the roll.

'As I said, just whatever you can manage.'

The girl opened the till and took out some small bills and coins and handed them over.

'Thank you. Appreciate it.'

'You OK?' the girl said. 'I can help you with more than change if you need it. I can call someone? Police?'

'No, really. Looks worse than it is. You can help me with one thing though. Now I'm cashed up, for my first purchase I'll take a full English and the biggest coffee you can do, please.' She handed back the requisite amount.

'No problem,' the girl said with a knowing smile. Leila took a seat a little way back from the window. She could see out but anyone outside in the blinding low sun would have a hard time spotting her at a casual glance. Her order was passed back to the kitchen and the girl moved on to her next customer, a young woman again buying takeaway coffee and cake on an industrial scale. It was a popular café, and with the right kind of people for Leila's taste. People on their way to work – office juniors mostly, doing the drinks run, up too early, concentrating more on getting their bosses' sufganiyah or kichel right than on a dusty stranger – gave her a sense of anonymity. It was good to fade into the background for a while. It was essential.

She needed information as much as she needed help. She would call Michael at home – but not from here. She was not going to drag this nice little business with its friendly owner and on-the-clock clientele into her mess – she would need to find a public phone. Of all the people who were looking for her, Michael was the only one she really trusted right now. It would still be early – two hours behind her time here – which would improve her chances of catching him before he went into Scotland Yard. She needed to speak to the man, not the counter-terrorism agent.

Breakfast arrived – a full English more English than anything she'd had at home for years. It only occurred to her as she stared at this thing of beauty how unlikely it was that she would have got sausage and bacon out here. But she had, and it looked fabulous. Fried tomato, two fried eggs and a portion of baked beans, over-cooked and slightly dry, exactly as she liked them. And a pot of coffee. Not a cup or a mug of weak instant dish-water, but proper freshly-brewed stuff. The elixir of life.

As she ate she tried to get the facts of the last few days straight. The ice that had locked away the memories of everything that had led her onto that pilotless plane over the Sinai Desert had mostly melted in the heat of the events of the last twenty-four hours. But she still had no memory of the days between being in London in the early hours of Saturday morning and waking up on the plane on Wednesday morning. Four days. While it was good that her longer-term memory was now clear, the black hole of those four days was worrying.

Fortunately, she couldn't have done a lot in that hole in time: whatever she had been drugged with at Epping Airport had not been capable of wiping out existing memories; it simply prevented her from forming new ones. In such a drugged state she would not have been doing much more than talking – but she undoubtedly had talked. Whoever was behind her abduction had finished with her by the time the pilot bailed out over the Negev shortly before she came round. So she had told them what they wanted to know, or at least convinced them that she had told them all she knew.

But why Israel? They could have interrogated her in London. They could have killed her and dumped her at sea anywhere along the British coast and no one would ever have known. So why fly her all the way out here to dispose of her?

The only answer was that she was collateral to another operation. They were coming here anyway and using the time involved in travelling to do what they needed to with her. Disposing of her out here was not an integral part of the plan, it was mere pragmatism, convenience.

And there was only one operation that could possibly have been important enough to justify such an insane level of expense and risk...

As dawn broke on Saturday morning she had shot the weapons expert Raha Golzar as she hid in the boot of Donald Aquila's diplomatic Lexus. The woman Black Eagle had bombed a London hotel and taken a building full of hostages to break out of jail was dead. Job done. Black Eagle's ambitions to bring Russia into their fold had been thwarted, at least for now.

But there was much more to it than that. Something that might explain Leila's own unexpected presence in Israel.

Raha Golzar had a long and complex history, and that history intersected perfectly with Leila's situation right now. Golzar's last job before being snatched by SIS agents working with the CIA fifteen months earlier and finding herself in a British jail awaiting extradition and trial in the Middle East, had been here in Israel. Jerusalem, at the crossroads of world, was where she plied her trade in counterintelligence recruitment.

So had Black Eagle come back to Israel with Leila in tow because Raha Golzar was still alive? Had she somehow survived the shooting? Had Donald Aquila's plan worked out, and Golzar was now back here to pick up exactly where she left off more than a year earlier? And had Leila been brought along in case she could be persuaded to use her own particular set of talents and contacts to ensure that this time nothing would go wrong?

The only crumb of comfort in this was the fact that Black Eagle had, in the end, gone to so much trouble and expense to dispose of her. She might have given them something, but she had obviously resisted their attempts at recruitment.

She had to know whether Golzar was still alive, and if she was still here in Israel.

And there was only one person she trusted to get her anywhere near a truth as dangerous as that.

18

The phone rang just ten minutes before the alarm was due to wake Michael Lawrence for another day. Not that he would have needed the alarm clock any more than he needed the phone to wake him. He'd dozed off a little after 2am and woken again soon after 4. It was already getting light and his chance of sleep had gone again for another night. He lay still in the hot airless bedroom, unwilling to get up and start another day. With their principle player, DS Reid, absent, whereabouts unknown, the job of investigating last week's attacks was proving far tougher than it should have been. He was in no great hurry to start in on it once more. But staying in bed offered no peace. His mind was on and churning. It was, yet again, trying to make a meaningful picture out of a jigsaw puzzle with most of the pieces missing – and quite a few extra pieces that had no place in this puzzle to begin with.

The Prime Minister had taken a temporary leave of absence, retreating to Chequers to lick his wounds after the humiliating failure of the peace talks and the murder of his daughter, Ruth. Aaron David had flown on to Washington and Abu Queria (minus one of his aides killed in the Mapleton siege) had returned to Ramallah. Operation Orchard had been initiated to look into the events surrounding the riots that Black Eagle had so skilfully fomented on the streets of London to cover their operation, and Thames House was trying to shore up their position of having no idea that any of it was going to happen… that they had no idea Black Eagle even existed until Donald Aquila and his men had so dramatically exploded onto the scene.

With Leila Reid at the centre of this maelstrom, Michael himself was under almost intolerable pressure – legal and professional – to supply answers. He also hoped he might find a way to save his troublesome friend in the process. He'd brought her into this; he had a moral obligation if no other to do what he could to get her out again.

The sun shone through the crack in the curtains and he propped himself up on one elbow to look out into the bright clear morning just as the phone rang. He glanced at the clock – five fifty-six. A call at this time of the morning was not going to be good news.

The phone buzzed again and Michael picked it up. His wife was still asleep. She always slept through his alarm, so she was not going to be woken by the soft purr of his phone.

'INTERNATIONAL' was all the display said. No number, no name. He swung his legs out of bed as he answered the call.

'Michael,' a voice said.

'Leila?' He walked quickly to the bedroom door.

'I don't have long, I'm on a payphone.'

'Where?'

'Be'er Sheva.'

'Are you OK? Leila, what's…'

'That's why I'm calling. Michael, do you know anything? Do you know how I got here?'

'To Israel? No. They're trying to make a picture out a lot of unconnected bits, but none of it makes any sense.' He glanced back at his sleeping wife and quietly closed the door behind him. 'Why did you just disappeared after Mapleton? Where have you been for the last four days?'

'Slow down. I have no idea. But I'm going to find out. Michael, they told you I'd crashed that plane deliberately…'

'And you picked a hell of a place to do it!'

'I had no idea where I was. I'd still be guessing exactly what I flew into. You've got to believe that.'

'I do, and we can sort all this out once we've got you back. You're not with the IDF now?'

'I'm not sure I ever was. I'm not sure of anything right now, but no, I got away. Long story. I'm on my own and so far it doesn't look like I've been followed.'

'Can you get to Tel Aviv?'

'Undetected is going to be a challenge, but at least I'm in civilisation now so there'll be transport…'

'Go to the Embassy. I'll make some calls, prepare the ground.'

'What does that mean?'

'It means right now I can't be certain what you'll be walking into. But it's still your best – probably only – option. If you hand yourself in, we can get you through this.'

Leila didn't speak for several seconds. In the background he could hear the low murmur of voices and the rattle of an old diesel engine, a bus maybe or a truck.

'Leila?'

'Yes,' she said. 'OK. I've got to go: I'm out of money.'

The line went dead.

Michael jogged downstairs to the study. To his boss, to his department, to the intelligence services in general, that call would have answered nothing. To Michael it answered the most important question of all. Leila was still theirs. Whatever he had heard in that final conversation from Epping Airport, Reid had not defected. The logic of his certainty was not strong, it was a gut feeling, and if Leila had taught him one thing (she had taught him a lot, but most of it was not immediately pertinent to their current situation), it was to trust a good intuition. It was possible that she would have called him even if her intentions were duplicitous, a way of getting back in as a double agent, but he'd have known. It would have been in her voice – a hardness, a slight tightness he heard when she was interrogating some of their tougher customers. No one else would pick it up; no one else knew her like he did, had seen her in enough contexts to be sensitised to the details.

And maybe more importantly, more convincingly, was the fact that Leila would have known he'd have seen through her lies. She would not have risked calling him, risked him seeing her duplicity. He was, in fact, the last person she would have risked exposing herself to.

Unless, of course, it was a clever double bluff.

He flopped down into his leather desk chair and leaned his head in his hands. Whichever way he looked at this, there was always a counter-argument. It was four minutes past six in the morning and already he felt exhausted.

He dialled Commander Thorne's desk number at Scotland Yard. It rang three times and went to voicemail. He hung up without speaking. He brought up the phone's directory again and paused. If Thorne wasn't at the office there was no point trying his mobile. He needed someone who could act now. He had to get Leila back on British soil where she could persuade those who needed persuading that the last four days had been as much a mystery – and a nightmare – for her as they had been for everyone who was searching for her. And time for that was short.

He went into the kitchen, put the coffee machine on and dialled the main CTC switchboard. The phone was answered quickly.

'This is DCI Lawrence,' he said.

'Yes, Sir.' Of course it was. His caller ID would have told them that before the phone was even picked up. He rubbed his hand across his eyes.

'Put me through to tech. Whoever you've got there.'

'Connecting you, Sir.'

The line rang again, then a man answered, speaking as if through a mouthful of food.

'Good morrow! Fielding fielding your call!'

'Sam? It's DCI Lawrence.'

A pause. Food being quickly swallowed. 'Sorry,' Fielding said. 'I was expecting an internal. Been a long night. How can I help you, Sir?'

'Can you lift the call logs from the phone I'm using now?' he said.

'Sure. Give me a minute. What's your password, passcode, whatever?'

Michael gave him the six digit code that unlocked the iPhone when his fingerprint mysteriously refused to do the job. The phone went silent; the display went blank. Then Fielding came back on the line.

'Got it,' he said. 'What am I looking for?'

'The last connected call before Commander Thorne's voicemail was an incoming international number. It's a callbox somewhere in Be'er Sheva. Get a location, then contact Thorne and tell him it's where DS Reid is right now.'

'The Commander's not due in until eight,' Fielding said.

'Then call him at home. Don't take this to anyone else. He'll want to act on this himself and Reid's not going to stay put for long.'

'I'll get on to it.'

Michael ended the call. The percolator bubbled and he poured himself a mug of coffee and returned to the study.

Five minutes later the phone rang. It was James Thorne.

'Good work on Reid,' he said. 'Fielding's got a location. Unfortunately, SIS have no one on the ground in Be'er Sheva. Of course they don't. They're sending an agent from Tel Aviv, but best case it's going to be an hour before he can get there. What did Reid say?'

'Very little. She claims she has no idea why she's in Israel or how she got there.'

'And you believe her?'

'Without question.' *Almost* without question. He would question his own name before that first coffee had worked its magic. But his gut reaction had been that she was telling the truth, and right now she needed at least one person who would stick to that conviction.

'Do you know where she's heading?' Thorne said.

'I told her to make her way to the Embassy in Tel Aviv and we'd bring her in from there.'

'She agreed?'

'That might be presuming a lot, but I think she'll realise it's her only option.'

Thorne was silent for several seconds then said: 'You know her better than anyone. How would you handle this?'

'Let her take the initiative. She's clever, she's resourceful and she's being hunted. We've got very little chance of intercepting her in Be'er Sheva. SIS are too far out, and other interested parties are far closer. One way or another, by the time our people get there she'll be gone. So our best chance is to let her come to us in Tel Aviv. And that means giving her free passage to get to the Embassy.'

'Not try to pick her up? She'll be taking the bus or the train. There's a limited number of options, and we can probably cover them.'

'Even if SIS found her, they'd have no chance of being able to contain her. She'll be vigilant. If anyone suspicious gets on the train – or even more so the bus – she'll bolt. Plus, as I said, she's got more than just us looking for her. The more options we close off, the more danger she'll be in. Let her go to the Embassy unhindered.'

'OK. I'll brief the Ambassador, get them to put extra security on stand by. It seems she's managed to escape from the Israeli military. Which means she'll be armed...'

19

It took a little over an hour and a half to get to Tel Aviv by bus. Leila positioned herself three rows behind the driver – if anyone got on and started to quiz him she was close enough to use the element of surprise to bolt for the door. It didn't give her much of an advantage, but it was better than being trapped at the back, and less obvious than sitting right by the door itself. Her only problem was the red rucksack. Her constant companion for days now was impossible to disguise, yet she was reluctant to give it up. She kept it between her feet, one hand wrapped firmly around the grab-strap at the top.

The journey seemed interminable, and the bus was full by the time they got to the outskirts of the city. But she'd got lucky. No one who got on paid her any attention and there was no one waiting for her at the main bus station. She mingled with the disembarking passengers and allowed herself to be carried along with the slow flow of people heading out of the station, then took a roundabout route into the central business district and found a tourist information booth. No one followed her and there was no one listening as she got directions to the Embassy. The middle-aged woman who highlighted the busses and walking routes on a free tourist map didn't look suspicious, and made no joke about why this scruffy, dusty English woman with a mostly-empty old red backpack would want to go all the way across the city to see one of the dullest buildings in the area, but she would remember the encounter. Leila was beginning to leave a trail that would not be hard to follow.

The British Embassy was easy enough to find in the Old North area of the city, almost on the coast overlooking the brilliant blue Mediterranean. From the map she could see there was a large marina and a park to the west, long beaches to the south (which might allow some chance of escape if necessary), and a river blocking her path to the north (which certainly would not). East would take her back into the labyrinthine streets of the city. Now she was on the ground, several large international hotels made their monstrous presences felt around the Embassy in a way the map could not convey. The area would attract a useful blend of business people, tourists, day-trippers and contractors, a mix she could get lost in.

She approached the Embassy from the east, walked past it on the far side of the road, stopped, and walked back almost another block further north, out of sight of the building. She had seen enough to know that the place was not ringed with troops waiting for her.

On any other day, she would have gone straight up to the front gate. It was British sovereign soil. The IDF – or whoever it was who was looking for her – would not be able to touch her. She would also have an effective defence against whoever had killed her escort out in the desert. But today was not just any day. Michael had advised her to 'hand herself in', and that one unguarded phrase was enough to make her nervous. The British had been told she had crashed the plane in a highly restricted zone. Given that she could not account for the reasons behind this herself, she might be walking into as much trouble here as she had left behind last night. At least for now, out here on the street with its busses and taxis and people, she was free, she was anonymous and she still had some degree of control. One wrong move now and that could change, fast, and potentially for a very long time.

She crossed the busy six-lane highway away from the Embassy. Up a series of shallow concrete steps she entered the light cover of the park, then headed south again, across a small service road and into a thick band of trees and shrubs that shielded this side of the park from the road. Along the main highway to her right were apartment buildings: two multi-storey monstrosities, then a row of lower modern dwellings. On her far right were two huge hotels, and between them and the apartment blocks the road dropped down through a tunnel, somewhere beyond which lay the main central business district of the city. Behind her she could hear the sea lapping at the walls of the marina. From this relatively sheltered vantage point she could see the corner of the Embassy and get an idea of its routines before she committed herself.

It looked like a prison. Vertical shade slats mounted on the outer edge of its four balconied floors looked like bars. Spiked railings ran along the road edge, behind which were massive concrete blocks, lending it the subtle but powerful look of a fortified compound. An armed guard stood in a little guard house tight against the corner of the building. Once she was inside, escape would be impossible if she was walking into a trap.

It was now ten in the morning. A few men in suits and women in sober work attire came and went from the Embassy. However official they looked, the guard checked their papers whether they were arriving or leaving. When two backpackers arrived, they were subjected to questioning and a careful inspection of their papers that lasted more than five minutes. Eventually the gate was opened and they disappeared into the dark interior of the building.

A man dressed in jeans and a white t-shirt approached the guard station. Leila couldn't sit here all day waiting for something to happen. If it was going to happen, she would have to make the first move. She dodged her way back across the road and moved up behind him. He produced his passport. The guard radioed his colleagues inside the building and there was a long pause. Beyond the tinted glass of the sentry box Leila could see movement inside the main building, but no detail. All the windows were dark and only shadowy forms moved inside. After a couple of minutes the guard's radio crackled and the gate opened to let the visitor in.

Leila stepped up.

'I need consular assistance,' she said.

'Passport please,' the guard said. English accent, impossible to place. He was late forties, slim, fit, immaculate uniform, radio clipped to his epaulette, side arm in a holster at his hip, mirrored glasses. Probably ex-military. 'Passport?' he repeated.

'I've lost it. That's why I'm here.'

'Travel permits?'

Leila shook her head. The guard's stance implied he was looking casually over her shoulder at the street beyond, but that was the point of the glasses. He had her locked in eye contact even if he was the only one who knew it.

'You're a British citizen?' he said.

'Yes.'

'Name?'

'What's the point? I've no way of verifying it.'

The guard turned his head slightly, looking at her more obviously now. There was no question, no challenge. Just a look. Leila raised one eyebrow.

'You're not going anywhere until I know who you are,' he said.

'I'm British. I need help,' she said. 'And maybe I can be of some help to your Embassy at the same time.'

He stiffened a little and looked past her again along the street. This time his change of focus was real. He was searching for something, alert to threats. Definitely ex-military. Caution was in his DNA, and she had aroused it.

'You can help us?' he said. 'And how are you going to do that?'

'That's something I need to discuss with the Ambassador. He'll want to hear what I have to say.'

'Your name.' It was no longer a polite request.

'I was told to come here by British Counter-terrorism Command in London.'

Instantly his hand moved to the pistol on his belt. 'Put your bag on the floor and take two steps back,' he said. He took a step back himself. Leila slowly removed the backpack, placed it on the concrete between them and took two steps back. The guard's hand twitched on the gun, his mirrored gaze switching back and forth between the bag and her. She took another step.

'Hands on your head, fingers locked,' he said. '*Now!*'

'I work for CTC,' Leila said. She laced her fingers and placed them on top of her head, a gesture of submission she had seen so often in her old line of work. 'The Ambassador is expecting me.'

'Name. Now!' He flicked the safety clip off his gun holster and curled his fingers round the grip.

'Leila Reid,' she said. 'CTC Detective Sergeant. This is a matter of national security.'

'It's all a matter of national security,' the guard said. He made a move to draw the pistol, then stopped. His grip on the gun tightened as he glanced over her shoulder, along the street behind her. Something had caught his attention. 'Stay here,' he said.

'No.' She glanced round. Several people had stopped on the pavement outside the compound. Tourists with mobile phones pointing towards her, faces in the crowd, two men chatting at the entrance to the park now turning in her direction, watching in silence. 'You've got to get me off the streets and under cover,' she said. 'Right now.'

'Wait here!' the guard said. 'Don't move. And don't touch the bag.'

He stepped into the guard room and spoke into his

radio... drew his gun... looked back at the main entrance to the Embassy. He clipped the radio back onto his shoulder and looked out over the rims of his dark glasses. Their eyes met through the tinted windows of the booth. Out of the corner of her eye Leila saw movement deep inside the main building, shadowy figures, moving fast. She had no idea what, if anything, had caught the guard's attention outside the perimeter, but she knew that what was coming for her from within the building would be much more dangerous.

She stooped, grabbed the bag and ran.

'Hey!' the guard shouted. 'Stop!'

Car horns blared, a motorcyclist skidded around the back of a van that braked to avoid her. She pushed herself off the bonnet of a taxi that screeched to a halt as she zigzagged across the six-lane highway towards the park. The guard would be trying to get a bead on her. She heard him screaming at her again to stop, then a commotion, voices shouting behind the fence. As she darted across the central reservation she looked back. Three more guards, each brandishing standard-issue MP5 sub-machine guns, were wrestling the metal gate open as the gate-keeper tracked her with his hand gun. Military or not, he would know he had neither the accuracy nor the clear line of sight needed to get a shot off. He'd missed his chance; she kept running.

She was across the road and onto the safety of the far pavement before the Embassy's finest were even through the gate, but she'd made a serious mistake. In trying to cause a distraction with the traffic, she'd ended up on the wrong side of the road. As she had discovered last night, scrubby desert, even if it is being encouraged into the shape of a public park as this was, offered little or no cover. On this side of the road there was nowhere to hide and no chance of escape. She ran on a little way then darted back across the road behind a bus that had stopped in the chaos. Keeping close to a line of shops, she hid the red rucksack close to her chest and slowed, trying to blend into the crowd that had stopped to watch the commotion at the intersection. More car horns blaring behind her; more tyres smoking on the hot road. Heavy footsteps pounding the pavement across the road. From her current position the guards were still unsighted, but only for a few more seconds. Right now they were concentrating the park. It would not be long before they widened their area of interest. She was well clear of the bus now, and as soon as they turned around she would be in full view, with only the tunnel a hundred yards ahead offering any kind of cover.

And a dark tunnel was no kind of cover at all if she didn't know what was at the other end of it.

Twenty feet ahead, the last of the row of shops gave way to a blank concrete wall in front of a huge apartment block. Beyond that were older residential buildings behind a concrete embankment that got progressively higher as the road dropped away into the tunnel. She had no way back, but if she carried on she would be funnelled down into it. Her pursuers would get a clear shot at her if that was their intention... and she was coming to believe it was. Whatever else she had said, the only word the security guard had heard was 'terrorism', and out here that word came with an explosive charge. If she couldn't put some distance between herself and them, and quickly, they'd neutralise her first and figure out the backstory later.

She glanced back, turning slightly to crab sideways for a few steps in order to see the progress of her pursuers. Any sudden movement would attract attention. She could see the three Embassy guards, but there could have been more by now. One had made it to the corner of the park, another was almost across the main highway moving in a direct line behind her. A third was still at the central reservation. She paused where the low wall met an ornamental iron gate. Timing was the only thing on her side now.

A truck drove up from the road tunnel. There would be a moment when the two men on the road would not be able to see her when she moved and that bright red bag acted as a beacon to her position; she could only hope the trees in the park would help her out with the third. The moment came more quickly than she had expected. For an instant the hunters were blind, and she vaulted the wall and dropped down into a wide alley. Her bruised ribs protested loudly as the awkward landing knocked the wind out of her. Doubled over against the sudden assault of pain, she half-crawled into the covering gloom behind a large wheelie bin.

The alley contained just a few ornamental potted palms in urgent need of TLC, a couple of old bicycles and a line of bins, but she was out of sight, and that was as good as it was going to get for now. If she was lucky it might lead to what she guessed were the apartments' rear gardens and a means of escape. And if she wasn't, she was a sitting duck for anyone who looked over the wall, which sooner or later they would.

She heard several sets of boots pounding along the pavement beyond the wall. They slowed, stopped. They were on her side of the street now, and they would realise she could not have made it into – and back out of – the tunnel this quickly. Two sets of boots began to retreat. She looked around the edge of the bin. Through the gate she could see two of the guards standing at the end of the alley, their backs to the low wall. Both were still scanning the park across the street – one by eye, one through the scope on his gun. They spoke in low voices.

Leila slipped out from her hiding place and crept along the side of the apartment block deeper into the overgrown gardens between this block and the next one north. Ahead was another gap between the buildings that fronted onto the parallel street. But between her and it was a metal fence topped with spikes and thick with weedy creeper.

Behind her she saw the two men who had stopped by the gate cross the road again and jog up the slope into the park. Moments later she heard voices in the rear gardens of the block next to hers. Two of them at least. Reinforcements had arrived.

She scanned the fence. She had no way of knowing exactly what was on the other side of it, but she knew exactly what was on this side. If she delayed more than a few seconds, at least one of the guards would walk right into her.

She ran, jinked right to the remains of a tree stump, reached for the fence between two spikes and vaulted. It might have been the loud rattle of the fence as she plucked it like a giant guitar string, or it might have been the involuntary cry of pain as her ribs took yet another brutal landing, but her progress did not go unnoticed. Two sets of boots began to crash through the vegetation towards her.

She had, however, been lucky. The owner of this garden was a little more green-fingered than his neighbours, and she made fast progress up a neat gravel path and into the darkness of the alley between the buildings. She didn't stop to see how close her pursuers were, she just ran out into the quiet tree-lined street and turned right, away from the Embassy.

Thirty seconds later she had passed a dozen possible escape routes – gardens, side streets, alleys, underground car parks, steps up to apartments – but she hadn't taken any of them. Another hundred yards brought her to what she was looking for: a street of old shops, busy with locals and lined with enough covering trees and signs, parked cars and pavement cafés that she dared to slow to a casual walk. Here she had a chance of being able to disappear. Even if the men who had followed her through the gardens managed to track her this far – and she was sure they wouldn't – they'd be searching the maze of possible hiding places until the sun set.

For now, at least, she was safe.

But she was also alone. Her only ally – her own country – had turned out not to be an ally at all. It looked as if even Michael had betrayed her. He might have believed in her innocence, but he had taken their early morning conversation to those who didn't. The Embassy had been waiting for her, with an apparent readiness to use lethal force to bring her in if necessary. Only the fact that the message had been slow in filtering down to the lowly gate-keeper had prevented their trap from springing the moment she mentioned her name. And because it was Michael who had told her to go to the embassy, she'd walked right into it without suspecting a thing.

Being cut off from any official help was one thing. She could deal with that. What was of more immediate concern was that she was almost broke and she had no official papers. Without cash and a way to identify herself she had no way to proceed and certainly no way out of the country.

Unable to turn to her own government for protection now, she had only one person left who might help her make sense of all this, might buy her enough time and space to figure out a way to survive. She'd sworn she would never ask him for help again, but things had changed. She had no choice. With her own people bound by political expediency and swamped by rules and protocol, she would turn to someone for whom the law was meaningless. More than that, he saw avoiding it as an intellectual challenge.

20

She found an internet café on a side street just east of the main shopping district. It was busy with locals and tourists alike and no one paid her any attention. The café was busy and from the rear she would be able to see the door and some of the street without much risk of being seen from outside. She paid for half an hour and took a seat near the back with a mug of Lebanese coffee. It was too heavy on the cardamom for her taste but the caffeine was what mattered. She needed to get her mind back in gear, and fast. She might have been in a stupor, asleep or unconscious for four days, but she hadn't had much in the way of down-time for over twenty-four hours now. She was beginning to lose whatever clarity she had managed to get back after Black Eagle's drugs had worn off. Her past was emerging from its icy prison, and now her future was threatening to sink her right back into the dark waters. Nearly walking into CTC's clumsy trap at the Embassy had been a wake-up call.

She opened Google, switched it into Arabic, and started work. The keyboard was configured with Arabic, Hebrew and English letters and she navigated it easily enough to do what she had to do. At some point she would have to switch to writing in English, but the less time she spend doing so, the less of an obvious trail she would leave.

She needed a quick and simple means to make contact with the outside world – or, more specifically, Phillip Shaw. Highly intelligent but trapped by circumstance, Shaw had got to the bewildering foothills of adulthood with limited education and zero life chances. He'd retreated from people into a world of computers where he'd developed a special skill when it came to machines, and contacts with the kinds of people who had no respect for, and no fear of, social norms and rules. He'd managed to disable one of the world's most sophisticated security systems for the crucial few seconds it took Leila to get into Mapleton House and begin the process of ending the siege there on Friday night. And if he could get her into that virtual fortress right under the noses of British intelligence and the army, he might just be able to get her out of Israel.

Her computer knowledge was limited, but she had no trouble using Google. In under five minutes she had set up a temporary Gmail address. She'd also read enough to figure out a way to send an SMS message from the computer without downloading anything or signing up for anything. It would still leave a trace, but since Bone's phone was almost certainly being monitored anyway it seemed like a small compromise.

Whether Phillip would talk to her, of course, was another matter. His sabotage of the Mapleton security system was only one part of what that kid had done for Queen and Country last week.

Under pressure from Leila, Shaw had been instrumental

in discovering who had been behind the London bombing the previous week, and he had paid a high price for doing so. His mother and sister had been murdered by a Black Eagle hitman as they attempted to stop him finding out anything else.

When his mother had been killed, he had been taken into the protection of a Broadwater Farm gang headed by the fantastically laid-back Steven Glass, AKA Scaz Bones. She hoped the two were still together. As long as they were, Phillip was safe. On his own, Phillip was nowhere near safe, and that meant nor was she.

Phillip Shaw had his talents; fortunately Leila had a peculiar talent too. She had never had any trouble remembering numbers – phone numbers, dates, PINs, numbers associated with her job as an investigator. She could still remember passport numbers and National Insurance codes for suspects from years ago. It was a particular part of her brain that feasted on them, devoured digital information and filed it with such precise, intuitive logic that she found it as hard to forget a date as most people found it to remember one.

That memory was about to be put to its sternest and most critical test. As the ice had gradually cleared backwards through the Kensington investigation, she found one number floating clear as day in the watery memories. A number that would get her to Phillip, or at very least to his minder Scaz Bones.

Bones had tapped the number of one of the Waterboys' phones into the old mobile he'd given her when she went to Mapleton House. She'd watched him do it, and the pattern of digits on the keypad had stuck. She'd seen it again on the screen when she'd sent through the single full stop message to Phillip, the agreed code that would start the countdown to him disabling the SHIELD alarm ring around the property. She'd seen patterns, pairs and clusters of digits that triggered other memories, given her a subconscious hook on which to hang this new number. The first four digits were more or less standard; the next four a Fibonacci pair; a single zero was followed by the year her brother had been killed. It was how her mind worked. Patterns, associations, logic. And it made it a simple matter of recalling those associated memories – recalling the stored movie of Bones handling the phone – to remember it with perfect clarity.

What was going to be more problematic was composing a message that Bones would take seriously enough to pass on to Phillip, and that Phillip would take seriously enough to act on.

She closed down the browser on the machine she was using, drained the last of the coffee and moved to a table that gave her a better view of the counter and the window looking out into the street. She typed in a web address into her new computer and switched to English on the screen.

Phillip, hope Steven is looking after you. Need some of that myself. Lost my way a bit.

Can we talk? chouette76b@gmail.com

She looked at it for a moment, then hit send. No point over-thinking it. They'd know from the fact that she'd used Bones's own Waterboys' number that it was her. If Phillip had not got back to her in an hour, either something was wrong or he'd taken her at her word when she'd told him the Mapleton job was the last thing she would ask of him.

She did one final internet search and stepped out into the hot dusty morning.

21

'Reid's made contact.'

Michael Lawrence took the seat across the desk from his boss.

'She arrived at the Embassy?' he said.

'Briefly,' Commander Thorne said. 'Something spooked her and she took off before they could detain her.'

'You told them to increase security. She'd have been wise to that.'

'Or someone tipped her off.'

Lawrence just looked at Thorne for a moment then said: 'So who's she made contact with if not the Embassy?'

'Steven Glass,' Thorne said. 'AKA Scaz Bones. Which means she's reaching out to Phillip Shaw again, God help us.'

'Shaw's told us she's been in touch?'

Thorne laughed. 'No. We got lucky. With the Peace Conference at Mapleton House, GCHQ obtained a warrant to trap all radio communications around and within the perimeter. On Friday there was an untraceable ping just before Black Eagle stormed the meeting: a single full stop text message. Obviously a signal for something: we all assumed it was something to do with the raid. Turned out the message was sent from the phone Reid was using, the one that was found at Epping, but GCHQ couldn't trace where the message went to. Pre-paid, anonymous cell. They've extended the same tap warrant to keep a monitor on that number in case it was ever reactivated.'

'In the assumption that it would lead to Black Eagle,' Michael said. 'But it was Scaz Bones's.'

'Twenty minutes ago Reid used the same number again. Text message this time, yes, sent for the attention of her old ally Phillip Shaw.'

'What did she say?'

'That she needs help. She gave him an email address, so she's expecting instructions from him.'

'Then she was more than just spooked at the Embassy,' Lawrence said. 'If she's reaching out to Phillip it's because she knows she's on her own. There's no one from here coming to get her out.'

'And your thoughts on that?'

'That we've pushed her into a dangerous corner.'

'For her or for us?'

'Knowing Reid, both. Is Phillip doing anything?'

'He'll be doing something, but we don't know what yet. We've got two of our people on the way to Broadwater Farm to pick him up. We also got the IP address of the internet café she sent the message from. Agents are on the way to check it out.'

'She'll be long gone,' Michael said.

'I hope that's not a hint of satisfaction I hear in your voice,' Thorne said.

The phone on Thorne's desk rang. He picked it up, listened, and replaced the receiver.

'Fielding,' Thorne said. 'Yes, Shaw's doing something. He emailed Reid an IP address two minutes ago with an instruction to open it in ten minutes. They're communicating on the net.'

'So we'll know where she is as soon as she logs onto it. Even if she's moved, we'll get the new location,' Michael said.

'So much good it'll do us. The city alone is twenty square miles. She'll have had half an hour to get from where she was – where we are currently looking for her – to where she'll pick up Shaw's instructions. On foot she could cover two miles in that time, giving us a twelve square mile area to monitor with just one agent on the ground and one driving like a bat out of hell from Jerusalem. On a bus, who knows? We can't afford to bring local police in, so it's down to our own people, and unless we get extremely lucky, by the time they get to where she has her chat with Shaw, she'll have moved again.'

'Can't we just intercept their chat?'

'With most people, yes. Shaw, unlikely. He'll have set something up. Fielding thinks it'll be a variation of a botnet – he'll bounce her around the internet until she's so far away from the original IP we might as well not have had it in the first place. And he'll do it in a way we'll have no way of following his route. Even if we did ever manage to follow her and read the conversation, she'd be long gone again.'

'With a whole new toolbox of ideas,' Micheal said.

'So we need to hope our people get to Phillip in time,'

Thorne said. 'If Reid's expecting to talk to him, that's what's got to happen. Except we will control the conversation. Otherwise we'll lose her completely.' His mobile phone pinged softly. He looked down at it. 'Mason and Connor have just arrived at Broadwater Farm with one uniform. After what happened on Friday, police are still not exactly being welcomed, but they say it's quieter than they'd planned for. If the boy's still in Scaz Bones's flat, they should have him before the ten minute deadline expires.'

'Then we've got her.'

Commander Thorne smiled. 'Then, as you say, we've got her.'

22

Leila took an eight minute bus ride south and jumped off on a tree-lined street a few blocks in from the coast. She walked back to an anonymous-looking café – a narrow family-run place with a friendly red awning over its modest sprawl of pavement tables and a sumptuous display of cakes and pastries in the window. Most importantly, and the thing that had caught her attention from the bus as she passed, the window also bore a hand-written sign advertising internet access. On one side was a bookshop, on the other a florist, with a boutique hotel across the road. A quiet street that the locals tried hard to keep for themselves and which only a certain kind of tourist ever took the trouble to find. The architecture was mostly still Tel Aviv-brutal, but the atmosphere was convivial and welcoming. She booked an hour on a terminal and ordered another coffee and cheese bagel. After a splash of cold water on her face in the tiny back washroom and with her hair tied in a tight ponytail, she looked reasonably respectable. Respectable enough not to attract too much attention or be remembered anyway.

Twenty minutes after she had sent her message to Bones's phone – and while Lawrence and Thorne were discussing her situation two thousand miles away in London – she logged back onto her newly-acquired Gmail account. There were three messages waiting: two welcoming her to the service and one with no subject and a return address that was a meaningless as her own.

Leila opened it. The body of the message consisted of just two lines. The top one was a string of digits – a pair followed by two groups of three and ending with another pair, each group separated by a full stop.

Beneath this was a less ambiguous instruction. '10 Minutes', was all it said. Ten minutes from when it was sent, and that was seven minutes ago. She had three minutes to decipher the coded message and act on it or she was likely to lose the only chance she was going to get to talk to Phillip. And with it, the only opportunity she was going to get to clear her name and get home.

But what the hell was she supposed to do with this string of numbers? They weren't grid co-ordinates guiding her to a location – the pattern was wrong, and Phillip was no geography nerd. He'd have very little idea where she was, and a physical location would be of no value to them anyway. They weren't a phone number – again the pattern was wrong, and as they had now established a means of communication online a phone number would be superfluous. So it had to be a computer code – that was his style, that was what he knew best. But a computer code for what? A socket address... some hackers' thing? Phillip knew she didn't know her way around computers.

A young man was sitting at the terminal next to her. She opened a new browser window and clicked through to a tourist site for Tel Aviv. She didn't read a word, but kept an eye on the man beside her. He was chatting to someone. He'd type, pause to read a reply, type again. He smiled a lot, chuckled at some ongoing private joke.

She had to risk it.

'Excuse me,' she said in Arabic. The man looked at her and shook his head. She hadn't expected a reply; she just wanted to avoid his first impression of her as being a British visitor. If he was questioned later, he would swear she was a white Arab.

'English? You speak English?' she said, doing a clumsy but passable impression of someone for whom it was not her native language. She'd heard the inflections often enough in her time in the camps of southern Lebanon.

'Sure,' he said.

'Can you tell me what this is?' She indicated the email screen with its cryptic message.

'IP address,' he said.

'Which means…?'

'Copy it into the address bar,' he leaned across and pointed to the top of the browser window – 'it'll take you to a website.' She saw him scan the other window, the Arabic-language guide to Tel Aviv, further reinforcing his impression of her being a rich but ignorant tourist.

'Oh,' she said. 'I never thought of that. Thank you.'

'You're welcome.'

Leila copied the string of numbers and pasted them into the bar at the top of the browser. An 'http' front-end was automatically appended to the string and the screen went dark. Leila glanced at clock in the bottom right of the screen. She still had around a minute to wait. The waitress behind the counter waved her over and she collected her coffee and what would probably the closest thing she would get to lunch, and returned to the terminal.

'You get it?'

'Sorry?'

'The IP address?' The man on the table next to her had paused in his conversation.

'Yes, fine, thank you.' She took a sip of coffee and stared at the screen.

'Where you from?' he said.

Leila shrugged. 'Around, you know.'

'Holiday?'

'Yeah.' Her fingers hovered over the keys as if she was about to launch into her own conversation, but she dared not touch anything and Phillip had not appeared yet.

'I detect a bit of Lebanon,' the man went on. He was leaning on one elbow, studying her. 'But there's something else. You've spent a lot of time in England.' He wagged a finger at her and grinned. 'London?'

'I travel a lot,' Leila said. 'I'm sorry, I'm busy here. Do you mind?'

'Sure, sorry. No offence. Can never resist an accent. Especially an intriguing hybrid.' He held his hands open in a pacifying gesture and returned to his own screen. Leila felt him watching her for a moment, then he returned to his online conversation. He'd remember her now. She just hoped he was either a linguistics student or a geek with a terrible line in chat-ups, but even at a glance she knew he was too old to be a student and far too self-assured and handsome to ever need chat-up lines. If she hadn't already opened the line to Phillip she would have moved on, and fast. That uninvited bout of small-talk was probably nothing, but it made her uneasy.

For almost half a minute she stared at her screen. She didn't dare do anything else. The computer clock ticked past the ten minute mark, and the seconds slipped by. She waited. Whatever this was she had copied into the address bar, she had activated something. She hoped the delay now was because in an anonymous flat in north London Phillip knew she was here and was working on getting them somewhere private to talk.

After fifteen agonising seconds the numbers in the address bar changed as the connection was rerouted. They changed again five seconds later, then again. Leila held her breath, fascinated, as a pair of boxes appeared on the screen with a digit between them. One box contained the number 7.37, the other 7.38. The number in the middle began to count down from ten... nine ... eight.

What was this? Was she supposed to choose one of the boxes? Which one? They didn't mean anything. She stared at them, her pulse thumping in her neck.

7.38 meant nothing at all to her. 7.37 was the time she went over the wall at Mapleton when Phillip had disabled the SHIELD alarms. Four, three, two...

She clicked on 7.37.

An old-fashioned smiley emoji flashed up for a second before the screen once more went black. The numbers in the address bar changed and she was presented with two new boxes: PSLRSG and GWNABR. This time the counter started at nine.

The right box meant nothing, but she recognised her own initials in the left one. And Phillip Shaw's initials… and Scaz Bones's, or at least Steven Glass's (Phillip always referred to his friend as Steven, never by his street handle). She clicked left at three seconds and was presented with the smiley. Blank screen. The IP address changed…

Phillip was drawing her through a maze. The questions were deliberately easy, but she was given very little time to think about them. No time to work out the codes; she had to act on instinct. Only someone who already knew the answers would be able to follow him down the rabbit hole. Stop to work them out, stop to look something up or consult anyone and the time would expire. One slip, one wrong answer or a missed deadline and she would be thrown out of the system. Blank screen, connection broken, you're on your own.

On the next screen the two boxes were ROSS:SNOW and ROSS:CRACK, six seconds. Bones had framed Mark Ross, their former IT specialist, with rocks of crack cocaine in his flat. She clicked Crack. Easy. Smiley. Her heart was beating hard and fast now.

PIZZA, CURRY, four seconds. Really? She'd eat both. The Kashmiri at the end of the road was one of the best Friday night eateries in her area, a regular, but Phillip couldn't know her preference for Modur Pulav after a long shift. OK, think simpler…Pizza at the Waterboy's safe house the night before the siege? Two seconds… Risk it. Pizza. Smiley. New IP.

There was a long pause. No new question. So far what

he'd asked her could either have been picked out of debrief notes made when they had interviewed Phillip after the siege – and they would certainly have done that – or they were just simple word puzzles. So far there was nothing truly telling to signpost her way through this labyrinth. And that last question... Pizza or curry...? Either answer could have been correct. Would it really have mattered what she said, or was this whole game just a way to keep her online and fully focussed long enough to trace her? Was Phillip sitting in his flat, alone and in the dark, playing what to him was little more than a computer game... or was he somewhere else? Was he in another concrete bunker, being directed across a bolted-down metal table...?

The cursor blinked and two new boxes flashed across the screen.

PICASSO, BANKSY, the text said. Three seconds to decide.

She stared at the screen, unaware of anything else around her. Phillip didn't know anything about that, but it was far too specific to be random. Her Picasso drawing, the owl her father had given her. Her mind raced. Phillip couldn't know, could he? Only a tiny number of people knew – owning an original Picasso was hardly something you made public these days if you wanted to keep it hanging in your front room. So who did know...? Michael Lawrence? Or the Black Eagle agent who had broken into her house, ransacked it, taken nothing? He'd left her little owl leaning against the wall...

Where was Phillip? What secret bunker was he being held in while he drew her into the light... or into a new darkness? Who was sitting across that steel table, directing her friend and ally, watching as they zeroed in on her position? CTC or Black Eagle...? James Thorne... or Donald Aquila?

Two... one.... It was a huge risk. Picasso.

The screen went blank.

And stayed resolutely blank as the seconds ticked by.

The IP address changed again but for five more seconds nothing changed. Then the most terrifying question of all appeared: CAFÉ or HOTEL? Three seconds.

Whoever was on the end of this connection had found her. If it was Phillip, he had drawn her to the centre of the labyrinth and now wanted her to confirm her location. Tell the truth and he would trust her; lie and he would vanish forever. If he was working under the direction of CTC, the truth would get her arrested... get her into a deep well of trouble she had no way of getting back out of. So far she barely understood this mess herself. She would have no chance of clearing her name if she was picked up as a defecting agent now. But if Black Eagle had got to Phillip, that truth would get her killed. Thorne or Aquila... either way, agents would be converging on the two locations – the internet café and the hotel across the street – right now. All they needed was confirmation that she wasn't using routing software to disguise her true location. Clicking on the right answer would draw a target on her back.

One...

Café.

No smiley. The screen was dark.

23

Leila looked round. No one was paying her any attention. The linguistics geek next to her was still chatting to his funny friend somewhere out in cyberspace. The street outside was busy but normal, a few pedestrians, dappled shade from the trees, sparks of desert sunshine reflecting off cars as they passed. She turned back to the blank screen. A new window appeared, empty except for a flashing cursor in its top left corner. She watched for several seconds as the cursor blinked expectantly before words began to trace their way across the emptiness as if typed by fingers from another world.

> Welcome to the dark side, DS Reid.

Her hands hovered over the keyboard.

Two more words appeared. > You there?

> That you, Phillip? she typed.

> Ye. no one can see us.

> Are you alone?

> Stevens gone for coke and chips ;) why are you in — there was a long pause — Israle?

Leila's hand hovered over the keyboard in a moment of doubt. Phillip may have known she was in Israel from some embedded code in her email, or some other random bit of hidden data, but equally, it might indicate he had been compromised... In the end, what tipped the balance was the casual, easy mention of Steven Glass – AKA his minder and friend Scaz Bones. Phillip was perfectly capable of lying, but if he'd been sitting opposite CTC or Black Eagle agents, he would have just denied they were there. No need to add such telling detail. She hoped. She typed, slowly.

> I don't know. I'm in trouble. Need your help.

> ?

There was a lot she needed, but it all came down to two things. With Phillip's international network of hackers, she was hopeful that he would know someone who could get her what she needed most urgently.

> Cash and papers. Passport, travel documents. I can pay

The cursor flashed. For several seconds there was no reply. Then it began to move, fast.

> Got your bank detals here :) How much?

It had taken him seconds to gain access to her bank. He'd probably been harvesting data on her from the moment she walked into his life in the Waterboys' flat in Broadwater Farm on Thursday morning. She already knew he had accessed her personnel and biometrics data on the police computer. Now it seemed he'd got into her financials too. He probably knew more about her right now than she did herself.

> Five thousand, she typed. Know someone who can help?

> Need a few minutes. I'll find someone. Wait.

The cursor pulsed on and off but no more words came. Leila took a bite of bagel and a slug of coffee to lubricate

the chewy dough down her dry throat. 'A few minutes'…
then what? She needed to start making her own plans too,
whether Phillip came through for her or not. She did,
mostly, believe Phillip was acting alone, which meant that
right now he was probably the only person who knew
exactly where she was, but GCHQ weren't stupid, and nor
were Shin Bet, Israeli Interior Intelligence. And Black Eagle
were probably smarter and better resourced than both of
them put together. With or without Phillip's help, she
needed to get out of here and as far away as possible very
soon. She dragged the corner of the window until it was a
small rectangle on the edge of the screen and went back to
the Tel Aviv tourist website.

* * *

From one of the many flats owned or controlled by the
Waterboys in Northolt tower, North London, Phillip
reached out to his fellow DemonAgent hackers. He had no
idea where any of them lived – none of the group knew
personal details of any of the others – he just knew from
experience that the middle east was as much a hotbed for
cyber terrorism as it was for the bullets and bombs variety.
If he could find someone in the right area, his friend DS
Reid would be in luck. No member of their group ever
refused a plea for help from any other. It was how they
survived.

The flat's front door burst open and the sound of Scaz
Bones's size eleven Nike hightops came down the short
corridor to Phillip's darkened bedroom.

'We got trouble,' Bones said. Phillip didn't turn around.

'Got the coke?' he said

'Police are coming in, right now, kid,' Bones went on. 'We got to get you outta here.'

'You shouldn't have broken into her house yesterday,' Phillip said. His fingers never stopped their flight across the keyboard. 'You knew one of them was there right before you.'

'Then you wouldn't-a known about that owl thing. You said that was what swung it for her in the end. Little detail, draw her in. But right now, we gotta go, OK? I don't think this is about no Picasso.'

'I just need a few minutes,' Phillip said.

'We don' have a few minutes. They musta traced the cell.'

'They'd have traced that text message before you even picked it up.'

'But the computer's safe, right?'

'No,' Phillip said. 'They've put spyware on it.'

'And you didn't get it off?' Bones said.

'Then they'd know I knew about it. I'm piggybacking off the neighbour's router.' His typing paused but he did not look away from the screen. 'Their detectors will narrow the signal down to a few flats. They know we're on this side of the building, but they can't be certain what floor. It'll take them a few tries to find it.'

'And then it'll be the wrong flat.'

'Upstairs... Or downstairs. I'm just waiting for a message.'

'Then it had better come quick, kid. We gotta get out.'

Phillip heard Bones retreat back to the front door and open it. He stared at the screen, waiting.

Then it came. A message from an agent in Tel Aviv. Phillip knew the screen name. He was a man known for hacking into the Israeli Secret Service's own hack into the telephone networks between Israel and the West Bank. His brother ran a telecoms and electronics store in Jerusalem. And the Jerusalem brother was an expert forger.

The front door closed again and once more Phillip's minder joined him in the darkness of the bedroom.

'They're downstairs now,' Bones said. 'Sixty seconds and I'm taking you out even if I have to put you down. Reid told me to look after you, and that's what I'm gonna do.'

Phillip typed. His contact replied. A furious conversation scrolled across the screen.

Below them there was a dull thud. Two men shouted. The flat downstairs had been breached and the CTC officers were moving in to make an arrest. It would take them thirty seconds to realise they were in the wrong flat, another minute or so to home in on the right one.

Phillip typed, line after line of short sentences. Bones glanced at the screen. He caught odd words, facts about Reid, things she and the forger could use to make contact. Then Phillip stopped. He closed the chat screen and opened another.

* * *

The screen on Leila's computer spooled out one final message. Short, to the point.

> Go to Jerusalem, Canaan Communications at — there was a short pause then an address appeared on the screen one character at a time.

> he's ecxpecting you around 1200.. Get personal details in conversation. Don't have to make sence. He knows stuff about you. Use detail's to confirm you are.

Leila read it twice, fingers poised over the keyboard. It was an address of someone Phillip trusted, and that was good enough for her. And it was close – Jerusalem was an hour or so away – easy to get to, easy to vanish in, easy to use as a springboard to get her out of the country once she had the right paperwork. He'd done well. She typed.

> Thank you. How's things at your end?

There was no reply.

* * *

'You done?' Bones said. Voices shouted in the corridor outside the flat. Someone hammered on the door of the flat next door.

'Just need to kill this lot.' Phillip initiated the machine's suicide routine. It would not have time to erase the entire hard drive, only the most recent files. That would be enough to put a firewall back up around Reid, buy her some time, and neither he nor Bones would be telling the police anything until they knew for sure that their friend was out of danger.

The front door burst open under the force of the portable battering ram. It didn't put up much opposition.

'Armed police! Stay where you are!' Boots pounded along the hall, through the empty sitting room and along the corridor. Two plain-clothes officers were in the bedroom in seconds, guns drawn. A third, in uniform, covered the door and corridor beyond. As the first officer in barrelled Bones against the wall with a Glock 17 pressed up beneath his chin, his colleague ripped the computer's mains cable from the wall, more concerned with the machine than the kid sitting in front of it. Phillip watched with a detached amusement. He'd never been right in the middle of an actual raid before. Bones was spun round and cuffed, and the officer who had been guarding the door dragged Phillip from his chair and threw him against the bed. He hauled his arms behind his back and cuffed him.

From the moment the door burst open to the two men being immobilised and the computer neutralised barely ten seconds had passed. Ten crucial seconds in which Leila, lost and alone two thousand miles away, lost the only person left in London who was truly and unquestioningly on her side.

* * *

The cursor blinked at the end of Leila's final word. She was satisfied – for the time being at least – that Phillip had been straight with her. He knew her location but had sent her into the murky backstreets of Jerusalem forty-odd miles away for her next traceable contact. CTC would not have done that; there would be too much risk of losing her, or her causing all kinds of other trouble along the way. And Black Eagle would already be here if they had been directing Phillip's end of the game. Her brain still wasn't entirely free of whatever Donald Aquila had given her back at Epping Airport to soften up her mind, but her gut told her Phillip was on the level, and for now that was good enough. She could imagine him sitting in semi-darkness in one of the Waterboys' flats, already onto something new. He had his life back, at least for as long as Michael kept his word and made sure he was safe, and as long as Scaz Bones could stay out of jail and give him somewhere to live. And as long as Black Eagle had more pressing matters to attend to… like a rogue agent, alive and fighting in their own back yard.

Leila took one more look at the address of Phillip's forger and closed the browser window. She opened Google and typed in the Jerusalem street name Phillip had given her. Clicking on the map on the right of the results screen brought up a schematic of Jerusalem's Old City and its spaghetti-like tangle of streets and alleys, most of which were little more than unnamed dotted lines. Canaan Communications had a useful little marker on it and she found the names of a few roads leading in its general direction. Start at the Damascus Gate in the north and head south and east. She closed the window but had no idea how to clear the history from this public machine, the residue of their off-the-grid chat. She hoped Phillip would already have taken care of that at least. It was more of a problem that one particular street in Jerusalem was lodged in the search history. She had been careful not to search specifically for Canaan Communications itself, but if (no, she knew it was not if, it was *when*) this computer was analysed, she had left a vital clue behind with the street name.

She took one more bite of the stodgy bagel, swilled it down with a mouthful of almost cold coffee and made her way out through the now-crowded tables. As she got to the front door she glanced back. The man on the table next to her was watching her. He nodded a goodbye as she turned and stepped out into the thick heat of morning.

She prayed she had enough cash to get her to Jerusalem and enough time to conclude her business there before they picked up her trail again.

Whoever 'they' were.

24

James Thorne walked the long echoic corridor to the Home Secretary's office in the Whitehall. There was only one item on the agenda for their covert meeting: Leila Reid, and her imminent and growing threat to national security. Phillip Shaw had been taken into custody an hour ago. So far he was saying nothing, and his computer had been erased just far enough that tech forensics had declared it an evidential write-off. All they knew for sure was that Shaw had told Reid something. He was saying nothing now, and no one was under any illusion that he would be able to keep saying nothing – or nothing true and useful – long enough for Reid to disappear. Or worse. Whatever her plan was in Israel, it was likely to be moving into its final stages and this kid would be able to send them up blind alleys or run down the clock in obstinate silence until Reid had done whatever she was going to do. With or without Shaw's cooperation, she had to be found – and stopped – as a matter of priority.

Emma Whitehouse was on the phone when her secretary showed the CTC Commander into her office. She glanced up at him and motioned for him to sit, then carried on listening with rapt attention to whoever was on the other end of the line. While she made a few notes on the file in front of her the secretary again knocked and entered, this time bearing a manilla folder of documents. He placed them on the desk, nodded to Commander Thorne, and left.

'This is quite a mess your Detective has caused,' Whitehouse said as soon as she'd ended the call. When Thorne did not respond – there wasn't much he could say to that – she continued. 'That was US Special Liaison.'

'The CIA know about this?'

'Reid made herself very visible to them during the Mapleton investigation. And they like to keep tabs on what happens in Israel. So I hope, since you've come to see me, you already have some plan to minimise the fallout?'

'I'll get to that, Home Secretary-'

'Acting Prime Minister,' Whitehouse said. 'I may not have moved into his office yet, but be under no doubt about the scope of my brief.'

'Of course, my apologies. I'm here because new evidence has come to light that suggests we might be dealing with something much more than just a defecting agent.'

'Evidence?'

'Reid contacted Phillip Shaw this morning.'

'The hacker? The boy in Broadwater Farm that brought down the entire SHIELD security system on Friday night?'

'Phillip Shaw is the tip of an iceberg of hackers. A socially inept kid who considers Reid to be his friend; a kid with no concept of the difference between a computer game and reality, but all the talent to play international politics like it's a scene from… what is it they all play these days? Minecraft?'

'I take your point. She's an arch manipulator, he's a classic patsy and he's got something she wants. Tell me you know what they were talking about in this 'contact'?'

'No. We had problems finding him at Broadwater Farm, and we were unable to back-trace their conversation. He was using a sophisticated botnet to get her so far off-grid...'

'Yes, yes. You found her then lost her again. The question is why now? Why are they in touch now?'

'We can't be specific, but we know she was asking for help. Six's bungled attempts to bring her in quietly at the Embassy mean she's out of options as to where to get that help – she's not likely to trust any of us again after what those idiots pulled in Tel Aviv. So she needs another way out.'

'And you think Shaw's facilitating one?'

'If we're lucky that might be the extent of it.'

'And if we're not 'lucky', Commander?'

'The elephant in the room is why she's in Israel. And why the Negev. There are no active, legitimate British operations there, so... what?'

'You're convinced she's working with Black Eagle now?' Whitehouse said.

'There's no proof, but on the balance of probabilities...'

'...there's even less evidence to suggest she's not.'

'That is how I see it, yes. Before she picked Golzar up from Holloway she herself suggested that she accompany Aquila and Golzar to wherever they were going. It seemed magnanimous at the time – our very own mole disguised as a human shield if you like – but in the light of current developments it looks like it might have been a bluff. A bluff aimed at us, not Black Eagle.'

'So why Israel?'

'The problem we have is that she chose to ditch her plane a few miles from what we all know – though none of us are at liberty to say – is a nuclear facility in the Negev.'

'And we're not talking about a power station, are we?'

'No. Our tech analyst thinks it's a weapons silo that even we didn't know about. I didn't entirely follow his reasoning: it's not my field. But he seemed convinced, so we're taking it as a significant line of enquiries.'

'For Six, surely.'

'Reid's ours, and this stems directly from a CTC investigation. Anyway, Six have got enough of their own inadequacies to worry about. We can handle this internally, at least for now.'

'I hope you're right,' Whitehouse said. 'So you think she was trying to draw attention to the facility – to expose it to the public gaze?'

'Maybe. But I don't see Reid as a new Edward Snowden. I think she's been put into the field in the same capacity as Golzar was two years ago. Black Eagle lost their chance to court the Russians then; they lost it for good when, or maybe I should say *if,* Golzar was shot by Reid. But if Reid is now carrying nuclear secrets, and God knows what else, they've got their bait back.'

'Where does Shaw fit into that?' Whitehouse said.

'Last week Black Eagle mounted a high-profile operation to free Golzar. They blew up a hotel, brought the capital to a stand-still, took over the Mapleton Peace Talks…'

'Yes. I was there, Commander. Your point is…?'

'It didn't work. They didn't cause the ripples they were

aiming at – Iran, China, Russia. So they've changed tack. Forget the big showy stuff, mount a small, pin-point operation. An operation that relies on intelligence, not muscle.'

'Shaw?' Whitehouse said impatiently.

'We suspect since Reid turned up in Israel that Shaw has been feeding her stolen information, and now it's starting to become clear why. He trusts her, wants to please her even, so he's giving her what she wants. What Black Eagle wants.'

'Tell me you were monitoring him!'

'Up to a point, yes. But to monitor someone like Shaw would take far more resources than we believed he warranted at the time.'

'So it looks like you were wrong about that too. He's the source of the nuclear leak.'

'In the light of this new evidence, that would be my conclusion, yes. Apart from being under Reid's spell anyway, his type always are – left-wing 'activists' with a sixth-formers' naive hatred of 'The Establishment' – anti-nuclear, anti-Israel, anti-government, anti-common sense. It's Minecraft on a global playing field. Reid wants to make a point to Black Eagle – to prove she's worth protecting and funding – and Shaw gets to play his games to facilitate it. But I stress, this is based on new evidence, and we had no reason to suspect anything of this nature until today.'

Whitehouse waved her hand dismissively. 'And your conclusion as to what their latest contact was about? Assuming he's already given her the nuclear secrets.'

'The original operation failed. He set her up with enough information to get into trouble, and now it looks likely he's directing her on the ground to get out of it.'

'We need to keep a tight ring around this,' Whitehouse said. 'Whatever you say about this being outside Six's brief, I'm going set up a meeting with David Bates. SIS can run the operation on the ground in Israel. You run things here. Keep it that way for now. All we're doing is looking for her; we have no reason to suspect her of anything other than a poorly planned flight in a restricted military zone. Whatever else your people already know, keep a lid on it.'

'Nothing to US Special Liaison?'

'Absolutely not.'

Commander Thorne leaned forwards in his seat. 'You know that even if we do find her, we're not going to be able to get her back, Prime Minister. If she's defected to Black Eagle, we've lost her.'

'We got Golzar out of Israel fifteen months ago,' Whitehouse said.

'Which is precisely why we're not likely to be able to do the same thing again. Mossad won't stand for it.'

'So what do you propose?'

'We need an executive order to take her out of the picture.'

'Are you talking about a state-authorised assassination? On one of our own agents? For God's sake, Commander, that's simply not how we do things here!'

'I fully agree: if SIS can capture her, that would be the best outcome,' Thorne said. 'If they can't, we can not allow her to run riot in the middle east.'

'SIS will capture her. However long it takes, OK?'

'With respect, I beg to differ, Acting Prime Minister.

With what Reid knows already, plus the financial and logistical resources Black Eagle can provide her with, she could start a war. And if, as I suspect, she's co-opted Shaw and his merry band of hackers as an army of blind agents in the game, she could literally turn the global status-quo on its head by the end of the month. You think asking her nicely to come home is an option?'

'There's a lot of options between asking her nicely – the tone of which I rather resent, Commander – and sending out an execution detail. In any case, Morgan will never sign off on it, and technically he is still PM. He's under the impression that she saved the lives of the delegates at Mapleton.'

'She also caused the death of his daughter in the process. He needs to be persuaded. And if he's not in any fit state to make that judgment.... SIS will have people on the ground that can act discretely.'

'I can't order the termination of one of our own people without better evidence than you've brought me so far.'

'I'll get you evidence. We've got Shaw in custody. He's not talking yet, but I think I have a way that he might be persuaded. Sooner or later he'll give her up, and when he does, we need to be ready to act. I don't need to remind you that if we are not seen to be taking robust action, the CIA will.'

'You don't need to remind me of anything, Commander Thorne.'

'My apologies. But my point remains: Reid is the first major Black Eagle infiltration we know about in the British intelligence services, and the Americans are not going to let us play with it for very long. Because if we fail to deal with it, this is a cancer that could bring down more than just our current government and it could cost us every intelligence and strategic ally we have left.'

25

Leila arrived in Jerusalem a little before 12.30, broke, late for her meeting at Canaan Communications, and apart from what she remembered of the map she had looked at in the café, having no idea where she was going. Even if she had known, that neat little map had given her no idea of just how chaotic this ancient city really was. She walked through the Damascus Gate at the north end of the Old City and entered another world. The bus from Tel Aviv had taken an hour and cost her almost everything she had left – the express train would have been much quicker, but had the disadvantage of being much more expensive than she could afford and being effectively a long inescapable prison even if she had been able to find the fare. In an emergency she could have disappeared from the bus; it would not have been so easy from a fast train.

Now, in Old Jerusalem, she really could disappear for a while. It seemed that all humanity was here, spanning more than four thousand years of history. White, black, middle-eastern… Jews in traditional immaculate black suits and white shirts… Palestinians, bearded men and head-scarved women, draped in layers of loose, bright clothing from neck to floor. And among them, almost unseen by the locals, ambled hundreds of tourists. Against snatches of Arab songs piped in on cheap speakers a Babel of languages from every corner of the world rose and fell like a restless sea of sound. Open-fronted shops selling everything from t-shirts to carpets, meat and fish to local art jostled with seemingly random pop-up market stalls piled with fresh fruit and vegetables, nuts, olives, cheese and sweet treats. Old, wise and wizened vendors sat on upturned crates and watched their younger counterparts collar anyone who looked their way, ready to make a deal – hustling, eager, charged with an optimistic energy that made these ancient walls hum.

Here and there on the more major thoroughfares soldiers kept watch but there was no air of menace and no one paid her any attention. She turned left along the Via Dolorosa (she thought that was correct) and probed several side alleys until a name struck her as familiar. She eventually found Canaan Communications in a claustrophobic back street of ancient limestone buildings, shops and cafés, cheek-by-jowl with residential flats. By the time she found it, she was over an hour late.

An old-fashioned bell jangled as the door brushed past it. Inside was cool and quiet after the chaos of the street. Shelves of electronics – everything from dusty DVD players to laptops, ham radios to used CCTV systems – covered the walls. Boxes of old electronics hobby magazines and battered books lined the base of the walls on each side. A young man, mid-twenties, black hair cropped short, open-necked brightly patterned shirt, was leaning on the counter at the back of the shop working on some kind of circuit board through a huge magnifying lens. In the glass display cases beneath him were boxed mobile phones and computer components. Leila wondered how much of it was legit. If ever there was a shop that embodied the term 'black market', this was it. The man looked up at her through the wisps of smoke from his soldering iron.

'Shalom,' he said without expression.

'Shalom,' Leila replied. He smiled.

'British?'

She nodded. 'I'm looking for a mobile phone,' she said. The man examined her for a moment, switched the soldering iron off and blew the smoke away. He stood up from the stool he was perched on and actually seemed to lose a few inches in height.

'That right?' he said.

'A friend is sure you'll have what I'm looking for.'

'Operating system?' he said. 'We've got your standard iOS, Pie, Q, even do you some Lineage mods if that's you taste.'

'Blue Butterfly might meet my needs.'

'Blue Butterfly?' He grinned at her, showing a full set of very white teeth even in the low smokey light of the shop. 'Bare bones?'

'More of a fillip to my browsing habits.'

'Curious choice of word.'

'You look like an educated man.'

He studied her for a few seconds then shook his head. 'I was about to close for lunch, Miss,' he said.

'Sorry. I had intended to be here an hour ago, but you know what Jerusalem's like.'

'And you, apparently, don't,' he said with a grin. 'But you'll learn. OK. Lock the door, turn the sign over. I think I might be able to help.'

Leila engaged the Yale lock and flipped the sign to Closed. He motioned for her to follow him through a bead curtain behind the counter and into a dingy room containing racks of components and part-built computers. As the curtain rattled back into place he rounded on her, fast. From somewhere he had produced a small black pistol. Leila didn't recognise it, but at a range of less than six feet the make was irrelevant. Accuracy would not be an issue.

'Let me see your teeth,' the man said.

'My…?'

'Open your mouth.' He waved the gun at her.

Leila opened her mouth, and leaned her head back so he could get a good view. It was the missing upper-16 molar he was after. Phillip had told him about the blue butterfly tattoo; he would have told him about the missing tooth too.

'Guess you can't fake that,' he said. He slipped the gun back into the belt of his jeans and turned to a small door at the side of the room. He opened it, flicked a light switch and stood aside.

'Down there. Sorry about the scare. Pays to be careful in my line of work.'

'No problem,' Leila said. 'Caution like that works for me as much as you.' She stepped through another bead curtain and down the narrow curving staircase. The man (she still didn't know his name, and knew she never would), closed the door to the store room and followed her.

The basement was much like the shop, only more so.

Shelves of electronic components covered every wall, except where a huge Chubb safe was mounted in the far corner. A corkboard of receipts, diagrams and restaurant menus was propped on a shelf above it. In the middle of the room was a desk, lit by high-intensity LEDs suspended from the ceiling. Phillip's forger was already decanting scalpels, letter sets, inks and papers from a drawer onto a cutting board in the pool of light.

'My man in England says you need papers,' he said. He span the dial left, then right, then left again and opened the safe. He rifled through a box of papers and took out a deep blue British passport. He threw the little pistol into a box on the bottom shelf.

'You want to go modern with a traditional blue,' he said, 'or are you still old-school EU?'

'Whatever I need to move around freely here and get out,' Leila said.

'We'll go blue. Old EU one really would have a few more stamps in it than I can be bothered faking right now. Keeps your costs down and my interest up. I hate doing the stamps.'

'You can't leave it completely blank...'

'I wasn't going to. I'll put a couple of neutral ones in: Australia, Canada, fancy Kenya? Of course. You look the sort. Countries that won't offend anyone but will make you look like you've been somewhere.'

'Phillip told me he'd have cash wired to you,' Leila said.

'Five thousand Sterling arrived from your account a few minutes ago. I can let you have two-g in Shekels, eight hundred in Sterling.' He took out two bundles of notes from the safe but didn't hand them over. He placed the cash and the blank passport on the cutting board. 'You'd get a better rate at the bank, but what can I say?' he said. 'There's risks.'

'That's fine.'

'Shekels you can take now, enough to get you started. After I take my expenses, I'll give you the balance and the Sterling when you come back. Passport'll cost you a thousand Sterling. You won't need a visa, but you'll need to carry an entry card at all times. That's two hundred. You travelling into the Palestinian territories?'

'It would be useful.'

'Gaza, you're on your own. No money'll buy you a way in there now. But even the rest of it, I wouldn't try to move much beyond the main city areas – East Jerusalem and Ramallah. There are Israeli checkpoints throughout the territories and the further off the tourist track you go, the closer they'll examine your papers.'

'Cities should be enough.'

'Why you want to go there?'

'It's in an early stage of planning.'

'Wise answer, but have a better one when you get to the checkpoints. You speak any Hebrew?'

'Not a word. Fluent in Arabic though.'

'Keep that to yourself. You start speaking Arabic at the checkpoint, especially coming back across, you'll be in a small dimly-lit room for hours. And these papers won't stand up to that kind of scrutiny. Right, sit there.' He pointed at a stool in the corner of the room. He drew a pale curtain across the wall behind her head and took a camera from a drawer in the desk.

'Look dumb,' he said, 'it's a passport.'

In seconds he had clicked off a dozen shots. He hooked the camera up to a computer and began to process out the best of the images. A high-end printer whirred on the floor.

'When we're done here, Phillip'll falsify records to show you entered Israel a week ago as a tourist. That way you'll be able to get out again. I'll give you a standard entry card: if you're asked you came in through Ben Gurion. Got it?'

Leila nodded.

'Know where you're going when you've done your business here?'

'Not yet,' Leila said.

'You'll be fine entering any third country from here as long as it's in Europe. Just don't try going directly back to the UK because they won't have any record of you. Go to Germany, something like that. From there the EU borders are so porous you'll get home without anyone checking anything too carefully even if you're not EU any more. Why you do that? Ditch the Union?'

'We hate the French. We're not that keen on the Germans either.'

He laughed. 'Yeah, makes sense.'

He shook the photograph dry then put on a green visor like the ones used in smokey casino movies and sat at the desk. Working through a magnifying glass bolted to the side of the desk, he set to work.

'Name?'

'Sarah Connor,' Leila said.

He looked up at her and gave her another of his bright-white grins.

'Resistance fighter. I like that. It'll be lost on most of the people who examine your papers, but it's fun. You enjoy your work.'

He took a stamping kit from the drawer and began to assemble the details of her first dummy entry stamp. The photograph was already attached to the back page of the passport. He passed her a slip of paper and a pen.

'I'll need an address, phone number, date of birth. That should do it. It'll go on the entry slip too. Can be real or fake. Fake it if you can remember it, but don't risk it otherwise. It's academic anyway. As long as something's filled in on the form the border guards and random soldiers who might want a quick look won't be checking the accuracy of it.'

Leila began to write. She strayed just one street east of her real address and used a mobile number from a phone she'd had stolen in a theatre six months ago. She knew from countless interrogations that when most people make up their biographies they either go completely fictional – in which case the story bears no scrutiny whatever – or they pick real details that they don't know enough about. It was almost impossible that she would be quizzed about her fictional self, but if she was she knew the details of the street, the local cafés, what film was showing at the cinema along the road, could even describe the scars that still remained from mini tornado that swept through the area three years ago. Details like that can save lives. For the same reason, the date of birth was her brother's, which had the added benefit that it gave her a slightly more favourable year than reality would have. She handed the scribbled notes over to the forger.

'Get yourself a skirt,' he said while he worked. 'Always dress modestly and don't drive on Shabbat in any of the orthodox zones. You'll be stoned. Thinking of which, don't get stoned. Even Phillip won't keep you out of jail if you're caught with anything illicit.'

'I wasn't planning on it. I've got business to attend to, then I'm out of here.'

'You in any trouble that's coming to visit me after you go?'

'You'd better hope not.'

'What did you do?'

'I crashed a plane near a nuclear facility in the Negev, escaped from military custody, was indirectly responsible for the deaths of at least two Special Ops soldiers, plus sundry other unidentified operatives. Oh, and then I stole a car and when I'd dumped that in the desert, I rode into town without paying my bus fare. All in all I'm probably the most wanted woman in Israel.'

He laughed. 'Sarah Connor... I can see why Phillip likes you, and he don't like anyone. Weird kid, even by DemonAgent standards. My brother says it's like he's talking to a machine over there in London...' For almost half a minute Leila watched him, this tiny, intense man conjuring up his own brand of magic art that would become her key to escape and survival. He paused, examined his work through the magnifier then looked up at her again, seemingly surprised that she was still there. 'OK, Sarah Connor, you can bugger off now,' he said. 'Come back at six. Get yourself some clothes while you're waiting.' He handed her a few notes off the roll of shekels on the desk.

'Five hundred. You'll get the rest when you come back. And go to this hotel.' He turned to the cork-board behind him and took a dog-eared card from it. He looked at it thoughtfully for a moment then handed it over. 'Owner's a friend, very discrete, but check in now. He's popular. You might find somewhere you feel safer tomorrow.'

'Safer?'

'Somewhere I don't know about. I'm going to wipe any trail back to you as soon as you leave here this evening. You should do the same. Firewall, you know? But I'm paid to take the risk on the forging; I'm not going to get myself killed protecting a fugitive. If they ask me, I'll stay schtum. If they lean on me, I'll talk. So make sure I don't know where you are, just in case.'

Leila tucked the card and the cash into her pocket.

'You know where I can get a gun?' she said.

'I don't deal in that shit,' the forger said, looking up through his green visor at her. 'IDF catch you out there carrying, they'll shoot you, no question. Jerusalem's technically demilitarised. Fuckers are even more twitchy here than they are out in Tel Aviv.'

'Then how about that mobile phone I came in for?'

'That I can do. I'll have one for you when you pick the papers up. No charge. Kids out here'll drop anything over a year old, so there's no shortage of old anonymous stuff. Come back for the rest at six. Now bugger off.' He smiled and turned his attention back to the cutting board.

Leila walked back out into the dingy side street. Phillip had done well.

26

Leila didn't check into the hotel the forger had recommended. It was too obvious a link between them, and she knew that however careful he was, he was likely to be on someone's watch list. She walked a quarter mile or so from Canaan Communications to a street that was, if it was possible, even more run down, and found a cheap back-packers' hostel. At fifty dollars a night The Hebron Gardens was hugely overpriced (and it didn't have a garden), but it was anonymous, it was close to where she needed to be, and it was full of the kind of transitory visitors who would not give her a second glance, let alone remember her the next day.

A huge woman sat behind a glass screen in the converted hallway of the old house. A scruffy mongrel dog watched her from the office beyond reception, but the owner barely looked up from her magazine as Leila enquired about a room for a couple of nights. The woman shrugged, made some noise that was probably affirmative and passed a clipboard through the partition. Leila filled in her details – made up on the spur of the moment – and handed the form back. The woman reeled off the house rules, took one night's money, and handed Leila a key for a room at the top of the building. She didn't ask for passport, ID documents or even query why Leila's only luggage was one small red rucksack with seemingly very little in it. Idle stupidity could be a wonderful thing, Leila thought.

She left and made her way to the first budget clothing shop she could find. She would keep her jeans and faithful leather jacket, the latter mainly because it had a useful set of pockets and there was very little else on offer to compare. Amongst her new super-budget ensemble she bought a headscarf – just in case – a long-sleeved shirt and the most modest skirt she could find as per the forger's instructions. It was a thing she would never have been seen dead in in England, but it would serve its purpose. It was generously cut and between it and the light walking boots she was wearing, she would be able to move quickly and freely if she needed to. She also bought another pair of jeans as back-up. Only when she tried them on in the shop's pokey changing stall did she see just how much punishment her current Diesels had taken. No wonder the waitress in Tel Aviv had asked her if she'd had a hard night.

Back at the hostel she took a quick shower in the filthy shared bathroom on the top floor, sloughing off the dust and sweat of her journey across the desert. She risked the soap congealed on the drainer by the shower head, but had no inclination to use the towel that the owner had generously provided on the towel rail. It looked like one the Hebron Gardens' resident dog had decided was past being good enough to sleep on. She dressed wet in her new, anonymous skirt and shirt. She dumped the rest of her

clothes in her room and went back out into the street with
the rucksack over her shoulder. (If someone wanted to steal
her clothes, they were welcome to them, but she wasn't
going to lose this bag or what was in it now. They'd been
through a lot together.)

She arrived at Canaan Communications at six as
instructed. The work lamp on the counter was on but the
rest of the lights were off and the closed sign was on the
door. She looked for a bell and, not finding one, pushed the
door. It was locked.

She checked the alley. There were people crossing the
junction behind her, mostly tourists, couples going out for
dinner or taking in the sights, but only a few locals were
within sight on the alley itself. She dropped her backpack
and crouched to find the lock picks. She had the old Yale
lock open in under fifteen seconds. The door rattled the old
bell as she pushed it open. She stepped in and closed and
locked it behind her.

'Shalom?' she called.

Silence.

'Hello? You here?'

A dim light shone up the stairwell beyond the bead
curtain. There was no sound of movement from below.
Something didn't feel right. She inched around the end of
the counter and tried to see down the stairs. She felt naked
without the reassuring weight of a gun in her hand.

She listened for a few seconds then slipped through the
beads. There was a single light on downstairs but she could
not see round the shelves at the foot of the curving
staircase. She took a step down.

Everything told her to back out now. Everything except her newly forged papers. She needed those to proceed, but there was more than that. If the forger had been caught, her Sarah Connor identity would already be compromised. More even than her need for documentation, she needed to know if the hunters were on her tail again.

Phillip's man was not at his desk. Nor were her papers. The cutting board, knives and all the paraphernalia of forgery had been cleared away. The only thing she didn't recognise from her last visit was a slightly tattered black nylon sheath from a combat knife. That the knife itself was not among the remaining junk on the desk did nothing to calm her unease.

She approached the table and listened again. The shop's front door rattled and a voice called out in Hebrew; there were other voices in the distance; electricity hummed and from an adjoining basement the very faint sound of Arabic pop music drifted in the stillness. The rest was eerily silent. Something was missing, but she could not pinpoint what it was right now.

Leila rounded the table to see if there was anything amongst the jumble of notes and cards on the cork-board that might give her a clue as to where the forger might be. And then she saw him.

His body had been tucked against the foot of the desk. He was dead. The table light had been positioned so that it illuminated his face, but it was not the gaunt, greying skin that told her she was too late. It was not even the pool of blood that surrounded his head like a halo. What put it beyond doubt was the missing Dustar knife that was sticking out of his forehead. The front four inches of the blade had been driven right through his skull and into his brain.

Leila crouched beside the body. There were no other signs of violence, just this one catastrophic wound. But it had surely not been the principal cause of death. The amount of force required to get a wide blade into a man's skull was huge, and he wouldn't have just stood there and let his assassin do it. The wound was a message. Whoever was behind this – Black Eagle, Shin Bet, CIA, even her own people – were making sure she realised they could act with impunity... and were not squeamish about their methods.

She stood up, less concerned now than when she first entered the building. If the assassin had wanted to kill her too, he would have just waited – unless the forger had not told him that she was coming back, in which case if she ran into him now it would just be bad luck. And even more important than her immediate safety was her longer-term future. She needed papers, or she needed to know if she would have to find another forger.

The passport-making kit had been cleared away, which meant that maybe the papers had been too. He would have put them in the safe, and as the safe was still closed, it was unlikely that the assassin had gained access to it.

Leila picked her way back to the foot of the stairs where she had been the last time the safe had been opened. She'd watched him do it, and although she had not consciously noted the numbers, she thought she could narrow down the possibilities from what she had seen. She stared at the dial and thought back to that first meeting. The dial had been on zero – very easy to remember as it was highlighted in red. The forger had spun it left a little way, right much further, then left, way back past the zero.

Left, almost to twenty, eighteen maybe. Right, fifty-five, fifty-six. Left late thirties.

If she'd watched him consciously, she'd have been able to narrow it down to a couple of digits on each side, maybe even the exact numbers, although she'd been a little too far away to read the dial with total certainty. As it was, her memory could probably get her to within three or four on each side. Which gave her around sixty possible combinations. At five seconds a try, she would be a sitting duck for three minutes. A small price to pay to get at what was in this safe.

She knelt by the enormous old Chubb and tried the numbers: 20-55-38. Nothing. 20-55-37; no luck. Someone banged on the shop door above her and called out again. Same voice as before, something in Hebrew, a little more agitated this time. She kept running combinations. The man upstairs wasn't going to break in, but he might decide to sit on the doorstep and wait a while, which would make getting out of the locked shop more of a problem than she wanted it to be. She span the dial again. On the ninth attempt, the lock disengaged. Nineteen, fifty-five, thirty-seven. She swung the door open and there, in the middle of the top shelf was a sheaf of papers, a British passport and two bundles of bank notes. She pocketed the money and examined the papers.

The entry card was so bland she was sure it would be fine. The forger had used the slightly fanciful information she'd supplied him with, written in a frighteningly good impersonation of her own handwriting. He'd even done a signature that would have passed most casual checks, and he'd never seen her signature. Phillip's guy was good. He was more than technically precise, he was observant, creative. How he had guessed how she would sign her name from fifteen minutes talking to her and a few scribbled words on a scrap of paper was impressive. Once again she silently thanked Phillip for getting her someone so diligent in his work.

Diligent in all aspects but one. She flicked through the passport, past a few entry and exit stamps to non-threatening countries around the world. It looked well-used and completely natural, but there was a problem, and it was a big one. In its current state, the passport was useless.

Her biographical details were all in place... but the photograph was not. He'd removed it again. There must have been a problem with the image, something he would need her on site to solve. But now that she was on site, he was beyond being able to do anything about it... and she had neither the time nor the expertise to do it herself.

'Damn it,' she whispered in the silence. She stared at that blank square where the picture should be, but there was really no decision to be made. No thought or plan could make the slightest difference to this situation. She threw the passport back into the safe and closed the door. Better not to have a passport at all than have one that would instantly be spotted as a fake by some over-inquisitive soldier on the street.

So what now? The entry card alone might be enough to enable her to move about freely inside Israel and some of the Palestinian Territories, but she would not be able to get out of the country. And she would be in trouble on the street if anyone demanded her passport, although she thought that was unlikely. Unless someone specifically recognised her – in which case no passport on earth was going to make any difference – she was just an anonymous tourist, unremarkable in any way. That was, until the local police discovered what was lying on the floor of this particular shop basement, and the state police filled them in with a backstory and a likely suspect.

She needed help on the ground, and under the circumstances she had no desire to bring another of Phillip's contacts into this. But there might be someone else. He had, until now, been just a name in a file, a player in a bigger game. And ironically, it had been this shadowy figure who had initiated the chain of events that led to Raha Golzar's rendition to Britain, and thus to everything that had happened in the last week... right up to Leila's current predicament. It would be a kind of poetic justice if it was he who helped her get out of this mess. With all other avenues now closed to her, he might be her best chance... if she could find him. If, indeed, he was still alive.

She picked up the tourist entry card and put it in her pocket. There was nothing she could do about the forger's dead body, but she did feel bad for this man's family – assuming he had one. He had died trying to help her and there was nothing she could do either to reward them or to soften the blow of how he had been killed.

She crouched at his feet and looked at him. She didn't even know his name. He'd had no reason to help her, but he'd given his life out of loyalty to Phillip. She wouldn't forget that. And she would never again sacrifice one of the good guys to achieve her ends. She needed to be smarter. She needed to climb out of this mess on the backs of the people who had dug this swamp in the first place. And the first of those was Hassan Hawadi, Fatah's slipperiest double agent.

27

'Phillip, we need your help,' DCI Lawrence said. He took a seat across the table.

Phillip had been brought into the anonymous central London building in the back of an unmarked car. He hadn't been processed (he'd seen processing on TV, and knew nothing like that had happened to him); he hadn't been put in one of those vomit-smelling cells (fly-on-the-wall TV was such a wonderful thing); as far as he knew he hadn't even been arrested. If he had been, he had no idea what the charge was.

A uniformed officer had talked to him but he had said nothing. Then for the next few hours he had been left alone in a small room where he sat on the floor with his back against the wall and a small plastic bottle of water between his feet. They were examining his computer, which meant they would be back sooner or later when they realised there was nothing on it.

And they were. He had been transferred to a large underground room with blank concrete walls and left there for nearly two hours. No handcuffs, no phone call, but no rough treatment either. He wasn't sure what the game was here. He rarely was sure what the game was anywhere, which is why he spent his whole life trying to avoid them, but here the rules – even the prize on offer – were a mass of contradictions beyond anything he could even begin to understand.

After the first hour two men had brought in a computer – his own computer from Bone's flat – and placed it on the table at which he was sitting. They left all the cables and went away without a word, leaving Phillip in this big space that had begun to make him more uneasy than any amount of police brutality ever would have done. He hated big, bright spaces where if you sat against one wall, the opposite one was too far away, and if you sat in the middle of the room, they were *all* too far away. It was like claustrophobia only the other way round, and this room seemed to have been designed for it. He stared at the lifeless computer. Tempting though it was to retreat into that world to escape the blank silence of this awful room, he refused to play their game.

Another hour later a uniformed policeman came in: Michael Lawrence – Detective Chief Inspector Michael Lawrence. Phillip knew the name. Leila had mentioned him, talked about him. There was something between them, a connection, but Phillip was still in no mood to cooperate.

'Can I get you a tea, coffee?' Lawrence said. 'Or a sandwich? Anything as long as it comes from the M&S Express next door. We might be here for some time.'

'I want a lawyer,' Phillip said.

'Phillip, you don't need a lawyer. And… your position is such that you are unlikely to be granted one even if you did.'

'So why am I here?'

'Officially, aiding a fugitive, impeding investigation, misuse of telecommunications, terrorist support…'

'Terrorist? I'd be in Guantan-what's-it-called.'

'Guantanamo's American. We do things differently. In your case, very differently.'

'Then I want a lawyer.'

'Stop the lawyer thing, Phillip. What you're officially here for and what you're *actually* here for are two very different things. If you work with us, all the legal stuff goes away, ended, forgotten. You go home. I want you to go home, but for that you need to cooperate.'

'Cooperate?'

'As I said, we need your help. With Detective Reid. Let's start by getting this computer working, shall we?'

'I cleared it. There's nothing on there.'

'We know. You did a good job! But humour me, OK? Just get it working.'

Phillip looked at him for a moment. He could refuse – this friend of Leila's was no heavy-weight enforcer even if he did have three letters in front of his name. On the other hand, having the computer on, even if just as a useless prop, would help to dispel the huge emptiness of this room. He began to plug it together as they talked.

'What can you tell me about Leila now?' Lawrence said.

'I don't know where she is,' Phillip said.

'Phillip, Mr Shaw, we're way past that. We know you communicated with her before we brought you here, and we know the nature of your conversation. You need to start being honest here: it's the best thing for you, for us, and for Leila.'

Phillip ran the mains cable to a socket in the wall and returned to his seat.

I need to start being honest...? he thought. DCI Lawrence was almost convincing, but Phillip knew there was no way his conversation with Leila could have been found or read. He'd bounced the exchange around assets in a vast botnet – even he had no idea which host would be selected for each node of the path. The switch was instant, randomly generated and untraceable. The system was so good that he could have got her where she was safe to talk in only a couple of steps. The silly questions were more about making sure he was talking to who he thought he was talking to (and reassuring her of the same thing) than disguising their path. There was no way on God's green earth that these amateurs could have followed them down into the darkness. Was there...?

He switched the computer on and waited for it to boot up. It felt good to hear the familiar fan whirring in the silence. The machine had obviously been investigated by their techs, but, as he suspected, it was equally obvious that his suicide routine had worked. There was nothing useful left. Anyway, if they had been able to reconstruct any of the conversation he'd had with Reid they wouldn't still be talking to him. Or at least not this nicely. They'd have sent him to Guantanamo (whatever the nice Mr Lawrence said) and would already have agents at Canaan Communications waiting for Leila to show up for her passport.

The computer finished its boot routine and a cursor appeared on the blank screen. Phillip gestured to it. 'I still don't know where she is,' he said.

'Maybe not by the most literal definition of the terms, no. But you need to know that you are not helping her now by staying silent. We need to get DS Reid – Leila – out of Israel, quickly. Diplomacy, borders, governments, rules, that's all just so much bullshit to you, a joke, but I am also very aware that Leila's not. Even after what Black Eagle did to your family you carried on helping her.'

'I didn't have anything else to do.'

'We both know that's not the whole story. She is in real danger, Phillip, and probably a lot more than she knows. Right now, you are our quickest and safest way of getting her back.'

'Are you her boyfriend?' Phillip said.

Michael leaned back in his chair on the other side of the table. 'No. Or… it's complicated. I care about her. And I know you do too, which is why I'm hoping you'll help us find her and get her out of the trouble she's in.'

'I'm not ratting her out.'

Michael smiled. 'No one was stupid enough to think you would. But you can talk to her. Bring her home. She nearly died in a plane crash because she had no one to talk her down safely. This time she's got you. She's not flying a plane now, but what she's doing is just as dangerous.' He placed the leather bag on the table and pulled out the phone Scaz Bones had received her original SMS message on that morning.

'There's no way to contact her,' Phillip said. 'As I told you already, I don't know where she is.'

'She'll contact you.'

'How do you know?'

'Because you're the only person she trusts. We need you to get back online with whatever system you used last time. Then we wait.'

The door opened and another policeman entered. DCI Lawrence walked over to him and spoke quietly. Phillip listened without much interest. He figured if they were going to let him hear what they were saying, it wouldn't be worth hearing. It seemed to mostly be about him anyway, and he knew that subject wasn't interesting at all. Lawrence looked back at Phillip as the new man showed him a mobile phone and seemed to scroll through photographs on it. They spoke for another minute or so, during which Micheal seemed to have convinced the new arrival that he, Phillip, was prepared to cooperate. Which was odd, because Phillip himself hadn't been aware of making any such promise. Only one final, whispered comment made his ears prick up. 'Shin Bet's giving us twenty-four, then the deal's off,' the new man said. Phillip liked the idea of a deal – a deal was a kind of game he could understand because no one started playing it until everyone knew the rules. And he liked time limits… they made the game much more interesting. He wasn't sure who they were talking about, but he could find out. He thought he could probably find out a lot about this mysterious Mr Shin Bet in the next twenty-four hours.

Michael Lawrence left and the other man took his place across the table.

'Mr Shaw,' he said. 'I'm Commander Thorne, Head of Counter-Terrorism Command. Thank you for agreeing to assist the recovery of our officer.'

'I didn't,' Phillip said.

'You will. We can work together, you and I.'

'Who's Shin Bet?'

'Nothing to do with this investigation. Shall we move on?'

'You give me something, I give you something.' Phillip grinned at Commander Thorne. 'So we can work together.'

'We've given you your computer. So let's get started, shall we?'

'I can't do anything with this,' Phillip said.

'Just get it set up with whatever you used to talk to DS Reid earlier and we'll take it from there.'

'You mean like an internet browser? Even you could do that.'

'Just get on with it. We don't have a lot of time, and if there's one thing I hate, it's wasting what little we do have. OK?'

'I prefer the other guy,' he said.

'The other guy has other business to attend to. So you've got me for a while. Consider it a promotion.'

Phillip allowed himself a wry smile. Thorne obviously thought of himself as a promotion. Phillip thought it was exactly the other way around. Michael Lawrence confused him. This whole situation, including Phillip's part in it, was personal; he was invested in Leila, maybe loved her, something anyway. And he was friendly. His motives were complex... no clear rules and no clear goal. Thorne was different. Thorne was a machine. Cold, thoughtful, official, bound by protocol. He was programmed by logic, and that made him transparent and predictable: not such a formidable opponent. Against someone like this it was all about power. Whoever has the biggest knife cuts the biggest slice of the prize. And Phillip knew he had the entire cutlery set. Thorne had no way of contacting Leila, and that was all he wanted.

He looked down at the computer screen and ran his fingers deftly over the keyboard, opening and closing windows but attempting nothing useful.

'And if I don't find her,' he said, 'you'll send me to prison.' Thorne looked at him. 'Misuse of telecom-whats-its. Maybe that's OK. I can get a lawyer. Get you thrown in jail for kidnap and shit.'

Thorne laughed and leaned forwards.

'Mr Shaw. DCI Lawrence might have told you that. That's not how this would go down. Shall I tell you how this would go down?' Phillip looked up from the screen.

'Do you know the name Holly Samson?' Thorne said. Phillip shook his head. 'Holly Sampson, six years old, resident of Duckett's Green, you probably know the place.' Phillip nodded. He'd never been there, but it was no more than a few minutes walk from Broadwater Farm.

'Nice girl, pretty, blonde hair, you get the picture,' Thorne went on. 'White. Remember that bit: white. Happy. Doing well at school. Until someone took a special interest in her. An unhealthy interest. Her body was found stuffed in a storm drain. She had been raped and tortured, the coroner calculated, for at least twelve hours before both her femoral arteries were torn open, again according to the coroner, with whatever the perpetrator had been using to rape and sodomise her. He thought it was possibly a claw hammer.'

Phillip shrugged.

'And we never caught the bastard,' Thorne said. He leaned towards Phillip across the table and spoke quietly. 'Or did we?' he said. 'A young black kid, messed up, retarded, no job, no friends except drug dealers twice his age. Fits the profile.'

'You think...? I don't know anything about it!' Phillip said.

'I know you don't. But you go to prison, on any little charge, rumours might start, a hint here, a word in the right ear there. You're in general population with loads of hard nuts, family men who haven't seen their kids in years. You know what they do to ordinary rapists? Add in paedophilia, extreme sadism, murder... You get the picture here?'

Phillip nodded slowly. *They wouldn't, would they? Could they?*

He looked back at the screen and decided he wasn't going to find out. One simple job here and he was out and away. This man Thorne was a machine. Cold, thoughtful, official, bound by protocol – in most respects not such a formidable opponent. But he carried the biggest knife of all. That knife was made of finely sharpened lies and his lies would be believed, because Thorne was a Police Commander and he, Phillip, was just a poor black kid who fitted whatever profile they wanted him to fit...

He trawled through the computer's remaining user files, more to appear to be doing something than because he was actually *was* doing anything. When he could pretend no longer he glanced up from the screen. Thorne was watching him with mild curiosity but no sense of urgency. He was a cat watching a mouse, playing without seeming to do anything, to care about anything. This wasn't even the game.

They were both waiting for the real game to start.

And twenty minutes later, it did.

The cell phone on the table rang. Michael had made sure Phillip's attention had been focussed on the computer, and as such he'd not given the phone any thought. He'd assumed it was just a prop, a reminder that CTC was in control, that they knew everything. But Thorne had not been so clever; Phillip quickly realised the computer was just a prop too, a way of keeping him busy and not asking too many questions, but until the phone rang he had been wondering what the main event would really be. Now it was obvious. Somehow they knew Leila would call, and they just needed all the actors on stage here in London when she made her entrance.

Phillip leaned forwards to pick the phone up. Thorne got there first. His hand hovered over it, index finger raised and pointed at Phillip.

'On speaker,' Thorne said. 'Talk to her as normal. If you even think about giving her any indication of where you are, remember Holly Sampson. OK?'

Phillip nodded. Thorne pressed answer.

For several seconds no one spoke. Thorne pointed at Phillip again.

'Hello?' Phillip said.

'Phillip?' Leila said.

'Yeah.'

'What's wrong?'

'Nothing. Fine.'

'You at home?… Phillip?'

'Yeah.' He looked at Thorne. 'Just closing the door. 'Sup?'

There was a long pause. Dead air. Maybe the connection had been broken or a hand placed over the mouthpiece. Then the sound of voices, footsteps. A song, a man singing in Arabic through a cheap speaker driven to the point of distortion. Someone laughed.

'Listen,' Leila said, 'something went wrong. I need your help again. Contact someone for me, if you can find him.'

Phillip looked across the concrete table at his interrogator. Thorne nodded.

'Who?' Phillip said, his eyes fixed once more on the phone.

'There's a man in Jerusalem calls himself Hassan Hawadi…' Phillip glanced up at Thorne. Thorne smiled for the first time.

'Go on,' Phillip said.

'I need to get in touch with him – arrange a meeting.'

'Do you know any more about him? Just a name's going to take a while.'

'He was peripheral to an investigation a few years back.'

'One of yours? Counter-terrorism?'

'Yes, but don't go that way! If CTC get wind that I'm looking for him you might as well put a tracker on me.'

'I can't help you.' Thorne pointed at him. Phillip got the message. 'Not without more info,' he said. 'Give me something to hook into.'

There was another long pause on the other end of the line. Phillip could still hear background sounds but Leila appeared to be thinking about what he'd said. Maybe he'd said enough. Maybe his friend would realise if he was putting up this much resistance after helping her without question before, there was a good reason for it. Maybe she would decide there was a better way.

Or maybe not. He heard her take a deep breath before she spoke again. 'He's got – or had – contacts in the CIA and Fatah, so that's going to be your best way in. One or the other will get you to him, but I can't tell you which is going to be the best place to start. Just try to avoid searching both if you can. I don't think either side really knows what he's doing, and it's useful to keep it that way. It's also likely he's got contacts in Black Eagle. He betrayed them fifteen months ago so it's not likely he's working with them directly, but he will be of ongoing interest to them... Above all, he needs to be convinced I'm working alone. Talk to no one about him.'

Phillip looked up again. Thorne made a rolling gesture with the index finger of his left hand: keep talking.

'Why do you need to find him?' Phillip said.

'It's better if you don't know. Are you sure you're OK? You sound different.'

'I'm OK.'

'Is there anyone there with you?'

'No.'

'This call will be being monitored,' Leila said. 'CTC will close in on you very soon, so what you don't know can't implicate you. All I can give you is a name. Just please, find him and tell him I'm looking for him, fast. Hassan Hawadi.'

Thorne waved a hand under Phillip's nose and he looked up. The counter-terrorism chief drew a finger across his throat and nodded. Phillip took this to mean he should just agree to Leila's request and get off the line.

'OK,' he said. 'I'll find him. I'll call you…'

'No. This phone's useless now. They'll be locking onto it.'

'So how will I contact you?'

'How quickly do you think can you do it?'

Thorne held up two fingers and mouthed two words.

'Two hours,' Phillip said.

'I'll be at the Dolorosa Café, near the Garden of Eden Bazaar—'

'Woah! If they're monitoring this line, you've just told them your location!'

Commander Thorne glared at him.

'Let me worry about that,' Leila said. 'If anyone approaches, I'm smart enough to know the difference between one of your people and one of ours. I'm almost certain someone here's watching me, and if not, they're very close, so they've not got the element of surprise on their side. And I've been doing this a long time, Phillip. Just get a message to me there, two hours, no more, no less. I'm sorry, truly. I didn't want to get you caught up in this again. This is the last time, I promise. You're out of this mess now.'

'Two hours,' Phillip said. Commander Thorne ended the call.

'I'm going to need my computer,' Phillip said. 'Properly this time. Without all your cheap spyware shit on it.'

'Don't worry about that,' Thorne said. 'As Reid said, you're out of this now.'

28

Fifteen minutes before Phillip's two hour deadline, Leila stood along the street from the Dolorosa Café, watching. She had no idea how – or even if – Phillip would be able to get a message to her, or what message would come. Given enough time, she would back him to be able to fix a meeting, though in two hours that would be a big ask. She hoped at least he would be able to give her a location. Or even just confirm that Hawadi was still alive and somewhere in Jerusalem… Without him, her chances of getting out of Israel, let alone clearing her name, were slight to non-existent now. Hawadi was the key to all this.

The street was busy. The Old City had the same kind of tourist foot-fall as any major city in the world, but its streets had been built for another age. An age where the widest vehicle was a donkey cart and the closest thing to a tourist attraction would have been a good crucifixion. It meant she was inconspicuous, but it also meant she had very limited sight-lines to anyone paying her undue attention.

When the two IDF soldiers who were standing diagonally across from her had looked her way five or six times without apparently seeing her, and no one stood out from the crowds as having passed her more than once without good reason, Leila walked over to the café. She had taken a huge risk giving Phillip her location over a line she was sure would be monitored by CTC or GCHQ, but maybe she had slipped through the eye of that treacherous needle, for now at least. Maybe both organisations were still so tied up in the details of her unexpected appearance in the Negev that they hadn't got around to watching Phillip as closely as they should have been. Whatever the reason, no one stood out as an intelligence agent in this crowded bazaar.

She took a table in the window and ordered a pot of coffee. The waitress barely acknowledged her presence either when she took the order or when she returned with the tray bearing a silver jug of aromatic coffee and a glass of rosewater. The bill bore only the single line, scrawled in Hebrew, that Leila had seen the girl write when she took the order.

So she waited.

The two soldiers ambled past, chatting. People came and went from the café. Time ticked by and the she slowly sipped the coffee down to its sludgy dregs. The two-hour deadline had passed and no message had come. She would wait a little longer, but the longer she was here the more the balance of benefit slipped against her. The arrival of a useful message became less likely, but her being spotted in this very public setting became dangerously more likely. She sipped the sweet and too-strong rose water and waited.

Two boys entered and scanned the tables. They spoke to an elderly couple – Leila had noted the American accents as she entered – and moved on. The café owner said something and the smaller of the two boys bowed extravagantly to her. It seemed to be some kind of show, a hustle, a way of singling out a target, but it seemed harmless. Leila watched, ready to move if they came too close and started to draw attention to her, but the smaller of the boys was already making his way towards her.

'Hey, pretty lady,' he said. He took the seat opposite her and pulled a long silk scarf, a pocket watch and a pack of playing cards from his pocket. He looked about ten years old, small, olive-skinned, eyes that had seen a lot more of the world than a ten year old had any right to see. His friend stood a little way away, looking out of the window.

'I'm waiting for someone,' Leila said.

'I do a trick for you,' the boy said. 'Amazing, amazing!' He deftly shuffled the cards and fanned them from one hand to the other.

'No,' Leila said. 'Please, I'm waiting…' Getting up and leaving now would unleash a wave of noisy protest. They'd found their target and the quickest way to get it over with was to play along and hope no one but her cared about the show.

'Say stop when you pick a card,' the boy said. He rifled the card, flicking rapidly through the pack. Leila just watched.

'Come on, pretty lady,' the boy said. 'You pick card. Good trick.'

'OK.'

He flicked through the pack again, too fast to see any of the cards properly. This was clearly a scam. The way his older friend shuffled from one foot to the other behind him was a big giveaway. This was a shake-down, Jerusalem style, but Leila was now just curious enough to let it play for a while. She could watch the street just as well with this tiny kid sitting opposite her as she could alone, and his presence (and the mildly amused looks of several of the people on nearby tables) made it marginally less likely that someone would rush in and drive a seven inch combat knife into her head.

'Stop,' Leila said. 'That one.'

The boy pulled the card out without looking at it and placed it face down on the table between them. He took the pocket watch and placed it on the card. The watch had stopped at eleven o'clock.

He then covered both with the silk scarf and waived his hands over the little mound, mouthing something Leila was probably not meant to hear over the noise of the café. He removed the scarf and watch and pushed the card a little further towards her.

'Put it in your pocket,' the boy said. 'No look! No look!'

Leila dropped the card into the outside pocket of her skirt and looked at the boy.

'Your card, it has magic,' the boy said.

'And what's it going to cost me?' Leila said.

'Ten shekels.'

'Ten? This had better be some good magic!'

The boy was harmless. Better than stealing for a living. At least he was providing some entertainment, and the coffee had already cost her twice that.

Suddenly the older kid leaned over and whispered

something to his magician friend. Both boys looked out of the window. The two soldiers were back.

'Ten shekels, ten shekels!' the older kid said. He held his hand out across the table.

'He hasn't finished the trick!' Leila said.

'Come on.' The magician gathered the cards, watch and silk scarf into his pocket and got up. Both boys pushed their way through the café and disappeared into a back room, probably the kitchen. Leila smiled. They were doubtless employed by the management to improve the tip-rate. At least until the IDF showed up.

She glanced at the clock above the serving hatch. It was now twenty-five minutes past Phillip's deadline. No one had approached her, no phone call to the management, no message on the order pad, no one had even acknowledged her existence. He must have run into a problem. Or maybe he'd already had a problem when she called him. He had sounded different, more hesitant than usual. She had a feeling the phone had been on speaker too, although given Phillip's dislike of phones he probably had his own superstitious ways of using one.

So how long should she wait? She drained the last of the rose water and looked out of the window. The crowds were beginning to thin out. A man was packing away crates of fruit from the shop opposite. The two boys emerged from a door beside the café and as they passed the fruit seller he threw a couple of oranges their way. The little conjuror, the Old City's very own mini David Copperfield, span his orange on the tip of his index finger then threw it to his friend. His friend didn't even react. In the split second between the fruit apparently leaving the kid's hand and heading to his accomplice, it vanished. A simple deception – distraction, point the audience's attention in the wrong direction, sleight-of-hand 101 – but it was exquisitely done. The fruit seller roared with laughter and several passing tourists pointed and aimed smart-phones at the pair. The boys skipped off down a side alley. Neither looked back in her direction.

As street entertainers they were good, but for once their shake-down, their real money-spinner, had failed. No ten shekels for their trouble, and the magician now had an incomplete pack of cards. He'd taken his pile but forgotten she still had one in her pocket – the magic card that was going to stun and impress the naive English lady. His scam wasn't going to work again if anyone – a slightly less naive English lady for instance – insisted on examining the pack for authenticity before he started.

She reached into her pocket with a smile.

An incomplete pack. Her finger rested lightly on the playing card and the smile fell from her lips. She felt a chill run up her back and she scanned the street for the boys. They were nowhere to be seen. The fruit seller went about his business, piling boxes into his tiny street-side lock-up, the soldiers chatted as they wandered away, a young couple negotiated with a market hawker for a carved olive-wood cross.

She took the playing card from her pocket and placed it on the table in front of her.

Phillip *had* contacted her. He'd just done it so secretively that even she hadn't realised it was happening. Deception, diversion, sleight-of-hand 101.

It was an ordinary playing card, a King of Hearts, a little tatty around the corners where it had no doubt been marked back when that little Arab kid with his broken English and cunning mind really had just been a street scammer making the best he could of a crappy start in life. He'd lost his card, but she had no doubt Phillip would have made sure he'd been handsomely paid for his trouble. Probably from her bank account.

The King of Hearts. But not just a random card: drawn in one corner was a clock face showing twenty past twelve. The kid might have only been ten, but he'd pulled an impressive trick managing to get this exact card to her while making her think she'd chosen it at random. No one watching would have suspected anything. She turned the card over and examined the patterned back for any further clues, but there was nothing.

The King of Hearts at twenty past twelve. What the hell did that mean? If Philip was behind this – and she had no doubt he had been – it was clearly a very specific message, but it meant nothing to her. Nothing at all. Was she supposed to meet someone at 12.20? If so, who? A King, a romantic poet, the husband of the local jam tart baker?

And where?

Phillip knew her, knew how she worked. He would have made sure she had all the information she needed to move forward with her plans or her escape, but the only clue she had was a playing card with a crude clock face drawn on it. Which meant that right now she had no clue at all.

29

Back at the Hebron Gardens hotel Leila examined the playing card again. It contained at least three important elements: it was a king, it was from the hearts suit, and it had a clock on it showing twenty past twelve. She couldn't understand how these elements coded enough information to tell her both when and where the meeting was to take place. Phillip knew how she worked, knew she thought deeper than the obvious. Having the time simply drawn on the card was overkill, so it was a diversion, a visual sleight-of-hand. A circle with two hands could hold much more information than just a time if she could figure out the code. But if she assumed the 'clock' did not refer to the time, what did?

She smiled. The kid used a pocket watch in his trick. It served absolutely no purpose. She had thought he was improvising, or just using this old prop to increase the mystery. But the watch didn't work. It had stopped at eleven o'clock, and he'd made very sure she saw it. That was the code for the time: simple, direct, effective... and cleverly, it had now disappeared just like the magician's flying orange. If she was searched now, that one piece of crucial information was missing. Only she knew the time of the meeting.

If the time scheduled for the meeting was eleven o'clock, she had less than three hours to figure out where it was to take place. Everything else she needed had to be on that playing card.

The king, taken literally, could refer to someone high up in either of Hawadi's main patron organisations – the CIA or Fatah. Neither of which was probable. It was highly unlikely that Phillip would have been negotiating with anyone significant in either organisation. Even if he had been, anyone with king-like power wouldn't need to send coded messages to fix a meeting. They could just have snatched her off the street and taken her to Hawadi's safe house. Or killed her for looking. So the king was not a person... it was something else, something less obvious.

And what of the hearts? That wasn't random, a one-in-four chance, either. Nothing about this was random. Did it refer obliquely to someone she loved? Not her brother: he had been killed in Iraq ten years ago. Both her parents were dead too – her mother from cancer when she was fifteen, her father from good old age and infirmity six years ago. Was the heart her boss and on-off lover, Michael Lawrence? Possible, but then it would not have been the king. He was second-in-command at CTC, a kind of queen in this coded language. And that more or less exhausted those possibilities. Leila didn't keep a lot of love in her life.

Hearts: love. That was all. Phillip somehow knew about her Picasso drawing, and may have been making an oblique reference to something artistic, but hearts in modern art led pretty much to Robert Indiana. Leila couldn't stand his work, Phillip would almost certainly never have heard of him, and even if there was some connection, the name was meaningless as a clue to finding Hawadi – if he had emigrated to Indiana, USA, under the patronage of the CIA, she was in serious trouble. And Phillip wouldn't have needed to be so creative to tell her that. He'd just have sent her the ace of spades – poker's dreaded Death Card.

So what the hell was he trying to tell her with this King of Hearts?

She dropped the card onto the bed and went over to the window. There was something she was missing. She was making this too complicated.

On the street below a couple walked hand in hand through the warm evening. They looked lost, absorbed in the history and romance of this ancient city.

Hearts… OK, if not love, what else? Something more literal and clinical than that: one of four suits in a game of cards… the so-called 'second' suit in poker. Used to break deadlocks.

Second suit. This playing card was the king of the second suit.

The pair turned into the Via Dolorosa and were gone, treading in the footsteps of Christ on his way to crucifixion. Or so the story went. Everything in this city dripped with symbolism and mythology. Layer upon layer of meaning… ancient stories written and rewritten over millennia. The Talmud, the Bible, by implication the Koran, each steeped in esoteric meaning, each coding mystery into the ancient stones of this city.

The bible.

She picked up the card and looked at it in wonder. King of the second suit: "Second King".

At twelve twenty.

She ran down to the reception desk and banged on the glass partition. The owner looked up from her TV in the back room. The dog didn't bother.

'Have you got a bible?' Leila said.

The woman heaved herself our of her armchair and waddled into reception.

'A what?' she said.

'A Bible. Old testament.'

'Wait a minute.'

She shambled back into her room and was gone for several minutes. When she came back she was brandishing a tatty, coverless book.

'Ten dollars,' she said.

'I don't want to buy it,' Leila said. 'I just need to check something.'

'You do it here, and make it quick. I'm busy.' The woman slid the glass partition open and handed the book over. Leila flicked quickly through it with no idea where Kings was in relation to all the other many books of this densely printed volume. Her hostess watched with barely disguised disgust. Joshua, Judges, Ruth... Samuel managed two books, then she hit the Kings. Second King, chapter, chapter, chapter.

The clock face on the card read twenty past twelve. But it wasn't a time for the meeting: it was a chapter and verse reference. Chapter twelve, verse twenty. For a moment she could not take in the words, strange names from a strange ancient world she had no knowledge of at all. 'His servants arose and made a conspiracy and struck down Joash in the house of Millo, on the way that goes down to Silla.'

Could it still exist? Could this be where Phillip was sending her?

'Do you know where this is?' Leila said. She pointed at the verse. 'The house of Millo? On a road to Silla?'

'I'm not tourist information,' the woman said. 'They can direct you in the morning. Have you finished?'

'Yes.' She handed the bible back through the narrow opening in the screen. 'Please, I don't have time to wait for tourist information. I need to know now. Is the house of Millo still there?'

The woman took a deep breath and let it out through her teeth.

'It's still there. Just outside the Old City.'

'Can you direct me to it?'

'It won't be open now. They do tours in the daytime.'

'I'll figure that out when I get there. Where is it?'

'South wall of the old city. You shouldn't go wandering the streets on your own after dark. Not round those parts anyway. And that's free information.'

'OK. Thank you. Maybe I'll go in the morning, but so that I won't have to disturb you tomorrow, could you just tell me where it is… now?' She kept the end of the sentence to herself: *before I reach in there and stuff that bible down your fat throat you lazy bitch…*

The woman shrugged. Maybe Leila's face had mimed enough of the last few words to make her realise the only way to end this was to cooperate. Teasing tourists was obviously fun, but only up to a point.

'You know the al-Aqsa mosque?' she said. Leila nodded. She had a vague idea and it wasn't exactly easy to miss. 'Below that's the City of David, through the Dung Gate. Millo's a pile of stones, like a foundation. It's really not much to see without a guide to tell you what you're looking at.'

'I think I'll know what I'm looking at when I get there. Thank you.'

She turned for the stairs then stopped. The glass partition was beginning to close when she put her hand against it.

'Have you got any stationery?'

The hotel owner raise an eyebrow.

'Couple of envelopes, two sheets of paper and a stamp,' Leila said. 'That's all.'

'Go to the Post Office in the morning. On your way to Millo, remember?'

'I might be dead by tomorrow morning.'

'Yeah, you might. Wait here.'

There was a lot of noise of shuffling papers and heavy sighs from the room beyond reception. The woman returned a couple of minutes later with two mismatched, rather crumpled envelopes and a few sheets of lined paper torn from a notebook.

'I've only got stamps that'll make ten shekels. Where are you sending it?'

'Ten shekels will be fine. Thank you.' She handed a twenty over and finally got a hint of a smile from her hostess.

Back in her room Leila sat on the bed and wrote two

short letters. She folded the first into one of the envelopes, addressed it and put that and the second letter into the remaining envelope. She thought for a moment, wrote the address and attached the collection of small denomination stamps.

The letters were her security. She'd cracked the puzzle of the playing card. She knew where and when to meet her contact but she was troubled by the reference to the assassination of the unfortunate Joash in the bible verse. She had no idea who he was or if he was relevant, but the allusion was unsettling. Maybe she was overthinking it. Not every word had to mean something. It was amazing Phillip had found a bible verse that coded so much relevant information at all.

She looked out of the window at the blank dark face of the building opposite. It *was* amazing Phillip had found such a perfect bible verse. She tapped the letter on her knee. It was amazing he had found anything in the bible at all. His mother had been a good woman, no doubt a first or second generation Caribbean immigrant in whom the word of the Lord ran deep and sonorous, but could Leila really believe she had educated her son in the ways of the Old Testament? Something didn't fit. It wasn't that the cryptic clue was too clever to have been thought up by young Mr Shaw, it was just that the source material felt wrong. The timing felt wrong too now that she broke it down. In under two hours he'd found Hawadi – not exactly a man to leave his calling card in every public phone box in Jerusalem – had fixed the meeting, worked out an obscure code to tell her about it, found the mini-David Copperfield to perform the sleight of hand with the playing card, and done the whole lot without alerting anyone to his plan. Was that possible? He had the contacts, somewhere in his maladjusted mind he had the intelligence and guile, but could he really have done it, alone, from a flat in north London that quickly? Had he been working with someone else for the last couple of hours? Had he been working on this *at all*? At eleven at night, with the site closed to the public, she would be walking into a certain trap. Whoever had killed the forger almost certainly knew she was here. Did they now know exactly where she would be in another two hours… and that she would be fatally exposed and without backup?

She had no choice. She had to make the rendezvous. Hawadi was her only hope now, and maybe even more so if Phillip had been compromised. She might be walking into a trap, but when the alternative was to live in this dump with its sullen owner and stinking over-priced rooms until Black Eagle or the CIA or Shin Bet caught up with her, she'd take the chance.

She changed into her new jeans and slipped into her faithful old leather jacket. With the letters safely at the bottom of her rucksack she headed out into the night.

30

She arrived at the entrance to the ancient City of David at just after ten minutes to eleven. It had been a short and easy walk, her only delay the five minutes it had taken to find a letter box in which she had dropped the envelope that she hoped might save her life tonight. The warning not to be out alone after dark had been meaningless. There had only been a few locals around, and on the whole they either looked right through her or looked the other way. There had been no sense of threat on the short walk from the inexplicably named Hebron Gardens hotel to the equally inexplicable Dung Gate in the south of the old Jewish Quarter. If anything, the biggest source of disquiet came from the eerily quiet and dark alleys, but Leila had never been much concerned with ghosts. Tonight it was the living that waited at the end of this journey that were the real threat, not the silently echoing footsteps of this city veiled in night.

The gates that led to the main tourist centre and on up flights of steps into the complex were locked. There was no one around. The huge walls at the top of the hill were lit up with floodlights, and streetlights on high poles cast pools of yellow light on the road where Leila now stopped. Behind her the ground dropped into barren scrubby wasteland with a dense rash of housing hugging the slopes of the valley's far side.

She was being watched. There was no doubt about that. Even if Phillip had set the whole thing up on his own – which seemed increasingly unlikely – Hawadi would have someone out here to make sure she was coming alone. To make sure she was (as Phillip would have tried to convince him) not a vanguard of some private army bent on righting one of the many wrongs Hawadi had done in his career as a mercenary, fixer, swindler and political chameleon. She could see no one, but there were a thousand places someone with a sniper scope could hide even in the brightest light of mid day. In the shadows of night, they were the real ghosts of this ancient place.

She was disinclined to enter the site. For one thing, she had no idea where Millo itself was located, and for another it was highly probable that the place was monitored by more than just the snipers across the valley. Five minutes after scrambling over the fence she would be in a police van – or worse – on her way to a very difficult interview.

So she sat on a low wall as close to the main entrance as she could and waited. A few cars passed, a group of people walked along the other side of the road and entered a gated building. They did not seem to notice her.

A clock struck somewhere in the city above her, a mournful sound in the desert silence. Others joined it. As the final stroke of a bell somewhere across the valley died away, a phone rang. It was quiet but it was close and she could see no one on the road or within the complex behind her.

She looked around, trying to locate the sound. On her right was a gnarled old olive tree, not much younger than Millo itself judging by the enormous girth of its trunk. She stood and peered up into its branches. The gentle burr of the phone continued. She reached up towards the sound and felt along the tangle of branches where they emerged from the huge trunk.

The phone buzzed against her hand and she grabbed it, lifted it down. Pressed answer.

'Open your jacket,' a voice said before she could speak.

'Phillip sent you?'

'Open your jacket.'

Leila looked down and saw a tiny red dot on her chest. She followed the laser sight back to a point high up on the city walls. She opened her jacket with one hand, transferred the phone and did the same with the other side.

'Place your own phone on the wall and take two steps backwards,' the voice on the phone said.

She complied. She thought for a moment of backing out, trying to find another way – that steady red bead was deeply disconcerting – but there was no other way. If a meeting had been set up with Hawadi, she was only going to get one shot at it. The door had been opened and she now had no choice but to walk through it.

'There is a taxi waiting for you one hundred meters north of your position,' the man said.

'Go on,' Leila said.

'Keep this phone on. Get in the taxi. Do not speak to

the driver. He has no connection to us, but he knows where you are going and will give you final instructions on arrival.'

'Confirm who sent you.'

'We will be watching your every move. If you speak to the driver for any reason, if this phone connection is lost or if you try to signal to anyone at any time, the taxi will be destroyed. Hand the phone to the man who meets you at your destination. If he does not confirm you are alone, or we do not hear from him, or there is anything to indicate you are not playing straight with us, you will be shot. Start walking.'

Leila looked around. The thin strand of laser light traced a broken line through the dusty air, its end-point on her arm now. She turned north and started walking. The light tracked her around the corner and within sight of the taxi parked facing her another fifty yards away. She moved into the shadow of the old city wall and the light could not follow her any further. There was no sign of anyone else watching, but someone would be. Somewhere out there across the parched Kidron Valley a rifle sight would be tracing her every step. Or maybe not: that was the point. Even if the sniper on the city wall was the only man out here, he'd sown enough doubt and paranoia in his quarry that she had to assume there were hunters waiting in every shadow.

She reached the taxi. The driver had been watching her, unseen behind the headlights. He jumped out to open the rear door as soon as she arrived. He smiled but said nothing. Leila got in. The driver got in, started the engine and drove back along the road heading south. He turned onto a wide freeway towards the new city and Leila was immediately lost.

After fifteen minutes the taxi turned onto a dusty, barren road past a new development of residential towers. She was sure they'd passed the other side of those awful modernist monstrosities a few minutes earlier. In front of them the far side of the valley was dark, punctuated only here and there with the warm yellowy glow of lights from houses and she was beginning to think she was to be taken out of the city by a long and disorientating route. Or maybe the taxi driver was as lost as she was. He took a right turn into a tree-lined residential street that she had definitely not seen before.

On one side were expensive-looking houses built of local limestone and softened by showy bougainvillea and cherry trees. The leaves and bright pink papery flowers of the bougainvillea looked black in the streetlights, the shuttered and recessed windows of the houses like dark eyes, watching. Across the street were a few shops, then a high-rise block of flats. An old man sat on a bench smoking, a dog asleep between his feet. There was no one else around. The driver slowed, examining the block of flats, then stopped.

'Fifth floor, flat five-eight,' he said without turning. Leila leaned forwards and took the roll of cash from her back pocket. She peeled off a twenty shekel note and offered it to the him.

'Your friend paid me,' he said. He glanced at her in the mirror, not taking his hands from the regulation ten-to-two position on the steering wheel. Leila dropped the cash onto the passenger seat beside him anyway. He'd done his job. She was still alive. She reached for the door handle and saw a flash of red dance across the dirty glass. The light flicked across her face and she followed it back to the roof of a building in the distance. There were other hunters out here.

She put the phone to her ear.

'What's your problem?' she said.

'What did you give the driver?'

'I paid him, that's all.'

'He'd been paid.'

'A tip then! OK?'

'The driver will be stopped. If any message is found, you have just signed his death warrant. If you speak to him again, if you make any sign, any more towards him, I will kill you both right now. Get out of the car.'

Leila stepped out into the dust and heat. From the deep shadow of a parched acacia she looked up at the flats. When she turned around, the laser had gone. She approached the barred door of the building.

As soon as she reached it, the door lock buzzed and she pushed it open.

31

Leila jogged up the five flights of stairs to the top floor and along the corridor to the rear of the building. There was a TV on behind the second door; the other flats were quiet. There had been two estate agents' boards outside. Maybe whoever lived here didn't think much of their neighbour in the last apartment on the right. Flat five-eight. The door was open an inch or so and through it seeped the acrid smell of French cigarettes mixed with the spicy, woody tang of cheap aftershave. She could see nothing useful from where she stood – a triangle of light from the hallway spilled across a wooden floor, but beyond that the room's own light was dim, and her angle afforded only a view of the back of a room divider and one corner of a tall chest of drawers. The door had been left ajar, so she pushed it open and stepped in.

She left the backpack by the door and rounded the cover of the room divider slowly and deliberately, holding her hands out in front of her so that whoever was hidden within would see she was carrying nothing more deadly than a phone. She immediately recognised the room's sole occupant as Hassan Hawadi himself, even though she had only ever seen him in grainy surveillance photographs, and he was, even now, partially hidden in a haze of smoke and the dim light of a single lamp.

He sat in an armchair at the far end of the long sitting room with his back to the windows, a small man in a big man's body. His short legs and torso would put him at about five-foot five, Leila thought, but he had done a lot of filling out. His belly spilled out over the waistband of a pair of crumpled pale brown trousers. The matching jacket hung open to reveal an open-necked shirt, off-white and equally crumpled. The top three buttons were undone and a mass of thick black fur crept around the edges of the pale linen.

In his left hand, resting on the arm of the chair, was a stub-nosed Ruger revolver. He tracked her across the room with it as she approached. A fan wafted warm perfumed air around the room, its blades clicking slightly on the bent safety guard that covered them.

She handed the phone to Hawadi and sat down in a battered armchair opposite him. He mumbled a few words in Arabic then listened. The lights from the building across the street were muted by the tinted windows and the landscape beyond them was solid darkness. The room was silent except for the steady click of the faulty fan as Hawadi listened to the phone and Leila studied the man who was probably going to be her last hope of getting out of Israel alive. She didn't like her chances. He clicked the phone off and grinned disconcertingly at her.

'Miss Reid,' he said. 'Either you are very desperate or very foolish.'

'Who says it's either-or?' Leila said.

'A little of both then,' he said. 'Foolish-desperate, desperate-foolish.' He made a see-saw motion with his free hand and his grin grew wider as his piggy eyes bored into her.

The soft shapelessness of his face made it hard to guess his age. She knew it to be mid-forties from the files, but in this low light he could have been a chubby teenager. A day's growth of beard crept high up his olive cheeks and down his neck. Small, black eyes, deep-set and surrounded by skin the colour of bruised plums gave him the look of a malevolent panda. His lips smiled; his eyes did not.

'A little of both,' he repeated. A gold tooth glinted just off-centre amid the top row of yellowing and irregular teeth. 'You are hardly in a good position to be seeking my help then. I assume help is why you went to such trouble to seek me out?'

'I believe we can be good for each other,' she said. 'I have a problem, and you have a solution.'

'That is good for *you*. Why would *I* be interested?'

'Because if you help me, you stay alive.'

Hawadi's hand tightened around the pistol's grip. He shifted uneasily in the chair and the leather groaned and creaked under his weight.

'You are in a dangerous corner, Miss Reid. People have been asking about you. People from all shades of opinion. And your first move is to threaten me? Why are you so sure it is not you who is going to die here tonight?'

'I'll come to that,' Leila said. 'First, are we alone in here?'

Hawadi tipped his head left and right without ever taking his eyes off her. 'Do you see anyone?' he said.

'And you're not so stupid that you'd bug the place,' Leila said.

'I keep my own counsel, Miss Reid. I am a very private man.'

'There's no one next door?'

'Take a look if you wish. I'm sure you would be able to pick their locks. But I did not come here to play games. You talk to me or you leave.'

Leila nodded. 'One moment.'

She walked behind Hawadi, taking a wide circle and moving slowly enough for him to be able to track her with the gun without becoming alarmed. She had no intention of checking the flat next door. If Hawadi had been lying, she would have known. But it was likely there were people interested in this meeting that even he didn't know about. Simple counter-surveillance techniques were unlikely to defeat them, but as her instructor had drummed into her when she first joined the force *'start with the basics and work up.'*

So she started with the most basic thing she could. She took the fan and pushed the already bent guard a little further into the blades. What had been a stuttering click turned into a steady clatter. Pulling the electrical flex to its maximum length, she leaned the fan against the window where its rattle was further amplified. She also drew the curtains.

'Now,' she said as she took her seat again opposite Hawadi, 'you are going to tell me how I can find Raha Golzar.'

Hawadi laughed. He laid the pistol flat on the arm of the

chair and leaned forwards to hear her better over the clatter of the fan behind him.

'Is that why you have come here?' he said. 'Miss Reid, Golzar is dead. Two times. First by stealth–'

'At your hand,' Leila said. 'Fifteen months ago you were brought in to arrange a meeting – in this very apartment for all I know – between Golzar and the Russian FSB. But the CIA paid you more. We know all about your involvement. You lured her into the trap that ended in a psych ward in England–'

'First by stealth,' Hawadi repeated, 'when your own agents made a botching up of shooting her, and then by your own hand when you did what they could not. Last Friday you shot her like a dog as she lay in the back of Mr Aquila's car. Do you not remember?'

'Not all of it, no, but I've pieced together enough. And it all points to the fact that she's not dead.'

'How so? Is she Lazarus, risen in Jerusalem?' Hawadi grinned broadly.

'Let's say that once again she dodged the bullet, it seems. And I have reason to believe she's somewhere close.'

'You English are not so good at political assassinations these days, it is true, but why do you doubt yourself so profoundly, Miss Reid? You do not seem to sort for such self-doubt. What detail have you not told me? What detail makes you sure enough that you failed to kill her that you come here to seek my help?'

'Black Eagle flew me here on a private plane from England,' Leila said. 'There was evidence that a patient had been attended to in the cabin. Blood-stained towels, bandages, empty vials. I believe that was to bring Golzar back to Israel, or Jordan, Lebanon, a place to restart their negotiations. If they could keep her alive.'

'And why do you think they succeeded?' Hawadi took a pack of Gitanes from the sideboard next to him, flicked one out and held it unlit between his lips. His grip on the pistol and his steady gaze on his guest never faltered.

'My guess,' Leila went on, 'and maybe you can confirm this – is that for the missing four days of my last week Donald Aquila had been trying to persuade me to fill her shoes in case they couldn't save her. I was their bonus prize from the Mapleton operation. They thought they could turn me, and God knows what they did to try to do it. Apparently they failed. So when they were sure they *had* saved her, and that they'd never turn me, I became an inconvenience. They put me back on the plane, sent me skywards and assumed I'd stop being inconvenient shortly afterwards.'

'Then I'm sorry to disappoint you, but it seems that you know a lot more than I do already.' Hawadi lit the cigarette and breathed a column of smoke out into the room. He was, Leila realised, creating a literal and metaphorical smokescreen between them. What was calculated to be a casual, even dismissive, gesture masked something deeper. Something important.

'I do know plenty, you're right,' she said. 'I'm just missing one crucial detail: where is she?'

'And you think I, a legitimate businessman, would know?'

'I think you, as a shrewd trader in secrets and lies, are selling yourself short, Mr Hawadi. I'm sure you know plenty too. And now you're going to tell me.'

Hawadi laughed but raised the Ruger from its prone position on the chair arm once more. 'If, as you think, I have connections, a negotiating position, with this Black Eagle organisation, why are you so confident that I will not pick up the phone and have them pay us a visit right now? Deliver their 'inconvenience' back to them and earn myself a good wage for my trouble? Or just kill you myself and make sure?'

'Because I bought insurance before I came here tonight.'

'Insurance?'

'There's a letter. Two letters. Both are in the postal system right now, out of anyone's reach, impossible to find or stop. The first is on its way to a friend at an address your people would not be able to intercept. The only person who can stop him receiving it is me. Which is to say, he will have it in his possession if I do not get back to London before it does.'

'So?'

'Contained within this letter is a short note and a second sealed envelope. This too bears an address. All my friend has to do is carry it a mile or so from his office and hand it over. And he will. Against all his professional judgment, he will. If I disappear out here, he'll owe me that much.'

'And this second letter?'

'Is addresses to the Ambassador of the Mission of Palestine in London. It details your involvement with the CIA and how you have been feeding Fatah state secrets to them for years. It also implicates you in the staged assassination of Raha Golzar, your knowledge of Black Eagle and anything else I could think of to make your life as difficult as possible. Or shall we say, impossible?'

'You have no proof!' He dropped the half-smoked cigarette onto the floor and crushed it under his foot.

'Do you really think I need any? Even if only half of what I've said is true, my guess is Fatah secret service will be able to extract a perfectly adequate confession from you to fill in the blanks. Adequate enough to send you to the gallows, or however they execute traitors these days. For you they might even decide crucifixion would be apt.'

'You bitch.'

'Good. Now we understand each other. Be very sure, Mr Hawadi, that if you do not help me, or if I fail to return home before that letter is delivered, there will be nowhere on earth for you to run. So, how do I find Golzar?'

32

Half an hour before DS Reid delivered her ultimatum to Hassan Hawadi in flat five-eight of an anonymous Jerusalem apartment building, James Thorne and David Bates sat in semi-darkness of Bates' office at SIS HQ in Vauxhall Cross. Open on the desk was a lap-top on which Bates was video-conferencing Scott Rees, SIS's 'cultural attaché' in Tel Aviv. Emma Whitehouse arrived just as Rees was hanging up on a cell call. He unmuted his end of the video call.

'Reid's just got into the taxi,' Rees said. 'She's smart. For an atheist. We had a wager that a bible clue would be beyond her.'

'She'd have known something was wrong if we'd made it any simpler,' Thorne said.

'Fill me in,' Emma Whitehouse said.

'The plan's proceeding, Acting Prime Minister,' Thorne said. 'Reid's on her way to meet Hawadi now. Whatever they talk about, we'll hear it all.'

'And you're still working on the assumption that she's going in her capacity as a Black Eagle agent?'

'It's looking more and more likely.'

'Then someone needs to explain why we ran such a compromised operation! Bringing a known criminal computer hacker into this?'

'Reid brought Shaw into this,' Thorne said.

'But why? If she's working for Donald Aquila, why didn't he facilitate the meeting?'

'Because for once – though doubtless not for the last time tonight – Reid over-reached herself. She failed in whatever plan they had in the Negev. Black Eagle abandoned her, so she's scrabbling to find a way back in. A way to prove her ongoing value to them, since she realises that after what happened at the Embassy she doesn't have a lot of other options. Aquila was never going to facilitate a meeting with Hawadi, so she did it herself. Or rather, she thinks Phillip did it for her.'

'And Hawadi? What does he know about what's going on with this?' Whitehouse said.

'He has no idea who is behind the meeting, and we went to lengths to keep it that way. The more he has to speculate, the worse his guard will be. He can't bias his truth if he has no idea which way to bias it. But he does know DS Reid by reputation, so he didn't take much persuading. Helped along, of course, with ten thousand US dollars wired to a private account. And he was allowed to keep his gun.'

'She's about five minutes out,' Rees said from the laptop on the table. 'I'll update you when she gets there.'

His face loomed large on the screen then the connection was cut. Thorne stood and walked to the window.

'I still think this is the best chance we're going to get to take her out,' he said. 'This meeting might have been arranged under our control, but we've very little control over what she does with the information she gets.'

'It's only that information that makes any of this worthwhile,' Whitehouse said. 'If we pull her out too soon, we lose what might be the only chance we'll ever get to penetrate beyond the surface of Black Eagle.'

'And we'll hear everything they say,' Bates said. 'We've got a laser listening device on the other side of the valley. Sensitive enough to pick up every word. She's not going anywhere that we won't know about.'

'And when she does move?' Thorne said.

'If her plan is to make contact with the FSB's man in Israel as Golzar tried fifteen months ago, we will extract her immediately. Blowing the lid off Israel's nuclear secrets benefits no one. But if she's got other reasons to talk to Hawadi, we let it play. The deeper she can lead us in, the more value we get out of the operation. And having Hawadi think he's got a British agent – even a defecting one – in his collection will do us no harm. Makes getting a real mole into his cesspit world a lot easier in the future.'

The laptop's screen brightened and Rees settled back into position.

'The taxi's pulling up,' he said. 'Hold…'

He muted the sound and put a satellite phone to his ear. The three people waiting in London could not hear the conversation; they just saw a look of stony concentration on the cultural attaché's face. He lowered the phone again and unmuted his connection.

'Problem?' Bates said.

'No. We thought she might be trying to communicate

with the driver,' Rees said. 'Seems she was just tipping him. She's entering the building now. We'll have ears on her as soon as she enters the apartment.'

They waited.

'She's entered the flat,' Rees said, 'made contact. She's got balls, I'll give her that. The little toad's going to have his work cut out with this one.'

Pause. Rees watched something on his screen that the others could not see.

'Hawadi has confirmed her arrival,' he said. 'The carry-phone we gave her has been disconnected as instructed. She's checking for bugs.'

'So the phone wasn't enough to convince her,' Thorne said.

'It was never likely to be,' Rees said. 'If it had made her drop her guard, it would have been a bonus, but we always figured she'd look for bugs too. She must at least suspect this wasn't amateur-hour cobbled together solely by her hacker friend on his home computer. Hold…'

There was another pause. Rees watched his screen. Another call on the sat phone. His brow furrowed. They saw him mouth 'shit' then the audio was reconnected.

'We've got a bigger problem,' he said.

'Which is?' Whitehouse said.

'She didn't even look for bugs in the room. She knew we'd be have our surveillance outside. She's placed a fan against the window.'

'And? What does that mean?'

'The laser's being bounced around all over the place. Short story: we've lost live sound on their conversation.'

'Can we still see them?'

'No. She's drawn the curtains. *Counter-surveillance For Dummies*. Draw the curtains! Hawadi wouldn't have known to stop her.'

'Or it was not in his interests to stop her!' Commander Thorne said. 'What's the one thing we know for sure about Hawadi? That he works for whoever pays him most! Reid walks in there claiming to have the entire resources of Black Eagle behind her, and we give him polite English tip of ten grand! As soon as Reid presents him with the cover he needs to make his own new deal, he's going to jump at it.'

'We always knew there were alternative outcomes,' Rees said. 'Hawadi might have decided that ten thousand was just about enough to allow her into the flat, but not enough to tell us what they talk about after she leaves. Hence external surveillance – and a further back-up of our people in place when she does leave.'

'But we've got nothing live?' Thorne aid.

'For now we're blind and deaf,' Rees said. 'We're getting the sound, but it's recording with so much background it'll have to be run through AI cleaners.'

'So you can still get something out of this mess?' Whitehouse said.

'The noise is regular, so we can clean it up. I'll have the recordings streamed over to GCHQ. I have to warm you that even with the kit they've got, best case is we might get a usable soundtrack in a few hours.'

'And the worst case?'

'Depends how badly you need it. It might be days.'

'How did this happen?' Rees said to no one in particular.

'We've got the best listening devices in the world and Reid can shut us out with a noisy fan?'

'She's not stupid,' Thorne said. 'That's what makes her so bloody dangerous.'

33

The only sound in the apartment was the rattle of the fan against the window. Hawadi had moved the pistol off Reid and held it loosely across his ample lap.

'Let's say,' he said, 'that I can find Raha Golzar. Alive or dead. Let's say I believe your ploy to sell me out to the PSS, and so I share that information with you. What can you do for me in return?'

'Isn't staying out of your affairs enough?'

Hawadi shook his head. 'Do you know who arranged this meeting here tonight?'

'I hoped you might tell me.'

'I was contacted earlier this evening regarding a business proposition, a small thing, nothing that would leave a trail. Nothing that could cause me problems, just business. Someone – you – needed information, and I could provide it, for a small financial incentive. I saw little downside to the arrangement. Sometimes one has to speculate in order to profit. Who was behind it was not my concern at the time – this was between you and them. I was led to believe I was just a businessman acting on a consultancy basis to grease the wheels of whatever game you are engaged in. And as long as you came alone, we would not have a problem. Even if your people had insisted on me giving up my little enforcer…' he twitched the pistol in her direction '…a lone woman was not going to give me any sleepless nights. So to speak.'

'I thought it was a friend working only for me in London,' Leila said, ignoring his gold-flash grin. 'But the arrangements were too sophisticated for him to have put in place so quickly on his own. It would seem someone else got to him.'

'And yet you came here anyway.'

'I had no choice.'

'Indeed. But they got to your friend, and in turn they got to me. I was not being paid for information: I was merely bait in a trap to draw you into their sights. This meeting is about nothing useful – to me anyway. So-so. OK… I was paid, I was used, that's life.' He leaned forwards to her. 'But now you are using an unfair advantage – a mysterious letter to your friends in England – to extort dangerous information from me? I don't like that arrangement. They are running both of us, Miss Reid. I don't like that arrangement at all.'

'No one's running me.'

'You may believe that, but it's exactly what is happening.' He leaned back and shook out another of his stinking Gitanes. He lit it and regarded her for a moment through the haze of blue smoke. 'Whoever got to your friend recruited you as a blind agent, Miss Reid, pushing you this way and that to lead them to their ultimate prize. The question is: what is that prize?'

'Right now, I have no idea. But I do know I need your help to give me enough time to figure it out. I can't prove why I'm in Israel, I've got British Secret Intelligence, Shin Bet and the IDF hunting me and I've almost certainly lost my only civilian ally in London. I also have no doubt that by now Black Eagle know their attempt to dispose of me failed, and I have no papers even if I could risk trying to cross the border. Finding Golzar is the only way to clear my name.'

'That does not sound like much of a plan, Miss Reid.' He blew a series of smoke rings up towards the ceiling and watched as they were torn apart in the fan's breeze. 'It's not really even half a plan. What do you intend to do with her once you have found her?'

Leila leaned forwards and rested her elbows on her knees. She spoke quietly, almost to herself, as she picked through her ideas to try to find a way to make sense of them... make sense of them to herself as well as to Hawadi.

'The peace talks in London last week rested on Prime Minister Morgan handing Golzar over to the Palestinians,' she said. 'That was Queria's price for attending. Morgan's motives were good, but he was heavily out-gunned by Black Eagle and a lot of people died to keep Golzar out of the game. So that's my plan. I'm going to finish the job I started last Wednesday morning: I'm going to get Golzar on trial for treason in the Palestinian territories, as Abu Queria intended.'

'And in exchange Fatah will facilitate your exfil back to Europe?'

'They won't have any choice. And it clears any suspicion

of my involvement with Black Eagle, or any other unfortunate business out there in the Negev.'

'You're a delicious enigma, Miss Reid. Are you arrogant to the point of insanity, or insane to the point of blindness?'

'Who says it's either-or?' Leila said.

Hawadi laughed and see-sawed his left hand again. 'A little of both then,' he said. 'You're putting a lot of faith in my ability to help you.'

'Not at all. If you don't give me what I want, you'll go to Ramallah in Golzar's place.'

'I have the enforcer, Miss Reid.' He twitched the little Ruger, his gaze fixed on her.

'And I have insurance, Mr Hawadi. I think in a few days you'll see that the pen is mightier than the sword. Or gun, in this case. Not as swift maybe, but even more effective.'

Hawadi crushed the remains of his cigarette under his foot and sat for a long moment watching her. Neither spoke. Leila waited. The silence was to her advantage. The more he thought, the more he would start to regret allowing himself to get trapped in this sticky web a second time. She could see it in his eyes, in the slight tensing of his posture as he realised, a little too late, that this meeting was further out of his control as he had thought. He might even have figured out what her ploy with the rattling fan was about, and how a lack of external surveillance on this meeting placed him in a very dangerous corner indeed. He ran his fingers through his too-black hair and gave her a thoughtful look. He placed the pistol on the table beside him and leaned forwards.

'Your letter concerns me,' he said. 'It is not impossible

that it might be discovered even if your plan does succeed. You might be delayed: there might be a parade in your honour, a banquet with Mr Queria, something of that nature. I need one further assurance.'

'I don't have a lot to offer other than sparing your life.'

'Oh, but you do.' His eyes twinkled in the low light. 'You are working deep cover. So deep even you do not know the full extent of your mission, or even who is running you. Codename Jerusalem Blind.' He grinned. 'Your paymasters will keep you safe, part all obstacles before you, cover your every move until they have you exactly where they want you. You are lucky. A simple businessman like myself can only dream of having such friends.'

'What are you talking about?'

'A new world order. Should you, and they, succeed, I believe it would be in my interests to align myself with... new forces. The CIA are maybe not so good any more for my long-term comfort. Old world politics is like an old bull elephant – it has the weight, but is not agile, commands no real authority. A new force is moving in on the herd.'

'You want me to make a formal introduction to whoever you think is behind this? Even though I have no idea who they are – or if they even exist?'

'Something along those lines. Assure me a meeting with your people, a time to demonstrate my worth, that is all. Then in time, I can work for them too, just like you. And I will be under the broad, comforting wings of their protection, just like you. Do that and I will see what I can do about finding Raha Golzar.'

'I have no way of contacting anyone. They're probably

right outside this building, but either you are right and they're running me blind, or they're waiting to take me down the moment this meeting is over. Either way, I go out there, I've got no leverage.'

'Then call them.' Hawadi reached into the pocket of his jacket and pulled out a heavy black phone like a child's toy walkie-talkie, with a short, fat aerial and a case that looked like it would survive a bomb blast. 'It's encrypted. Left here in the flat before I arrived, with instructions and a secure number. I was to contact them when you left here, tell them what you wanted, where you were going.'

Leila watched him for a moment.

'Who do *you* think is behind this?' she said.

Hawadi shrugged. 'Eliminate the likely and what you have left, however unlikely, must be the truth.'

'That is an appalling misquote. And it doesn't answer my question.'

'Who do we have? Shin Bet, Mossad: possible, but unlikely. They would have no reason to run an outside agent to get to Golzar, and it runs against their usual methods. PLO? Not enough resources, and they would be insane to run *any* operation inside Israel, even with the best plausible deniability in the world. If their aim is to get back to the Peace Table, why smash it up and set fire to it before they can use it? The Russians, Chinese, Iranians would not have the contacts or means to run an operation like this here at short notice. They, and our old friends the Americans, are also not spontaneous people. British Intelligence? You work for them anyway, so why risk an operation where so much could go so badly wrong?'

'Which leaves Black Eagle.'

'However unlikely... The ultimate irony. It leaves our old friends Black Eagle. You've seen what lengths they'll go to to get what they want.'

'But they've already got Golzar back.'

'But they haven't got *you*, at least not yet where they want you. Why do you think this meeting was so easy to arrange? You furnished them with the perfect plan! For historic reasons, I want to please Mr Aquila, and for their own future, they want to please you. It's a perfect menage a trois of diplomatic intrigue.'

'To what end?'

'My dear.' He leaned forwards conspiratorially. 'Running you on a blind operation to get back to England, right into the heart of the one secret intelligence agency they admit they have never been able to infiltrate? It's so beautiful. It seems, my friend, that you and I are not so very different after all...'

'You seem to be forgetting the fact that they went to a lot of trouble to kill me.'

'And failed, Miss Reid. They failed spectacularly. Maybe you have now passed their final, unpassable test. You are made of, how you say, 'the right stuff'. It is time to find out for sure.'

He tapped a six digit unlock code into the phone's keypad and threw it to Leila. 'Dial hash-1. Then maybe you will begin to understand what you have got yourself into, Jerusalem Blind.'

Leila looked at him for several seconds. Hawadi's theory was preposterous... except for one thing. When captured and under interrogation by Israeli military intelligence, someone went to a lot of trouble – and considerable loss of life – to get her out of their clutches. The British would have spent months grinding through diplomatic channels to release her. Only someone as ruthless and direct as Donald Aquila would have sent a mini army into the desert to take on an armoured transport operated by some of the toughest Special Forces in the world. Maybe it was to prevent her spilling what she knew about them… or maybe it was so that they could continue a mission they had previously written off. Maybe…

'Let's assume for a moment that you're right,' she said. 'Do you really think Black Eagle are going to 'protect' you after you betray Golzar, again? Or that they'll be able to intervene against the Palestinian Authorities if my letter gets to England before I do? They'll kill you anyway as soon as they know what I'm doing.'

'Maybe. But this way you buy me a few hours in the company of their powerful inner circle before they do find out. Enough, maybe, to prove my ongoing value to them. Between your letter to England and Black Eagle's rage at my betrayal, I prefer to deal face to face with the latter for now. So make the call.'

Leila dialled hash-1 and made the connection. It was answered almost before the first ring had finished.

'Hello?' she said.

'Reid? How did you–'

'Shut up and listen. Say one word before I'm finished and I hang up.' She took a breath. 'I know you're watching the building, and if you're as stupid as I think you are, you'll be scrabbling around with AI noise filters trying to pick the bones out of a near-useless recording of a rattling fan to work out what I know and what I've told our mutual friend here. You can't risk not knowing, so this is how we're going to end this. You are going to let me walk out the front door. You are not going to attempt to follow me.'

'We can't…'

'I told you to listen. Basic stuff, even for you. There is something I have to do. After that, you can do what you want. What I know, you'll know. Full cooperation. As a gift to you I'm also offering you a back-up, a second prize, in case something goes wrong for me. Get Hawadi into protective custody. He won't tell you anything yet, so don't even try, but I believe he will be of great use to you when this is over. Listen to what he has to say. Say yes if you agree.'

'Yes. What are—'

Leila cut the connection.

'They'll take you in when I leave,' she said. 'What happens after that is up to you.'

Hawadi reached a fat hand out for the phone. She paused for a moment then gave it to him.

'Let's get down to the real business of the evening, shall we?' she said. 'In the end your timetable is still the same as that of the postal system. Time's ticking. So find me Golzar. Please.'

34

In Vauxhall Cross, the screen on David Bates's desk sprang back into life.

'I've spoken to Reid,' Rees said from his office in Tel Aviv.

'Did she know who she was talking to?' Emma Whitehouse said.

'Impossible to be sure. She didn't give me much scope to say anything, but among the list of possible candidates she'll realise we're the most likely. She must know by now that Shaw couldn't have done all this alone. She'll also guess that the boy has been under surveillance since last week, and that we'd have intercepted their communication at some point. So it's a small leap of logic to realise that we're in this mix somewhere.'

'Which is probably to our advantage,' Commander Thorne said.

'How so?' Whitehouse said.

'Because she's got a history of out-thinking us. She'll be over-confident. She's got the might of this shiny new international organisation behind her now and her only pursuers are a bunch of bumbling English gents. And ladies, apologies.'

'Then we use her naivety against her, don't we?' Whitehouse said. 'And we keep the personal out of this, yes? Did she give you anything, Mr Rees?'

'No. We're no closer to knowing what she's intending to do, but she asked that we take Hawadi into our protection when she leaves.'

'Whatever he's told her is enough to put him in danger,' Whitehouse said. 'She gave no indication what it was?'

'Nothing' Rees said. 'She's asked for clear passage out of the building, so she obviously got what she came for. What do you want us to do?'

'Hold,' Bates said. 'We'll get back to you.' He muted their end of the connection.

'Acting Prime Minister?' he said.

'The only question we need to answer is "can we keep track of her if we let her back into the field?"' Whitehouse said.

'She's got no way out of the building that we won't have clear sight of,' Bates said. 'She's got no vehicle, nowhere to run. If Hawadi has given her a contact inside the Russian Secret Service, we need to know about it.'

'That's one hell of a risk,' Thorne said.

'It's one we can contain,' David Bates said. 'Russia is largely a friendly force within Israel. We know who their agents are and we'll know if she's attempting a meeting.'

'I agree,' Whitehouse said. 'If we bring her in too early, we've got nothing. She won't talk unless we've got so much proof against her that she has no choice. Even then... the more we know from our own surveillance, the better position we're in.'

'And if she does manage to escape?' Thorne said.

'She won't,' David Bates said. 'The apartment is right on the fringes of the city. It's nearly two AM over there. Even if she manages to get a car, following her is not going to be a problem. And if Hawadi has given her FSB contacts, she'll want to move fast. She won't risk trying to lay low. The storm she's caused with the Israelis already means she needs to conclude her business and get out of there. Remember, as far as we know she's got no way out of the country apart from Black Eagle. I'll contact John Nash, make sure GCHQ puts a hurry-up on the surveillance recordings. Finding out what they're talking about will go a long way towards making a plan.'

'And minimising the fallout,' Thorne said. 'For all of us.'

'OK,' Bates said. 'We agree to let this play out for now?'

'If your agents can keep tabs on her, with reluctance, we'll let it run,' Whitehouse said.

Bates reconnected with his counterpart in Tel Aviv and said: 'Have your men follow her. They won't have to be too discrete about it as she clearly knows they're there. Which means she knows she can't turn to the Shaw boy again – he's already sold her out once.'

'And her forger is… no longer in business,' Rees said.

'Forger?' Thorne said. 'That's what Shaw was fixing for her? Papers?'

'Did you interrogate him?' Whitehouse said.

'No,' Rees said. 'He was dead when we found him. Local police alerted us to some unusual activity. A witness said he thought he'd seen someone matching Reid's description at a place called Canaan Communications in the Old City.

Turned out the owner was an expert forger, but by the time we got there, someone else had done the last interrogation he was ever going to face.'

'Was it connected?' Thorne said.

'Doubtful. Our guy ran into someone banging on the shop door about seven thirty tonight. Said he was owed money from a gambling deal. I think Phillip's boy had made a lot of enemies. One in particular by the look of him.'

'Do we know what he gave Reid before he died?'

'No,' Rees said. 'No way of knowing.'

'It's not important for our immediate concerns,' Thorne said. 'She told Shaw something had gone wrong with their original plan, so it's likely she too knows the forger is no longer an option for her. So she knows she's on her own, and she'll suspect someone is sending a cleaning crew out in her wake to tidy up after her. So she's now desperate enough to try to go through with her plan any way she can before the cleaning crew get ahead of her, which means she might get sloppy enough to lead us right to the heart of it. But be careful: she's taken counter-surveillance measures already. She'll have a plan to give you the slip.'

'Let this run as long as you dare, Mr Rees,' Whitehouse said, 'but only up to the point we have proof of intention. Then take her out.' She looked at Commander Thorne, who met her gaze steadily. 'Alive if possible,' she went on, 'but no one's going to look too hard at what happens if it's not.'

'As Acting PM, are you sanctioning lethal force?'

'Lethal force,' Whitehouse said.

'Understood,' Rees said. 'I'll report when we have movement.'

35

Leila sat opposite Hawadi throughout his long conversation on the encrypted sat-phone. She made no attempt to follow the conversation. He spoke quickly and softly in a lilting South Levantine dialect. She understood enough to know he was playing straight, but too many words were blurred and unfamiliar for her to get all the details. He appeared to be talking to someone about Golzar's medical predicament. Places were mentioned, batted about. Her own name was mentioned, and the reply was met with a long silence from Hawadi. He cradled the phone in the crook of his considerable jowls and took a notebook from the table beside him. As he talked he drew lines, curves, stars, words in Arabic, on a blank page. She watched him for signs of deceit and saw none. He seemed unaware that she was even still there. That he was playing straight was her only concern for now. How he located Golzar, and through whom, was none of her business. The whole reason for wanting to meet him was that he had a contact book that would be the envy of every secret intelligence force in the world, and he had no scruples about using it for his own advantage. If he knew a driver who worked for the pharmacist who supplied the doctor who administered the morphine to Golzar as she lay in a secret bed in Jerusalem, who was she to question it?

When he had finished he dropped the phone back into his pocket and wrote a few final words on the scrap of paper.

'So she is still alive?' Leila said.

'Of course. As I said, you British are not so good at assassinations today. Although… in this case you were so close to her and still made such a poor attempt, a man less trusting than myself might say you never intended to kill her in the first place.' He laughed, but there was no humour in the sound.

'How bad is she?'

'You shattered her left leg, put a bullet in her liver and cut her a neat new parting down the middle of her scalp. She'll live. Maybe.' He made the now-familiar see-saw gesture with his left hand.

'And you know where she is?'

'She's being treated at a private compound south west of the city.'

'And they just told you that?' Leila said. He shrugged. 'Of course,' she went on, 'I have something Black Eagle wants.'

'Exactly: you. But are you certain is it enough? It seems to me that if you touch her, you won't get out of there alive. You know that, don't you?'

'Let me worry about that. My immediate concern is how I get out of *here*.'

'You told them you're going to walk out the front door.'

'It would be a short walk. Is there another exit?'

'There's a parking garage in the basement. You could drive.'

'A car would only delay the inevitable.'

'Sooner or later you've got no choice.' He tore a sheet of paper from the notebook and handed it over. 'The compound is about twenty miles out of the city, beyond the moshav of Narom. One bus a day, and it's not any time soon. You'll need to find a vehicle of your own at some point. I've drawn a map to get you started. The important thing is not to cross the Armistice Line or you'll get fouled up at checkpoints. In and out. From here, get onto the main highway heading west as soon as you can: this'll be a start, if you like dark twisty roads.'

She took the paper and nodded.

'Past Narom you'll find an abandoned village in the next valley. There's a maayan, a natural spring, there. Follow the stream that runs out of it – you'll need to be right on top of it to see it – until it crosses an old drover's track. If you miss it you'll be lost. A mile beyond the spring there's a house. It's not all it seems.'

'The car's still the big problem. Whatever they've got out there'll be faster than anything I could steal downstairs.'

'Then steal a motorcycle.'

Leila paused for a moment. 'Is there one?' she said.

'Kids on the other side of the building share one. An old yellow trail thing. You ride?'

'If it'll get me out of here, I can figure it out. Is there an alarm?'

Hawadi laughed. 'There wouldn't be much point. They're two brothers and their runty little friend. Trouble here, trouble there, all of them. They leave the helmet locked on the bike and the key on a piece of string behind the main water pipe. So they can all use it if the others are out. They like to think they're hard enough that no one would dare touch it.'

'They got that wrong. OK. When I leave here, give me a couple of minutes then use the old mobile to call your contact and someone will come and pick you up.'

'I won't need to do that. That bike will let you move quickly, but it's not invisible. Or silent. Noisy sons of bitches, those boys.'

'Then calling them will split their attention. They want me, but they want you too now. And there's not that many of them out there. Small advantages.'

'Add up to big wins. Why on the old cell phone?'

'Because I'm taking the sat-phone,' she said. She stood up and held out her hand. He looked up at her in amusement.

'It won't do you any good,' he said. 'It's a myth that satellite phones can't be traced. Make a call and they'll find you in seconds. They have, as you might say, got your number.'

Leila walked to the window and peeped out through a crack in the curtains. 'Wrong, Mr Hawadi. You are not the sort of man to leave geolocation turned on and you already told me with great pride that it's encrypted. They might, just might, trace the RF emissions, but my guess is out here sat-phones are not exactly uncommon, so having them pull my RF out from the background chatter is a risk I'll take.'

Hawadi turned in his seat and flashed his gold tooth in a

grin of genuine amusement. 'A simple key code lock will ensure it is of no more use to you than a cold fatayer,' he said. 'Unless I choose to unlock it for you, and why should I do that? Our business is concluded, and already I have paid far more for this deal than you yourself.'

'I was always rather partial to a fatayer, Mr Hawadi. Spinach and feta. Could never quite get the taste for goat though. And the unlock code isn't a problem. Two-nine-zero-four-seven-six. You tapped it in in full view.'

Hawadi held his hand up. 'I try to help you, and you throw it in my face. Your choice. Keep the phone.' He reached into his pocket and threw the phone to her. His piggy black eyes followed her as she walked back to the room divider by the door and dropped it into her backpack.

'Good luck and goodbye, Mr Hawadi. Keep them guessing long enough for me to do what I need to do and this will all work out.'

He lit another cigarette and bowed his head slightly as Leila left the room.

36

The bike key was where Hawadi said it would be. There were three motorcycles parked in the corner of the underground facility, only one of which was yellow. It was an ageing single-cylinder DR350, a scrambler with huge suspension travel and a high seat. Clipped to the defective lock on the back was an open-faced black helmet. No goggles. That could be a problem where she was going.

There was no rear exit to the car park. She was going to have to blast straight out the front into the view of the agent – or agents – across the street. She mentally rehearsed her route, or as much of it as she could. Hawadi's tangle of lines on the scrap of paper he had given her at least pointed her in the right direction out of this building. His romanticised tale of an abandoned village with a hidden spring told her what to look for. The twenty miles in the middle were largely a mystery. What she did know was that she was roughly south west of the city already, so if all else failed she would just keep going with Jerusalem behind her. Narom would be out there somewhere, and beyond it, her way out of Israel.

She put the helmet on and pushed the bike back out of its parking space. With it facing the exit, she swung her leg over the seat. She could only touch the tips of her toes on the ground if she wanted to put them both down at the same time. She leaned the bike over and kicked the side stand up… checked the position of the lights… turned the key and pressed the starter.

The bike sprang to life and she pulled the clutch in and engaged first. With only a little throttle she played the clutch out and the bike sprang forwards. This was a very different machine from her brother's old BSA Sloper that she'd learned to ride as a teenager down at their holiday home in Devon. This thing was feather-light and with enough power to raise its head and spit her right off the back if she treated it roughly. She crawled up the slope that led out of the garage. The bike's single cylinder engine throbbed noisily in the confined space.

She emerged onto the street and turned left, straightened the steering and twisted the throttle.

She had expected to be spotted, but she had not expected the bullet that pinged off the road a foot or two behind her and whined off into the night. She leaned hard around the corner to the main road opened the bike up.

As she glanced in the rear-view mirror a few seconds later, a car rounded the corner behind her and accelerated hard. For now she had an advantage. The roads were narrow, badly maintained and lined with parked cars. Perfect territory for the nimble trail bike and she pushed it as hard as she dared as she got the feel of it. It was nervous and twitchy at speed but it took the ruts and potholes effortlessly, and the acceleration was impressive. Minute by minute she stretched the distance between herself and the far more cumbersome car. She blasted the wrong way round a small roundabout – mainly because she didn't see it in time to take it properly – and the BMW fell further behind. But her current two hundred yard lead was not going to last long once they got off these residential streets. The BMW was easily capable of a hundred and fifty... and the little DR wasn't. The speedometer ran all the way up to 160. But that was KMPH, and it was a wild exaggeration even if this old nail had been brand new out of the showroom.

For ten minutes she wove through residential back streets, then quite suddenly she passed from urban modernity into another, far older, world. Trees replaced the houses, boulders the parked cars. The cracked and sagging road turned into little more than a track and her key advantage was lost. She turned the throttle as far as she dared and the old bike wheezed breathlessly up to 100 on the clock. Barely slowing through a village and struggling to keep her eyes open against the blast of cool air in her face, she scanned the area for anywhere she might get off the road. There was nothing. This was a rat-run road that served no purpose but to connect places at either end of it. There was nothing but scrub along its length, and nowhere to hide. She blasted past a lumbering truck with two tractors on its flatbed and glanced back. The black BMW's blinding halogen lights that had been growing steadily in the rear-view mirror were temporarily lost in the night. The road was narrow and passing places rare when it came to a contest between a truck and a large sedan. She had a few seconds when her pursuers were blind, and she used them to open the gap again.

As the seconds ticked by and her chances of ending up

on a main highway where it would be impossible to outrun the BMW increased, she became more and more convinced she had misread Hawadi's map. Or maybe that had been his intention. If she was being run as a blind agent by Black Eagle, as seemed likely now, getting her lost in the desert was the perfect win for him. They would pick her up – or pick her off – and Golzar would stay alive and well out there in the abandoned farm. Aquila got both prizes handed to him on a plate, and Hawadi earned the patronage (or the reprieve of a fifteen-month-old death sentence) of Black Eagle's man in the Middle East.

Quite suddenly the track changed from cracked and dusty deathtrap to a smooth paved road – still narrow, but maintained. Past a farm it hair-pinned down through a small grove of trees then straightened out as it ran alongside a main road. She glanced back up the hill and the lights of the BMW flashed through the trees above her. The steep hairpin would slow them momentarily, then they would have all the advantage they needed. The highway on her left was almost deserted, and this section was arrow-straight. Seconds later she was spat out onto it with no choice but to try to outrun a car capable of at least twice her speed.

The pursuing car closed the gap to less than twenty yards in under a minute, then held steady behind a blinding wall of blue-white headlights. Even over the wheezing scream of her own engine going full-blast she could hear the BMW's engine was barely ticking over. They had her exactly where the wanted her and they could keep her there as long as they stayed on this smooth road with its safety barriers along each shoulder. She had to get back onto rough tracks again, get back the one advantage that the bike gave her. If they intended to shoot her, right now she was as good as a stationary target. If they wanted to stop her, it was only a matter of time before they got in front of her and forced her off the road.

Watching the car in the mirror she rehearsed her next move. Nothing in front of her and only the BMW behind. Riding this agile beast hard and fast had given her a good feel for its balance and power, and she had a good theoretical idea of what she needed to do. She just needed a break – literally and metaphorically. Against the wind and dust in her eyes she scanned the shoulder for a gap in the safety barrier. Ahead the ground rose up to the road's level, where, logically, there would be no need for the armco. And two hundred yards later she got lucky. Open scrub on both sides – a break of fifty feet or so in the barrier, but she was past it almost before she knew it was there. No problem: she could use that...

She pulled into the opposite lane and slammed the brakes on. The front of the bike dived, the back snaked as the rear tyre lost grip and began to skid. Thrown forwards over the tank, her bruised ribs screamed in protest at the sudden unexpected insult. She braced her arms and held position as the bike scrubbed speed off, fighting to throw her off sideways having failed to pitch her over the handlebars. The car was almost level with her before the driver even had time to react. She eased the brakes off a touch, got both wheels turning, and stabilised the machine for her next move. Her first concern – that the pursuing driver would simply slam into the back of her and wipe her out without wasting ammunition – proved unfounded. The BMW continued on the right side of the road, the anti-lock brakes chattering and its nose so low the front spoiler was almost scraping the road. At more than ten times her weight, it was going to take a lot longer for the driver to slow his vehicle enough to do anything useful than it had taken her. She had a couple of seconds before the he would be able to pull the handbrake on and spin the car back towards her.

She leaned the bike over, gave it a fistful of power and held the front brake. The back wheel span out and the ribs down her right side sent another wave of agony through her so hot and deep her eyes momentarily watered up. It was a good thing. She blinked the wet grit from them and pushed the bike hard and fast through its tyre-smoking one-eighty spin. The instant she was facing back towards the city, she let the front brake go again. The little DR surged forwards. She kicked up through second, third, revving the long-stroke single cylinder engine in a way that even the noisy kids who annoyed their corpulent upstairs neighbour so much would never have dared. With the BMW screeching through its own about-turn behind her and her speed climbing rapidly, she leaned hard and ran the bike off the road and into the dusty land that stretched off into the darkness.

She didn't look back. She didn't need to. The car lights swung in a wide arc across the ground in front of her before bouncing wildly for several seconds and coming to rest. The driver would be unable to follow her any further, but he could still get a shot at her unless she put a good distance between them. She blasted over gravel, dry shrubs, water gullies, everything that came up. The bike was more than capable and even at nearly sixty-k and with stones showering out behind it, it never once threatened to throw her off.

Out of the pool of the BMW's headlights she slowed a little and turned her own lights off. To the agents watching her a quarter mile back, it would have seemed as if she had simply vanished.

Leila ran on into the desert. The eastern sky was beginning to take on the faintest hint of dawn. Hawadi's map had sent her slightly north then west out of town so she needed to follow as close to a southern route as possible now. Given the time she had been out here she figured she must be at least twenty miles out of the city, so she was on approximately the right arc to find her target. He'd described Narom as a moshav – a settlement of farms similar to a kibbutz – which meant it should be big enough to spot. The landscape was still hidden in darkness and a road sign might prove useful if she hit the settlement before dawn, but she dared not venture back out onto the main road. She slowed and rode on through the desert scrub, keeping the breaking dawn to her left. Fifteen minutes later patches of pine trees began to resolve out of the sky, ragged black shapes on a lightening sky. She slowed to little more than walking pace as the natural scrub was gradually replaced with cultivated orchards of fruit trees. There was a small settlement to her left, and here and there narrow dirt tracks lead to what appeared to be cultivated fields. Even at this early hour shadowy figures moved along the field edges and in the silence the slow thud of the DR's single cylinder engine would certainly be heard.

A mile or so further on she began to look for cover where she could hide out until it was fully light. This crepuscular gloom served her badly: as a moving and noisy target she was easy to see, but the combination of dust and her own lack of headlights made it almost impossible to see much herself. Out of sight of any occupied buildings she found a dilapidated old barn, ran the bike in through its rusting doors and killed the ignition. She tore the helmet off and threw it into the corner, glad to feel the cool air on her head after its sweaty grip. The only sound was the ringing in her ears from the wind of that insane ride and the sound of the occasional car on the distant highway.

She piled straw against the bike's front wheel and sat down against it. In less than a minute she was asleep.

37

She slept fitfully as the sun broke the horizon, throwing long shadows across the pale rocky scrubland and creeping up the slope towards the barn. The temperature rose, banishing the last of the dewy night chill and making the old corrugated iron of the barn's walls click as it warmed just as the DR's engine had clicked itself to sleep an hour earlier.

She woke suddenly, a jolt of panic bringing her mind to full attention in an instant. Low sunlight streamed in through gaps in the walls, illuminating motes of dust that danced in the breeze. Leila held her breath, watching, listening. Always a light sleeper, especially in unfamiliar surroundings, had it been the rev of a tractor coming to life in a nearby field that had disturbed her? Or had there been something before that... a sudden noise, masked by sleep and softened by distance? She looked out. A dozen or more people were in the fields below her. Two men were stacking pallets onto a donkey-drawn cart. The bang as one landed on the pile echoed around the valley like a muted gunshot.

She searched her bag for the last bottle of water she'd rescued from the downed plane. It was half empty and warm, but it was as close to breakfast as she was going to get. For almost a minute she watched the field workers. Another pallet slapped onto the pile and the uneasy feeling began to subside. No threat there, but as she looked out through the window on the opposite side of the barn she realised just how lucky she had been to find this place in the dark. Half a mile away down a rough farm track was the main road – probably the main highway she had nearly killed herself to escape a few hours earlier. Traffic was light, and the breeze carried most of its sound away, which is why she had thought it was much further away. If she'd ridden on for another two minutes without finding this barn, or if she'd decided to look for somewhere better, she'd have run right back onto it. If this was the main road running past Narom, the black BMW would have continued to patrol it until all hope of finding their target was gone. They'd have had no idea just how close they were to finding her.

To the west of the barn was a grove of old almond trees. She walked along its edge, parallel to the road, keeping below the ridgeline to hide her presence from the farm. A quarter of a mile from the barn she spotted a road sign below. She waited. When the sound of cars was at its lowest ebb, she slipped down the shallow scree slope, close enough to read it. It was a right-angled arrow, pointing left off the road. Above the arrow was a single Hebrew word. Fortunately, it was translated into English below. And the translation read 'Narom'. By chance she had almost driven right through the middle of the moshav without even realising it.

She returned to the barn and covered the bike with a sheet of rusting corrugated iron and straw. There was nothing she could do about the tyre tracks that still led across the dustier areas of ground, but out here there was also much more vegetation, through which she had left no trail. She hoped the breeze would take care of what little other evidence there was in the next few hours.

With the headscarf she had picked up in Jerusalem tied in place as token protection from the coming sun, she walked north for fifteen minutes, away from the road, away from the moshav, and across an uncultivated field towards the head of the valley. In the long convoluted shadow an old olive tree she paused and found the monocular she had used back in London at the bottom of the bag. The glass was badly scratched, but she could see that across the valley terraces of grape vines ran along the contours of the hill, broken at regular intervals by small windbreaks of fruit trees. Dry stream beds meandered through the sandy ground below her and here and there were tractor trails, but there were no buildings and no proper roads. More importantly, there were no people.

It took another half hour to pick her way across the head of the valley and through the grape terraces to the sharp ridge at the top of the hill. From here she had a clear view of the next valley: the valley of the lost village. The temperature was rising by the minute. Through the scratched lens she scanned the ground below. The lower slopes of the next escarpment was planted with almonds and olives. Above these, large areas of hillside had reverted to natural scrub punctuated with a few ancient and gnarled trees that stood dark against the pale morning sky like angry modernist sculptures. Again, the wide valley floor was criss-crossed with tracks but it showed no sign of recent or ongoing cultivation. And in the distance to her left was a cluster of ruined buildings, a dozen or so single-storey cottages, none more than precarious walls now, honey-brown against the parched vegetation. This was Hawadi's abandoned village, in which she would find a natural spring, and a house that was more than it seemed. Or so she hoped. Out here, it would be easy to find herself in the wrong valley and lost for hours.

The time on the sat-phone's display read 6:04. Time to make an early morning wake-up call. Maybe it would yield something useful, maybe not.

She had no intention of calling Bone's old mobile again. She was increasingly sure that something had been wrong with Phillip when she'd called him yesterday. Donald Aquila's henchmen had found his mother and sister as easy as flies on a wedding cake, and then wiped them out with the casual contempt of a strutting bride protecting her fairytale illusions. Bones would have done what he could to protect the boy, but Black Eagle had resources and determination that would have been past him or through him before he even knew what was happening. And Phillip had always been the key to finding their real target: the one that got away in the deserts of southern Israel. Phillip had been compromised, and with him the one phone number she had for him. All the phones had been compromised as far as she was concerned, but there was still one person who might talk quickly and honestly enough to make a call worthwhile.

She dialled the familiar number. The phone rang. And

rang. It was 4am in England. She'd give him a few minutes to stir – he always slept most deeply just before dawn. A minute or so to find the phone, switch his brain on. If he was there.

If… she shuddered despite the growing heat of the early morning… *if he's still alive.*

The ring tone cut out but no one spoke. She heard a breath on the other end.

'Michael?... Hello?'

'Leila?'

'Your early morning call…'

'Where are you? Sorry, stupid question. Leila, they'll be tracing this call–'

'I know. I need to know one thing before–'

'I can't help you,' Micheal said. Across the sterile digital connection it was impossible to be certain how much of that statement was anger and how much regret. But she knew it was all truth. Whether he wanted to or not, he couldn't help her now.

'You have to hand yourself in,' he went on. 'You have no other options now.'

'I'm going to, but I need some clue about who I'm dealing with here. The plan to go to the Embassy didn't exactly work out, did it? And I know someone was watching me to Jerusalem.'

'Are you sure you want to do this? They'll find you from the signal.'

'The phone's encrypted: I've got a few minutes and I need to know who I'm up against, who the hell I can still trust.'

'Leila, trust no one. Not even me. As a friend, yes, but professionally Thorne's pulling strings that lead right to the top, and everyone – me included – is just a pawn in a much bigger game. My guess is the only person who is clever enough and bloody-minded enough to still be loyal to you is Phillip.'

'No. The evidence suggests Black Eagle had got to him.'

'Really? We have no reason to think so…'

'The way he set up the meeting with Hawadi-'

'What? You met Hassan Hawadi? Do you know how that's going to look?'

'Never mind that. The point is that Phillip set the meeting up like I was going to buy a used car. And then there's the way they found and killed the forger, the questions Phillip used for the labyrinth…'

'I have no idea what you're talking about, but I can tell you Phillip Shaw's not with Black Eagle. He was picked up by CTC after that first conversation with you in Tel Aviv.'

'*After* Tel Aviv? Then that proves it! Someone *had* got to him. And if it wasn't you – personally – then it had to be Black Eagle.'

'Why?'

'He used a series of questions to get us somewhere we could talk. One of them was about Chouette – Picasso's owl. It was the clincher. The question that hooked me in to his labyrinth. Only you and the Black Eagle agent who broke into my house on Thursday would know about that. And if it wasn't you…'

'Slow down. I think there is someone else. I went to your place two days ago. Scaz Bones was hanging around. I didn't know who he was at the time – our paths had never crossed until he and Phillip were brought in yesterday, and then it made sense. He was there for the same reason I was. To find you. And his whole life depends on observation. We do it on the clock; his kind do it to stay alive. He'd have noticed that little owl, his old burglar's eye would have recognised the name and the significance. He was with Phillip when you talked, so they'd have cooked the question up between them.'

Something moved among the ruined buildings down on the valley floor.

'Just a minute,' Leila whispered. With the phone in on the ground beside her she scanned the village through the monocular. A pale brown figure, crouched and slow moving, passed across an empty window in a house that was little more than two ragged six-foot walls and a pile of bleached-out roof trusses. She waited. There was no other movement among the buildings, but someone was down there. She hunkered further down into the shortening shadow of the ancient olive and picked up the phone, keeping the glass to her eye, trained on the building.

'So Phillip's safe?' she said.

'What was that?' Michael said.

'I think I've got company. It's a way off. I'm OK. Talk.'

'I saw Phillip yesterday in Mason Court. Thorne was about to… *speak*… to him in Interview Room 3. Fortunately, I got to him first, poor kid. I'm sorry, Leila, but I tried to persuade him to assist in finding you.'

'Good. I'd rather you were trying to protect him than me. I can look after myself. Phillip needs someone.'

'Thorne's got the operation ring-fenced, especially from me, so I have no idea what he's done for CTC to help track you down. Or how satisfied Thorne is with his efforts. But yes, I believe the boy is in the safest place he can be right now. As long as you cooperate.'

'So CTC were behind what happened last night?' Leila said, more to herself than to Michael. 'Not Black Eagle…? That doesn't make any sense!'

'I have no idea what happened last night, Leila. But if you have reason to believe Phillip had a hand in any of it, yes, that would indicate CTC were the principal players. Beyond that…Thorne suspects my loyalties, so I don't know anything and what I could guess at might be dangerously wrong. After what you did in the Negev, however, I do have reason to believe you're in much greater danger than you realise.'

'IDF? Mossad?'

'Right now, no. And I do know Shin Bet's backed off for now too. Twenty four hours. They'd prefer us to clean up our own mess, deal with the details after you're no longer running wild out there. But as I said, don't even trust me. Thorne himself told me Shin Bet were cooperating, so if he's assuming I will tell you, it could be a bluff.'

'No, it makes sense. CTC want a show trial, prove to the world they're up to the job of keeping their house in order.'

'It may not be quite that simple…' There was a long pause. Again, something moved in the village. Another figure in desert cammo broke the line of a doorway for an instant. By the time Leila had the monocular on him, he'd slipped back into cover. There were two of them at least down there. And they must know – or suspect – she was up here. They were being careful to stay on the shadowed side of the buildings, hidden by darkness in the lea of the ruins except when they changed positions. They would have no idea she had the monocular, so they weren't being paranoid about being seen.

She heard Michael take a deep breath.

'Leila,' he said, 'I believe there's a kill order on you. Whatever you've done, whoever you're working for now, they're not going to risk a trial.'

'What? CTC are going to take me out? Can they do that?'

'I told you: this goes right to the top now. You need to find a way out of there before they find you. They've convinced themselves you've defected, and they're not going to let this run much longer.'

'I've found my way out, Michael,' she said. 'That's why I called you. I need you to get a message to the PM.'

'He's not the PM right now. Whitehouse is filling in, and she's the most gung-ho of the lot.'

'Get a message to Morgan, tell him to clear a way for me to get to Ramallah, to Abu Queria. The Peace Talks are not dead. In under an hour I'll have something that's going to get the balance of power back.'

'You're selling what you found in the Negev to the Palestinians? Leila, that's insane!'

'No! I don't care what's out there in the desert. I'm not even sure what it was I stumbled into, though from the macho military bullshit my guess is it was nuclear.'

'That's most people's guess...'

'Then they need to grow up. Nuclear weapons are about

as relevant as the bow and arrow in the modern world, Michael. The game now is biological – synthesise the right virus and you can bring the entire world order down in weeks. And even if you can't actually do it, whoever holds the highest card in the deck gets to call the deals. Golzar is alive, Michael! That's my way out of this!'

'She's still alive? And you know where she is?'

'I can almost see her. If my source can be believed.'

'You'll never make it! CTC, SIS, Cheltenham, they're all listening to every word of this.'

'I know. That's my insurance. If anyone's going to catch me, my preference would still marginally be the British, but only when I'm ready. They might know what I'm planning now, but they have no idea where I am. By the time they trace this phone – if they ever do – this will all be over. If they catch me before I get to the Mukataa in Ramallah, I'll already be carrying the proof I need to clear my name. And if Morgan – the real PM – can clear a path so they don't mess this up for me, I can undo some of the damage of last week's carnage. Or at least make sure those deaths were not completely meaningless. This is my way out.'

'That's not much of a plan, Leila. It's not even half a plan…'

'Funny. Someone else said that to me last night. And yet here I am.'

'Listen! It's not even half a plan because you're completely dismissing Black Eagle in all this. If Golzar's there, so are they.'

'I can deal with them. Let's say I have something they want too.'

'And so the circle is complete! That is exactly what drew a bead on your back the moment you disappeared from Epping Airport. Your willingness to engage with Aquila and his men is what has worried Thorne and Whitehouse from the start of this.'

'Trust me.'

'I do, Leila. The problem is, if my faith in you is well placed and you haven't defected, Black Eagle will kill you as soon as you get anywhere near Golzar. And even if they don't, I seem to be the only one who doesn't believe you've already betrayed your country. Emma Whitehouse will do Black Eagle's job for them as soon as CTC or SIS trace you.'

'Then I've not got much to lose, have I?'

'Leila…'

'Goodbye, Michael. Hopefully I'll see you in a couple of days. Talk to the PM. The real one, not the idiot you've got driving in the dark with the lights off right now.'

She cut the connection. Five minutes ago she wasn't sure whether this call would yield anything or not. She still wasn't.

She was left with two equally unpalatable possibilities. Either Michael or Phillip – or more likely both – had been co-opted into Black Eagle's plan and this conversation had just been another step in their ongoing and opaque plan for their pet Jerusalem Blind, or Black Eagle were not involved in this plan at all.

On the one hand, she couldn't believe Michael would knowingly betray her, but she could easily believe that he would be open to the right kind of persuasion if he truly believed it was her – Leila's – best chance of getting out of this. Lesser of two evils, two wrongs to make a right and all that. His insistence that Black Eagle were not involved in her meeting with Hawadi last night might simply be a well-meaning attempt to keep her alive and playing the game long enough to figure out the truth.

But if Michael had been right and if Hawadi had been wrong, and Black Eagle were not running her as a blind agent at all, she really had been out here on her own from the moment she woke up on that damn plane. In which case that compound out beyond the village was a whole lot more dangerous than she had thought. If the mini-army with the RPGs, diamond cutting wheel and acid spray out in the desert had been trying to finish the job they started at 22,000 feet over the Negev and not just discover what she had learned out there in the hidden underground fortress, she was about to walk into a fatal trap.

"When you have eliminated the impossible, whatever remains, however improbable, must be the truth." But what remained now were *two* improbable truths. And neither of them gave her much confidence in what was already a near-insane plan.

38

All was quiet in the village now. A lone buzzard rode the shimmering thermals beyond a thicket of trees a little way south of the village. Nothing else moved. Whoever was down among the ruined buildings was waiting, watching. Through the scratched lens of the old monocular Leila scanned every building, and she could see no sign of life. The problem was, as soon as she moved, they would see her. And she had to move. Her only chance of finding the spring that had presumably given this settlement life back in the day was to get down to the valley floor. Without the spring as a staring point, she had very little chance of finding Black Eagle's hidden lair.

There was almost no cover between her position on the ridge and the valley floor. The hillside was a mixture of bare rock and loose rubble, interspersed with patches of spiny grass, parched shrubs and a few intrepid trees. Apart from these odd pines there was nothing growing to a height of more than a couple of feet. Picking her way down the scree to the village in a direct line was not going to be an option. Skirting below the ridgeline to the road half a mile to her south would also achieve nothing: in most places the road was higher than the surrounding landscape, and walking along it would make her even more obvious than if she simply walked straight across the scrub to the abandoned settlement.

To her north, three quarters of a mile away, the valley floor rose as it narrowed. Cutting down from the top of the ridge into the head of the valley was an old track – presumably running back to Narom – and all along the track was an avenue of gnarled and unkempt nut trees. Not enough to give much cover, but better than nothing at all. She might make it.

She might make it as long as she wasn't carrying a bright red beacon on her back that could be spotted at a thousand paces. There was no colour out here at all except for her faithful red backpack. So here they would finally have to part company.

She put the lock picks and monocular in the outside left pocket of her leather jacket. The roll of cash – some brought from London, some given to her by Phillip's forger – went in the inside pocket. The spare jeans and t-shirt would serve no purpose now, so she left them rolled in the bottom of the bag with the empty water bottle. The skirt, however, might serve a purpose. She had no idea how long she was going to have to spend in Ramallah, and having a way to blend in modestly and discretely might give her one of those tiny advantages that had punctuated so much of this odyssey. As a cheap cotton thing it rolled down to almost nothing and slipped into her right pocket. With a curious reluctance she stuffed the pack that had been with her for a week now into the exposed roots of the old olive and kicked dust and stones over it to dull its garish incongruity in this bleached landscape.

For half an hour she moved slowly and deliberately from one patch of cover to the next, keeping below the ridgeline so that her silhouette would not make her approach any more obvious than it already was. Every few minutes she stopped the survey the village, but still nothing moved. A second buzzard had joined his mate riding the warm updrafts, flying in wide lazy circles just beyond the village. Their harsh, high-pitched cries sliced the morning silence now and then, but there was no other sound, no other movement below her. She hadn't imagined those two figures... so what were they doing? Had Hawadi tipped them off that she would walk right through the middle of this hamlet? Were they waiting for her to arrive, without having to make the effort of hunting her down on this morning where the temperature was already nudging the low nineties?

She dropped further down the valley's rubbly escarpment and met the old track just where it turned sharply to avoid the highest part of the ridge heading to Narom. It was a long route into the abandoned village, but a good one. To keep the track reasonably level, whoever had built it had taken the trouble to cut through the undulating land – sometimes to a depth of ten feet or more – which gave her long stretches where the village was completely out of sight. Where it rose above the surrounding land, overgrown pistachio and walnut trees gave some cover, and as she drew closer, wild, self-sown eucalyptus grew in dense clusters as they made the most of the relatively fertile ground on the valley floor.

Fifty yards from the first of the tumble-down houses she stopped. From here she would have to make it across open ground in plain sigh. In the narrow gap between two buildings there was a flash of movement again. A figure dressed in brown, with smudges of grey and black camouflage, his head completely covered, slipped from one patch of shade to the next. She caught only a fleeting glimpse, a snapshot impression, before he took cover again.

She scanned the buildings through the monocular, moving from wreck to wreck, examining every wall, window, doorframe, every tangle of fallen roof trusses, every blasted mess of shrubby growth. If he – they – were watching, she could not figure out how. Nothing broke the wall lines, no face in the cracks and empty windows, no rifle sight resting on a bleached-out joist, no smooth edge of a mirror peering around a pile of rubble. They were just waiting. Which may just have been a display of confident bravado – knowing she would come to them – or it may mean something else entirely. Maybe they weren't waiting for her at all...

With little to give her a true sense of scale it was hard to be sure, but the figure she had just glimpsed had appeared to be a very small man. Even crouched as he was to minimise his exposure, he was surely not much more than the size of a child.

She examined the area between the buildings again. Nothing. She picked up a rock and threw it as hard as she could towards the building. It landed well short, and provoked no reaction. Nothing moved, no one spoke. No curious face broke cover to see what this lunatic was doing lobbing rocks at an armed ambush. She stood, got a clear shot and threw a larger stone. Again it landed short, but this time there *was* a reaction to the thud and the shower of dust and gravel it threw up into the stillness and silence.

It was an inhuman sound: quiet, low and unmistakable.

'You wily old bastard,' she whispered and laughed under her breath. Another rock, same reaction – that plaintive, inhuman moan. Without bothering to conceal her approach she jogged down the slope to the nearest building and rounded the corner.

In the cool shade beneath the wall three goats sat contentedly chewing the cud and staring at her with their weird rectangular pupils. They seemed neither surprised nor concerned by the sudden appearance of their visitor. More had found shelter behind the next building.

'Leila,' she said, 'you've been in the city far too long, my dear...' A flock of ten goats, sensibly staying on the lea side of the walls and moving as little as possible had cost her almost an hour in getting down to the valley floor. There was not a single sign of human presence at all.

39

The spring was easy enough to find fifty yards or so from the last of the ruined houses. Where the ground was permanently fed with water flowing out of the hills a small woodland had grown up. The grass was greener and softer than the lacerating scrub on the rest of the valley, and goat tracks cut arrow-straight from their shady resting points to the clear, dark water. Leila crouched amongst the reeds by the pool and drank. Not the wisest decision, but if it was good enough for the goats, it was probably good enough for her. And it tasted fine. Better than fine. Cold and with a hard mineral edge, it was the finest water she had drunk in years. It was also the only water she had drunk in hours. The temperature was still climbing, the sun a blinding white ball in the cloudless sky. She had no idea what lay ahead, and this could be the only water she'd get for the rest of the day. And she'd left the empty plastic water bottle – the last of her salvage from the plane wreck – in her backpack... which was a mile back across the valley among the roots of an ancient olive tree.

The spring had been easy to find, but as Hawadi had warned her, the Black Eagle compound was not. Even finding where the stream exited the small pool was not so easy among the thick vegetation. It was hardly a stream, more a thin trickle of water that the desert had not immediately claimed as its own. A mess of tracks – some carved out by the goats, others the remnants of a time when this valley had been the centre of the local farming operation, snaked away from the pool. Any one of these paths could have tempted her to explore it on the assumption that it would lead to another settlement sooner or later. But Hawadi had told her to follow the watercourse, so she did. Fifty feet into the thicket of pines and eucalyptus trees the trickle ran out, leaving only a line of darkened earth. This in turn faded to nothing more than a channel of exposed rock. In flood times (which, she realised, could well have been in Biblical times), the slow, relentless trickle of water had carved out this channel, but now all that was left was smooth limestone, so bright where the morning sun penetrated the undergrowth that it was almost white, scar tissue from an ancient wound.

The rocky channel, choked along most of its length by grass and thorny broom, turned abruptly and ran west towards the lowest part of the valley floor. She followed it, increasingly aware that if she carried on like this too much longer she was going to end up right back at the main road she had done so much to avoid. Already she could hear the hiss of the thin traffic through the trees.

Then quite suddenly she came to a row of trees so straight and orderly that they could not be natural. The drover's track they bordered had mostly been reclaimed by nature, but this straight scar that cut directly towards the main road on her left and a deep spur valley on her right must be the one Hawadi had told her about. The one that led to the Black Eagle safe house. She was close.

From the cover of a broad pine she scanned the area through the monocular. To the south she could see momentary flashes of light as the sun glinted off passing cars. The sun was high enough now that shadows were beginning to flatten out, making any judgement of distance even more difficult. She followed the line of the almost invisible highway until it intersected the drover's track. Two huge concrete bollards marked the entrance to the track, and snaking between them was a chain heavy enough that it could have moored a cruise ship. One end of the chain was attached to the bollard, the other had been let down to open this improvised but highly effective gate. She followed the dirt path, scanning through the blindingly white rock rubble. An exposed area immediately below her position showed fresh tyre marks just before the track dipped out of sight through a thicket of young trees.

Slowly, silently, she made her way along the track away from the road until, quite unexpectedly, she found herself looking across a clearing of about twenty yards to a low dirty-grey building. Surrounding the single storey flat-roofed farmhouse was an eight-foot chainlink fence topped with razor wire. A gate across the approach road was closed, the two ends of its closing chain hanging loose. A Toyota pickup and a Mercedes C200 estate were parked beneath an awning to the side of the building; the Land Cruiser was covered in a matt film of dust, the C200 was clean, a more recent arrival. All the windows of the compound were shuttered, and the only door on this side of the building sported a skin of mild steel over the original wood. Nothing moved and even the buzzards were quiet now, flown off in search of prey elsewhere.

This was it. This was Black Eagle's safe house. It was a good choice, sheltered by the overgrown valley on three sides and completely open at the front. Although it would probably be invisible from the road, the old drover's track led in a straight line between the two. If there were guards on the roof it would be impossible to get within a hundred yards of the place without being seen. She trusted Hawadi a little more now. He could easily have sent her in through the front entrance, past those big concrete bollards and right into the sniper's alley that was the main drive. His preferred route had taken her two hours to navigate (allowing for goats), but he had given her the opportunity to get some understanding of the building and who might be in it before they even knew she was here.

Two vehicles. It didn't mean much, but it did indicate that this wasn't the headquarters of a private army, and whoever was here felt secure enough that they didn't even bother to lock the gates.

She was not, however, alone. Something broke the roofline for an instant. Maybe a foot, an elbow, a bottle, as the sniper lying face down on the ever-warming asphalt adjusted his position. Leila shrank back into the bushes. She held her breath, but there was no further movement from the roof.

She could not rely on stealth, the element of surprise, or superior firepower to gain access to the building. So when all other possibilities have been eliminated… She had only one thing on her side, and that was that Black Eagle were going to be delighted to see her. At least briefly. She was just going to have to announce her presence then wing it and hope. The best person to introduce herself to at this crazy party was the man on the roof. He could effect further introductions, if she could avoid him shooting her first.

It was impossible to see onto the roof from her current position, so she moved the back to higher ground and scrambled a few feet into a tree.

What she saw was both surprising and perfectly obvious. The sniper was there, accompanied by two almost comical breakfast guests. The object that had broken the roofline had been the tip of a giant wing. The buzzards she had seen riding the thermals as she crossed into the village had not been out for a pleasure flight. They had been scoping out a meal.

The two birds were picking through the scattered fragments of a pizza at the far end of the building – the antipasto before they started on the main course of Sniper Carbonara. The pool of dark liquid around the sentry's head clearly indicated that the pizza had been destined to be his evening meal but a bullet to the head meant it was still there for the keen eyes of the buzzards to find as the sun rose the following morning. A gun lay beside him, a rifle with a scope attached. He had been waiting for someone, but someone else had seen him first. She wondered if the sound that had awoken her back at the barn had not in fact been the slap of a pallet being piled onto the waiting trailer, but the single report of an assassin's rifle.

Then there had been a second shot. Two guards? Two kill shots from the cover behind the house?

The chain between the bollards at the entrance to the compound was down. The sniper, with his clear view along the old drover's track, was dead, probably hit from an ambush behind him. There was no sound or sign of movement within the building even though she could easily have been spotted by someone hiding in the gloom behind those weathered shutters. And the two cars parked under the awning at the side of the farm were no evidence of anything. This time yesterday there could have been more, and whoever had cleared the compound out in the early hours of this morning would have had their pick of transport out of here.

She had just found several more pieces of the puzzle lurking in an unexpected corner of the box, but they did nothing to make the picture any clearer. Nothing made any sense.

Hawadi could have double-crossed her and warned whoever had been behind their meeting that she was on her way to the compound when they took him into protective custody. If that had been Black Eagle (and despite her conversation with Michael, she still entertained the possibility that it was) surely they would not kill their own guards just to make it easier for her to gain access to the site?

But if Michael had been right, and this was a British operation, why were they not still here? Why clear out the compound in readiness for her arrival, then leave without their main prize?

Hawadi had been right about one thing: she was someone's Jerusalem Blind, a puppet in a game she was not meant to understand. They had drawn her here and her best – her only – course of action now was to play the game, see where it led. And if part of that game was to make it to the compound, there was no point in trying to be subtle about it.

She took the head scarf off and wiped away the trickles of sweat that sprang from her hairline and etched dusty trails down her face, then scrambled down the tree, along the high fence, and walked through the unlocked front gate to the steel-clad side door.

40

The farmhouse was dark and hot inside. As she had expected, the steel door put up no resistance. She had turned the hot, sun-baked handle and it had simply popped open. Whoever had been here in the early hours of the morning either knew she was close behind and wanted her to come on in, make herself at home, or they had cleared the place of anything interesting. Either way, locking the door was completely pointless.

She found herself in a small kitchen. Shards of sunlight streamed in through the old shutters, brightly illuminating narrow strips of the room while leaving other parts in near darkness. The room was nowhere near as derelict as the outside of the building would suggest, though it was hardly out of the pages of Ideal Home either. There were signs of recent use: plates and mugs piled in the sink, a half-empty jar of instant coffee beside a kettle, a cooker decorated with spatters of uncongealed food that could not have been there more than a few hours. And a smell of curry, thick and sweet, that lay over the colder antiseptic odour of disinfectant, which in turn lay over a deeper, metallic smell of fresh blood.

The kitchen gave onto a short corridor. On the left, in a darkened room that should have given a picturesque view along the drover's track towards the hills to the south, the sofa and armchairs had been piled against the far wall to make room for two narrow military-style cot beds. The beds were unmade and the room stank of cigarettes and beer. These were civilian guards living in a make-believe world of private armies and mercenary glory. They were Black Eagle's hired muscle, not their elite commanders. Whatever they were, they were not here now. The house was silent, and Leila became increasingly convinced that whoever had been here eating curry and trying to stay awake on cheap coffee was as gone as the sniper on the roof. But was everyone gone? And had her main person of interest – Raha Golzar herself – ever been here in the first place?

Both questions were quickly answered when she opened the door at the end of the corridor.

The bedroom had been made up as a parody of a private hospital suite. The wall to the bathroom beyond had been smashed through leaving a rough hole and the room had been cleared of everything except a bed and a trolly-table against one wall and two chairs against the other. An anglepoise lamp stood on the table, directed to the floor so that the corner of the room glowed in its yellowy light, but the rest of the room was almost dark. As with the rest of the building, the window shutters were closed and the lack of ventilation, coupled with the fact that this was clearly the room of a very sick patient, meant the air was hot and foetid with the smell of disinfectant and blood and an undertone of something like nail-varnish remover. It was a smell of coming death.

Leila approached the bed. On the night of the siege the only glimpse she had caught of the woman she shot – the woman who had been indirectly responsible for the whole bloody mess last week – was an arm hanging out of the boot of Aquila's car as he sped away. She had seen the admission photograph from Golzar's time at Low Newton Prison, but those pictures never look like the person concerned. And now, the face she saw in the bed was so heavily swathed in bandages that she probably wouldn't have recognised her own mother.

But this was Raha Golzar, no doubt about it. She lay under a white sheet, from which snaked a tube attached to a drip. Another line led back to a small pump – Leila assumed one delivering morphine – and a bundle of wires sagged between the bed and an ICU stats monitor, the screen of which was dark and lifeless.

The patient herself was not, however, lifeless – probably just drugged to near-unconsciousness. Her breathing was slow and rasping and what skin Leila could see beneath the bandages was sallow and waxy and drenched with a slick of sweat. Hawadi had told her that her clip of bullets back at Epping Airport had cut her a new hair parting – which accounted for the lavish medical turban – and hit her liver. At least two of the bullets had, apparently, shattered her left leg. There was no way to check. Even in the gloom and with the patient beneath a sheet, it was obvious that the left leg had been amputated above the knee. Only a single knee and foot tented the bed sheet below the waist.

'Leila Reid?'

She span round.

Silhouetted in the door was a man. Leila reached instinctively to her right hip for a gun that wasn't there. The only gun in the room was already pointing at her from less than twenty feet away.

'Don't worry,' the man said, 'I'm not intending to shoot you unless it's really necessary.'

'Then let's make sure it isn't,' Leila said. 'Who are you?'

'My name is Scott Rees,' he said.

Leila smiled. 'I don't believe it. British Secret Intelligence,' she said. It wasn't a question. It was a logical deduction. Between her time in the Foreign Office and the constant low-level rivalry between CTC and SIS, she could pick a spy at a hundred paces. Recruitment had been broadened in recent times, but this guy was old-school. Old *public* school, he came with the assured bearing of the military and the cocky veneer of bought intelligence and a deeply held certainty of his own importance.

Rees nodded slightly. 'These days I'm more of a…' 'Cultural attaché' in Tel Aviv.'

'A field agent put out to pasture. How ironic,' Leila said.

'Let's say I lean on the gate between the two. I still retain the licence, but these days I prefer to persuade a little more subtly. Hence…' He spread his hands.

'So what now?' Leila said.

'That depends on you,' Rees said. He stepped into the room and walked slowly to the chairs opposite the foot of Golzar's death bed. He sat down. Leila didn't move.

'GCHQ cleaned up enough of the signal to know your aim was to find Raha Golzar,' he said, 'but what no one is sure of is *why*. Signal-to-noise on that bit of your conversation meant we had to make a lot of guesses, and none of them made any sense.'

'She's my way out of here.'

'How so?'

'She's the leverage I needed to convince Prime Minister Queria to get me out of the country. She was important enough that the peace talks were contingent on Queria having her in his custody. Important enough for Black Eagle to bomb a hotel and foment riots on the streets of London to break her out of prison. That's some passport if I'm in possession of her.'

'I don't understand why you need her at all now,' Rees said. 'After SIS fixed the meeting with Hawadi, you must have realised you could have negotiated a way out with us.'

'Black Eagle were behind the meeting...'

'Is that what you think? No, your friend Shaw started the ball rolling, as you requested. He fed CTC, they fed us. If the warning bullet as you left Hawadi's apartment had been enough to make you stop and think for a moment, you'd be back in London now and we'd have dealt with Golzar. Could have saved us all a lot of trouble.'

'I was so sure...' she said.

'Then keep that to yourself. Telling the wrong people you thought you were working for Aquila and his people will not be a good look.'

'Not that I *was* working for them! But that they *thought* I was. They thought they were running me; I was using them as much as...'

'Double bluff. Hard to Prove, Miss Reid. Harder still when there are those in London who would be disinclined to believe anything you say. Remember, we assumed you were aiming at a meeting with the Russians, and while it would have been fun to see who Hawadi had hooked you up with, we could hardly let the exchange itself go ahead.'

'And then you figured this was about more than nuclear secrets…'

'We cleaned up the audio and realised you wanted to find Golzar. Which was interesting. So we let it play a while longer.'

'But once you knew where Golzar was, why risk losing me again? The whole thing could have been a bluff.'

'Now you're starting to ask the right questions. We've never had any hook into Black Eagle. Until last week, we had very little intelligence that they existed at all. You are the only person who has ever seen or spoken to the man who calls himself Donald Aquila. You're the only person with all the information, all the pieces that could be fitted together to make the complete picture. You investigated Hawadi two years ago, knew the depth and scope of his web of contacts. You'd spent time with Aquila, you were at Mapleton House, you had the ear of the PM, contacts in the Foreign Office, CTC, MI5… You're also one of the most devious and instinctive cryptologists any of us have ever seen. Only you could piece it all together and lead us to the root cause of everything that has been going on for the last fifteen months, all the deaths in London last week. How you're still only a DS with the Met is perhaps the biggest surprise of all. But there had to be a hidden agenda, a long game, and we were curious about how it all fitted together. We had to let you come here to complete the puzzle…'

'I just wanted to get home, that's all. If you bastards had trusted me from the beginning, I'd be back there right now, glass of wine in the garden, the worst I'd have to deal with is convincing you that I neither knew nor cared what the hell the IDF have hidden out there in the desert. If anything!'

'And yet here we are. They played us all, Leila, not just you. This went right to the top, probably in ways none of us will ever really understand. So where does that leave you?'

'I do what I came here to do.'

Rees was right of course: she didn't need to any more. She could negotiate a cleaner way out of Israel under the protection of SIS, but it wasn't enough. Through the heat and the dust, the constant presence of unseen hunters, the sheer desolation of knowing that but for one misfit computer hacker two thousand miles away she was completely alone, her mission had grown. Mission Creep they call it – as the snowball of intention rolls, it grows. Golzar had simply been her way out of this mess when she started. Now she could serve a much bigger purpose.

Rees was watching her from his seat in the low glow of the lamp.

'OK,' he said. 'I guess you've earned that much. You get to make your choice.' He smiled and threw her the gun. It was, she now saw, the gun that Hawadi had kept on her throughout their meeting. The little Ruger, with its scratched polymer grip and dull steel barrel was heavy, almost certainly fully loaded.

Leila raised the gun and pointed it at Rees's head. He didn't break eye contact.

'Aren't you going to tell me what a terrible mistake it would be to kill you?' she said.

'Why? Reid, if you kill me, your best hope is that Abu Queria will give you sanctuary in exchange for Golzar. But do you really think it would be that simple? Even when – if – Richard Morgan comes back, you've made too many enemies among the permanent staff in Britain. Queria can keep you alive; he cannot give you the life you think you want. You'll spend the rest of your days in Ramallah, constantly watching shadows and jumping at every footstep behind you. You'll never go back to England. Too many people still believe you have been trying to fix a meeting with the FSB to leverage a position with Black Eagle.'

'And you don't?'

'Would you be holding a gun if I did?'

'So you think you're the missing half of my plan? If I spare the British agent I must be on the level?'

'You're getting there. Question is: what about the first half of your plan?' He motioned to the almost lifeless body in the bed beside her.

Leila looked the SIS agent in the eyes for a long moment then swung the gun through ninety degrees. Alive or dead; it made very little difference. That's what she'd told Hawadi, but it wasn't quite the truth. Abu Queria didn't want what Golzar knew, he just needed to be sure no one else would ever gain access to it. Leila thought he had a point. There was also the fact that Black Eagle had gone to extraordinary lengths to break her out of jail in Britain last week. What would they do to get her out of Ramallah? The risk was too great that if Golzar survived, the events of the last week might go down in history as a mere prelude to the main event…

Alive, Raha Golzar was a deadly liability.

She steadied her hand and fired twice into the unconscious Iranian's body. She adjusted her aim and put another bullet in her head.

'Satisfied?' she said.

Rees stood up. 'Slightly surprised, but I guess you have, as you say, done what you came here to do. Now we need to move. I need to get you on a plane back to London before anyone else turns up here.'

'No, not yet. I need to deliver Golzar to the PNA first.'

'Really? You still think that's important?'

'It's *all* that's important, Rees. If I'd killed Golzar on Friday night, none of this would have happened. And if she'd ended up in Ramallah as your people had planned fifteen months ago, none of the events of the last week would have happened.'

'You can't change any of that…'

'But I can really piss Donald Aquila off, and that's a start.'

'And then what?'

'One step at a time. Right now, you're going to help me get the body into the car, then you're driving me to Ramallah. OK?'

Rees shrugged, but his half-smile told her all she needed to know.

Leila pulled the cannula and monitors from Golzar's body and wrapped the bedsheet around her. There wasn't a lot of weight to her… fifteen months in a psychiatric prison that had taken its toll, then there was the transfemoral amputation which saved twenty-five pounds or so, plus a week of extreme privation in the care of Black Eagle… and the Iranian had not been a big woman to start with. They laid her in the C200's large boot and Rees dug the car keys out of his pocket.

'Incidentally,' Leila said, looking up at the roof where one buzzard had again taken to the air. 'What did you do with the guards inside?'

'There was only one, and he had his music turned up so loud he didn't hear me take out his mate on the roof. He was so surprised to see me when I stuck my head through his kitchen window that he was dead before he even realised he'd been caught. I went back to the road to get the car, the chain at the bollards was down and there was no one else around. My guess is they'd already given up on the place, and their patient. Unlike you, Aquila had no use for Golzar unless she was alive and talking, and she was well past that.'

'You don't think she'd have made it?'

Rees stared at her in disbelief for a moment before a broad grin spread across his face. 'You thought there was a chance she'd survive, and you shot her anyway? Wow, not CTC's usual modus operandi. Shoot first, then wonder!'

'I've had a bitch of a week, Rees, and most of it was down to her. But if I'd bothered to think about it at all I'd still have made the same choice. Now come on, this place might be deserted now, but my guess is it won't be when those guards fail to report in, whether Aquila cares about his patient or not. I'd rather be in Ramallah by the time he comes to find out what happened. Remember, I'm still a very loose end for Black eagle.'

41

The trip to Ramallah took less than an hour. They were not stopped for papers – although Leila realised that she would not be so lucky if she tried to get back into Israel again alone. Without a passport and carrying only an entry card that would not stand close scrutiny, she was going to be stuck with Rees until she was back in London.

They drove through the traffic-choked streets to within a few hundred yards of the government compound on El-Irsal Street. After the shady tree-lined boulevards of Tel Aviv and the deep canyon-like alleys of old Jerusalem, Ramallah was an assault on the senses. Noisy, crowded, and built of bright stone (or painted an even more painful shade of white), it had an unreal quality about it – part third world, part other world, like a movie set for a film without a script.

Leila directed Rees to pull off into a dusty parking lot within sight of the Mukataa's blank white walls. Officially the national defence building, this place was as close as she was going to get to Abu Queria, or at least someone who might understand the value of the cargo they had in the boot of the Merc.

'I assume in your role as cultural attaché in Tel Aviv,' Leila said, 'a phone number for someone high up in there is not going to be a problem?'

Rees took out his mobile and scrolled through the directory.

'Our consulate-general is in East Jerusalem, but obviously we have contacts.' He pressed dial and handed the phone to Leila. 'This is his secretary and general minion.'

Leila stepped out of the car and closed the door behind her. Rees watched her as the call was connected to the British representative working somewhere behind that impenetrable wall. She talked for a few minutes then got back into the car.

'They were expecting us,' Leila said. 'Morgan did come through. Queria's not here, but his deputy's curious about what we've brought.'

'So you're going to drive in there and just see what happens?'

Leila laughed. 'I'm not totally insane. Morgan didn't fix this because he's being a nice helpful guy. I've never been under any illusion that he blames me for the murder of his daughter – amongst other things. All he wants now is to get me out of the picture, or at least back under control, any way he can. But I'm not going to make it that easy for him. When we're clear of here, I call in the location of the car and the people in there come and do whatever they need to do.'

'And I take you home,' Rees said.

'That is the main reason I didn't shoot you in the head when I had a chance, yes. You can clear the route ahead as an Intelligence operation. My guess is that was always part of your plan anyway, so we both get to win. And yes, I also realise you're almost certainly got your own agenda here, but frankly as long as whatever scheme you're cooking up keeps me alive long enough to get home, I really don't care what it is.'

'My job is simply to get you back to London for a debrief, and save everyone a lot of trouble here. There's those back home who still think you're running around with nuclear secrets, and they really don't want that.'

'Of course not. They want to know what I know. They're going to be sadly disappointed.'

'Not my problem,' Rees said. 'OK, no luggage, no resistance and no stupid questions. If it all stays that way, I think we can make this work. Now, whatever you got from Canaan Communications, leave it in the car. It'll do more harm than good when we get moving, and it'll be good evidence for the PNA as to who dumped the body of their Most Wanted right outside their front door. I'd rather they thought you were acting alone for now, keep SIS at arm's length from this.'

'Part of your real plan here?' Leila said.

'Just part of the missing second half of yours, Reid. Come on.'

Leila took the only piece of evidence Phillip's forger had given her, the entry pass in the name of Sarah Connor, and put it on the car's dashboard. They stepped out of the last of the car's air-conditioned coolness and into the blazing white-hot sun of downtown Ramallah. Rees locked the car and threw the phone to Leila. She redialled the number of

Abu Queria's British liaison and confirmed the location of the Merc and that its unexpected cargo should be picked up before the heat did too much damage to it.

A hundred yards back along El-Irsal Street Rees flagged down a taxi to take them to the bus station. As they got in a car alarm sounded from the direction of the Mukataa. The Merc had been opened. In a few seconds Golzar would be found and the unbelievable story that had landed on Queria's desk would be confirmed. With luck, the wheels of peace would begin to turn again.

As the taxi crawled through the city traffic Rees began to make his arrangements. Much of the conversation was in Hebrew and Leila tuned out and watched the dusty white city slip by. It was over, and her mind was beginning to slip back into the icy depths of unknowing. There would be time in SIS's extensive debriefs to make sense of it all, but for now she was happy to let the ice hold the memories and trust that this ageing ex-spy was going to do everything he could to ensure his prized catch would make it safely back to London.

An official car, maybe even the same Black BMW that had chased her through the desert the previous night, picked them up at the bus station. It avoided the complicated explanations that would be required when papers were checked as they passed back into Israel (especially in a Palestinian taxi), and it also meant the trail would go cold should their taxi driver be questioned. Leila had no idea why anyone should be questioned about these two English travellers, but Rees was a spy and some habits die hard. Not that she cared. The car was air-conditioned and she dozed in the all-encompassing luxury of the rear seat. A seat very much like the one she had woken up in two days earlier. Except this one wasn't at twenty thousand feet and climbing....

Just one thing remained. A niggling doubt that she could not quite put her finger on. Her danger-radar still pinged a faint trace of something. She had been run as a blind agent – Hawadi's ever-so-funny 'Jerusalem Blind' – but was that the whole story? And was it over? Just how deep and wide did the operation really go?

Something Rees had said lodged in her mind like a half-swallowed pill in the throat, but she couldn't quite find the memory now. A piece of the jigsaw that seemed to fit it's allotted hole, but turned out to have the wrong picture on it. An anomaly, a gap...

She slept.

42

Scott Rees might have been an out-to-pasture cultural attaché these days, but he obviously still had friends in high places. They had arrived at Ben Gurion airport in Tel Aviv less than half an hour before the British Airways A350 was due to take off for the five hour flight to London.

They made it on board as everyone else was buckling up, hand baggage stowed, newspapers and magazines at the ready. Even the not-so-clandestine Air Marshall seated in K41 (like secret agents the world over, Leila had a sense for them... their over-attentive attitude, the studied casualness) was satisfied that his life would be easy at least until they were at cruising height. He looked at Leila as she and her minder made their way to the back row of steerage, but one look at Rees satisfied him that all was well with these two very late arrivals.

Getting through check-in had been simple. Calls had been made, forms emailed, and by the time Rees led his charge into a security office at the rear of Ben Gurion, something close to extradition papers were waiting. Shin Bet were ridding themselves of a tiresome nuisance, far away from Israel, to where her innocent lack of knowledge about something that didn't exist in a place no one knew about would, at most, become a diplomatic bump rather than an all-out military and political incident. She would become someone else's problem. As such, her lack of passport was of no more concern to airport security than her lack of luggage or the fact that she looked like she had been living in the desert for the last few days. Which, in truth, she more or less had.

The only hitch was Rees's gun. Even SIS veterans flying their own national airline could not circumvent some rules. He dropped his weapon into an evidence bag which was sealed and passed to an armed guard. From there it would be placed in a bomb-proof, fire-proof, tamper-proof box in the hold, which was inaccessible from the cabin and safety-locked so that it could not be opened under any circumstances unless the aircraft was stationary. Ironic, considering the burly pseudo-businessman in K41 was carrying exactly the same weapon concealed beneath his Savile Row jacket.

She gazed unseeingly out of the window or dozed. After a couple of hours she awoke and looked down at the slowly passing vista of night-time Europe spread out below her. Although she didn't know it, the twinkling orange glow far below off the starboard wing was Frankfurt. Just twenty minutes earlier, in a hotel on Kennedyallee, Donald Aquila had received a phone call. Golzar had vanished from the safe house outside Jerusalem, both guards murdered, no sign of force, no evidence to follow. As yet he did not know she was spending her first night in Ramallah, or that she was dead (although he would have been astonished if she had survived the rest of the day, with or without someone helping her find the final out door). He had immediately suspected – known – that his nemesis Leila Reid had been involved in the Iranian's disappearance somewhere along the line. What he didn't suspect was that at that very moment she was closer to him than she had been since they parted in Amman three days earlier, albeit out of reach at 35,000 feet. Or that this time she was destined for a safe landing.

Leila knew none of this, partly because she didn't care what that orange glow was, and partly because her mind was still back in Ramallah with that anomalous piece of her crazy jigsaw puzzle of history. It was a piece that did not help her solve the puzzle at all, did not present her with a satisfyingly complete and understandable picture. The more she mulled it over, the more she realised that all this strange, blank fragment did was pose one huge and terrifying question.

Back in the rubble-strewn car park, cocooned in the last of the air-conditioned comfort of the SIS Merc, Rees had told her to leave whatever she had got from Canaan Communications on the dashboard. Perfectly reasonable. It was evidence best left behind. It was not even a surprise that he knew she was carrying fake papers – anyone in her position would have made it a priority to find something to legitimise her existence. What she had not registered at the time, and what now begged that awful question was how he knew where the papers had come from.

How had Rees known about the Canaan forger?

He'd as good as admitted SIS had been running her as a blind agent for twelve hours prior to their meeting in

Golzar's improvised hospital room. But Phillip's forger was outside of that time frame. He came at least six hours *before* SIS had picked her up at Millo for the meeting with Hassan Hawadi.

They hadn't picked up her trail as a result of her conversation with Phillip about finding the Fatah double-agent as she had been led to believe. They'd been way ahead of that part of the game. Phillip didn't know it. Maybe CTC didn't know it, but all the evidence suggested SIS had been on her trail since the moment she entered Jerusalem, maybe even since her first contact with the outside world in a Tel Aviv shopping centre. And when she stepped off their carefully curated route, threatened to find a way of slipping through their grasp with forged papers, they'd moved into get her back on track. Although there was no way they could have known what she was really doing in Israel (because the truth was, she was doing nothing more than trying not to be in Israel at all), they had made sure she kept to their plan by killing her only trusted ally in the Old City, and doing it in the most barbaric way possible. And Scott Rees had then made one more move to ensure she *stayed* on track...

Just how deep did this go? She still believed Aquila had been responsible for her leaving Britain under cover of darkness and anonymity, and that Black Eagle had put her on that doomed plane over the Negev. But had SIS been watching even then? Had *all* of this been part of an elaborate sting operation?

How long had she really been their Jerusalem Blind? And to what possible, terrifying, end?

43

The plane touched down into Heathrow at a few minutes past midnight. Leila and her chaperone were among the last passengers to deplane from one of the last flights to come in that night, and the airport was quiet. Rees ushered her through a back channel of immigration and into the main lobby. As he and his gun had to be kept apart airside, he led her to a door between arrivals and departures and looked into a camera above the door.

The door opened and a uniformed security guard looked Rees up and down.

'About ten minutes,' the guard said. 'Passenger bags come first, apparently. Come in.'

He stood aside and Rees moved to pass him.

'I need to use the bathroom,' Leila said.

'Then use it while I wait,' Rees said.

The guard looked doubtful. 'Back here she'd need to be accompanied. Rules, you know? Can you use the public ones across the way?'

Rees gave her a half smile. 'Don't even think about it,' he said. He took out his phone and stepped back to take a full-length photograph of his charge. He tapped a few keys and slipped the phone back into his pocket.

'Our driver's waiting outside. Now he knows who he's waiting for. Try to leave, you won't get far. So do what you have to do and come back, here, and only here. OK?'

'Fine,' Leila said.

'And you're on camera everywhere,' the guard said, warming to his role as ally of a British Secret Agent.

Not quite everywhere, Leila thought. *Not quite.*

As Rees followed the wannabe secret agent down his secret corridor into the labyrinthine back world of Heathrow Airport, Leila walked across the almost deserted arrivals hall to the public WC. There was no one else inside. She checked each cubicle – all empty – and slipped into the last one on the right and bolted the door. She hung her faithful leather jacket on the door hook, half aware that she was saying goodbye to it for the last time, and slipped out of her jeans, again for the last time. The rolled-up skirt she had stuffed into a pocket back in that lost Jerusalem valley was so flimsy it barely had the strength to hold a crease. It merely looked like it had been on a plane for the last five hours, which meant for her purposes it looked just fine.

The shirt, a useful contrast of off-white after the chestnut brown of the jacket, was also serviceable. A rough plait kept her hair up far enough to cover most of it with the scarf that had been her final purchase in the backstreet market of the Old City.

She heard footsteps approach as she rolled her jeans around her jacket and, after a moment's indecision, left them on the closed toilet cover. There was nowhere else. Rees was not going to take long to find them and realise she had left looking rather different to how she had arrived, but putting them in a cupboard – even if there had been a cupboard that wasn't protected by the one kind of low-tech locks she couldn't pick – would only have bought her a few extra seconds. Her time for believing in small advantages like a few extra seconds to disappear was long gone. She was going to need a lot more than that to get out of here.

And she got a major break when she opened the cubicle door. Two women – one about Leila's age, the other early twenties and carrying a baby's cot – were standing side by side, talking to each other in the mirror over the sinks. Obviously new arrivals, travel-worn and disorientated, they gave Leila an idea. She washed her hands, watching the two women for a moment.

'Excuse me,' she said quietly. The older woman turned slightly to look at her in the mirror. 'Could you help me? You don't need to do anything... I just need...'

'What is it, love?'

The younger girl placed the baby carrier beside the sink and disappearing into a cubicle. This was a job for her mother.

'It's silly,' Leila said.

'It's not silly if you're asking for help.'

Leila smiled. 'My husband... Long flight. Long story. Too much free vodka and...'

'I get the picture,' the woman said. 'You need me to call the police?' Leila felt herself being examined minutely, face-on now.

'No, nothing like that,' she said. 'I just need to get out of here while he's at baggage collection. And I'm a bit short of cash. Oh no! I'm not asking for money. Just… any chance you're taking a taxi in the direction of London?'

The toilet behind them flushed and the door opened.

'We are,' the young mother said. 'We'll get you where you need to go. I've been where you are. Bastards.' She nodded at the baby and turned the tap on full to wash her hands. 'But if you want to get out before he gets your bags, we'd better get on with it. Dad was just waiting for our last bits when we came in here.'

'Oh, thank you.'

'No bag yourself, love?' the older woman said. Leila shrugged. Her bag was under an olive tree two thousand miles away. 'Come on then. Stay with us. We'll get you where you need to go.'

The two women formed a protective escort as they walked out of the toilet and towards the main exit. The door to the secret corridor was closed and anonymous. Rees would – with luck – be twiddling his thumbs in there for a few more minutes yet.

A man in his late forties was waiting beside a suitcase-laden trolley. 'Dad', Leila assumed. 'Mum' whispered something to him and he led the way out of the terminal.

A dark grey BMW 5-Series was parked on the yellow No Parking hatching right outside the door. From her protected position between her two saviours, Leila glanced at the driver. He had his phone in his hand and was staring vaguely out of the front window. As his attention was caught by the movement of the four new arrivals and their baby, he turned to them. He looked right at Leila without even registering her. He glanced down at the phone – no doubt checking

Rees's photograph – and continued his silent and absent-minded vigil. Ten seconds later Leila was in the back seat of a taxi.

And ten minutes after that, she was on the M4 heading for London. By now Rees would have realised she wasn't coming back. He might have found her discarded clothes, but he would have no idea what she looked like now (or how she had managed to make any kind of transformation at all). His driver would swear she hadn't left the airport. For the time being, she was clear. Her freedom wouldn't last long, but she had only one more thing to do before she either handed herself in properly or made one final bid to vanish once and for all. Her only two goals since waking up on Donald Aquila's ageing private jet were to get home and to clear her name of any culpability either in the attacks of last week or the events that had followed in Israel. She'd managed the first and by now she cared very little about the second. She cared very little, but that was not to say she didn't care at all…

There was one more loose end to tie up, one more person she had to try to explain this mess to…

44

Leila had told her Good Samaritans that she was planning to stay with her sister in Kew until her husband sobered up and missed her enough to discuss a solution to their marital problems. Kew was not where she needed to be, but it was close and she had plenty of time to get from there to her final destination in Wimbledon. The taxi dropped her – without any money changing hands – right outside the locked and peaceful paradise of the Botanic Gardens. After ample reassurances that she would be fine from here, Leila watched the little family disappear into the night. There were still good people in the world – plenty of them. She just had the misfortune not to be part of that world any more. Her choices in life had led her into a murky world of lies and treachery. It was a world she had tried to escape before but had always been drawn back into. She had decided during that last taxi journey that this time it would be for ever. This time…

She sat beneath a tree and dozed on the edge of Wimbledon common waiting for the rest of the world to catch up with her. The house she had come to visit was one of the modest ones – it bore the Southside address, but not the gameshow-host and pop-star price tags of its neighbours. It had been in the family for a long time, tenaciously held onto through thick and thin. No police officer, however far he had been promoted, could ever afford an address like this now.

At seven thirty the front door opened. Two people came out onto the gravel drive: one got into the metallic blue Mini Cooper and drove north towards Parkside and her job at the private hospital overlooking the park; the other waved her off and began his constitutional across the park to get his morning paper. Same every Saturday. Almost every Saturday. There had been a few that Leila had interrupted, weekends when he told his wife he was away for work (or she really was away for work) but those days were well behind them now.

She had about forty-five minutes until he returned. Long enough to put the coffee maker on for when he got home. Long enough to decide finally what she was going to say, how she was going to end this.

At 8.15 she heard the key in the lock. The door opened and there was a momentary pause when the alarm failed to demand that it be disarmed.

'Hello?' he said.

Leila waited. She was in the sitting room at a little table in the corner. The front curtains were partially closed against the assault of the summer sun, and the steam from two fresh mugs of coffee shimmered in the narrow beam that forced its way through the crack.

'Hello?' he called again. The front door closed.

'In here, Michael,' Leila said.

He stood framed in the doorway, his morning Telegraph under his arm and his sunglasses hanging loosely in his left hand.

'Leila?'

'Obviously.' She smiled at him. 'Made you a coffee. And I kind of needed one after the week I've had.'

'How...?' He dropped the paper onto the sofa and walked over to her.

'How did I get out of Israel, or how did I get in here?' she said.

'The first is a bit much right now,' he said. 'Let's start with how the hell you got in here!'

She indicated the lock picks on the table. 'The only thing to make it out of Israel with me, all the way from that other life back in Mapleton House. You really should get a better lock, Michael, even out here in nice-ville.' He started at her. 'Oh yes, the alarm. Remember Hors de Terrain?'

Michael laughed.

'Yes, you do,' she said. 'That dreadful French thing we went to in Crouch End. All poetic angst and arty emoting? It rained. You dropped me off outside here, trying to find somewhere to park. Such a gentleman, considering your wife was in Berne for the weekend.'

'You remembered the alarm code from three years ago?'

'Remembering details like that answers your bigger question too. Detail got me out of Israel. Which is a good job, because no one at CTC was going to do it, were they?'

Michael shook his head. He picked up one of the coffee mugs and sat in an armchair near the table. 'You stirred up a lot of trouble, Leila.'

'And now? Where are we now?'

'I don't know much, but the last I heard was you were clear of the Israeli authorities at least. Mossad are happy your incursion into the Negev was what you claimed it was, and obviously they would prefer the matter was not pursued. I also got a call from Richard Morgan last night to tell me about your visit to Ramallah.'

'Did it do any good?'

'Too early to tell, but the fact that he told me and not his acting PM is probably a good sign. It means for now he wants to keep his powder dry, but he knew I'd talk to you sooner or later. I don't think either of us expected it to be quite this 'sooner'!'

'And Phillip?'

'Shaken but fine. I checked in on him yesterday. If the kid's capable of reflection, he seemed worried he might have helped what he called some bad people find you, but he's OK. Thorne put a lot of pressure on him, and I suspect it'll be a long time before he'll be helping us again.' He took a sip of coffee. Leila knew what was coming, and it was a fair question, if one she was not entirely willing to answer. Right now she didn't feel entirely *qualified* to answer it.

'And you?' Michael said. 'Your trip to Ramallah with Golzar – and no, I'm not going to ask whether she was already dead when you found her – proved you evaded Donald Aquila, but Six were on your trail. How did you evade them? How the hell did you get back here without papers, without money, without getting yourself shot?'

'Your first and last contact with Phillip was at Mason Court before Thorne interrogated him?'

'Yes. Leila, that doesn't…'

'It does answer the question, Michael. If CTC were not involved in my first contact with Phillip, our online chat, then it seems likely someone else was. I think someone knew where I was, what I was doing, where I was going, even then.'

'The security and intelligence services have known you were in Israel since you crashed in the Negev. And yes, I reported your first call to CTC…'

'It went deeper than that. Someone was running me as a blind agent, for even longer than Rees admitted. Hawadi almost had me convinced it was Black Eagle, but it wasn't. You convinced me it wasn't CTC. The fact that Whitehouse's kill order wasn't executed at the house in Narom proves to me who was behind all this. Who was pulling the strings.'

'Just back up a minute, Leila,' Michael said. 'Before you start making assumptions that could get you even further into this mess. Whitehouse wasn't behind the kill order.'

'Then who?'

'It had been Commander Thorne's preferred option right from the start.'

'Interesting. I knew he wanted rid of me, but that does seem a bit extreme!'

'I think he was dealing with a fairly extreme situation. But regardless of who was actually behind it, the question remains: how did you avoid it and get back here?'

'Scott Rees.'

'Six's Cultural Liaison, Attaché, whatever he calls himself out there?'

'Six,' Leila said. 'He brought me in. It was all planned. This was a tap on the shoulder.'

'A recruitment?'

'I'm sure of it. The exfil was so slick, everything in place, no arrest, no cuffs. He even gave me a gun. They went to so much trouble to find me and make sure Aquila's safe house was just that – safe – that there had to be something else. Something he'd even risk revoking the kill order for.'

'What?' Michael said, 'what's the end-game? Running you as a blind agent must have been a massively risky operation. What did they want from you that was worth all that? If the Israelis are satisfied that you weren't interested in nuclear secrets – if there even are any – it's not that. So what do they want?'

'Apart from my brilliance, my charm and my movie-star good looks? Rees told me back at Narom that I'm the only person who's ever had contact with Donald Aquila. No photographs, no background file. Until last week no one even knew he existed. I do, and this is where it gets really interesting. Aquila's already got me in his sights as a recruit to Black Eagle.'

'Six want you to go in as a deep cover agent...'

'Exactly. I'm their perfect spy. I don't need a legend because Black Eagle have been trying to recruit me since I screwed up their operation in London. Hell, Michael, I was so convincing even CTC – and my guess is that deep down, even you – didn't know for sure where my loyalties lay.'

'But Rees never actually mentioned any of this? Never explicitly asked you to join Six?'

'We never got that far.'

'And yet he brought you all the way back to England. What did you do out there to convince him to just let you walk out of Israel on a guess and a hope?'

'He made sure he had a little insurance before we left the country. He made sure I left evidence of my contact with the forger in Jerusalem – the *brutally murdered* forger. That was his first mistake: he mentioned the place by name; he knew about it. But Rees is old-school, careful. He put one more layer of security in place, that I didn't see until now. A brilliant sleight-of-hand. He made sure I was focussed on one goal – in this case getting Golzar to the PNA to ensure the way was open for Morgan to restart talks – while he conjured up one last damning piece of evidence.'

'Which is...?'

'I killed Golzar without a second thought, Michael. And it was a set-up. Rees gave me the gun; he was banking on me killing her.'

'Why?'

'It was Hawadi's gun. There are three sets of prints on it: Hassan Hawadi's, Scott Rees's and mine.'

'And he left it where it would be found...'

'The PNA have it. I stepped out of the car to speak to Abu Queria's liaison in Ramallah and I left the gun behind. When I got back, I didn't give it another thought, but Rees must have hidden it in the car. It'll quickly be established as the murder weapon, and the prints of all those concerned will be easy to trace. Hawadi, no one cares, and he's under the protection of Six now anyway. Rees has a legal kill licence. But me? My prints, the last ones on the gun? Extra-judicial killing, unless Six throw up a smoke-screen to claim that I was already acting on their behalf in a legal take-out.'

'OK, maybe Rees backed you into a corner, but killing Golzar as a way of getting you into Black Eagle as a mole? It makes no sense. Surely it's precisely why Aquila will never believe you've turned.'

'Wrong. Look at it from the other end. I killed Golzar to eliminate the competition. My guess is that Rees's plan was to have me taken from Heathrow to some secret bunker. None-too-covertly, SIS would interrogate me, and I'd resist. CTC would put me out to pasture somewhere, nice and public, maybe even with another press scandal attached. All that, Black Eagle are going to be curious, Aquila is going to be beside himself to find out what's really going on. Sooner or later he'll find me, and this time, rationally, I'd have no reason to refuse his invitation, because it's exactly what I'd been courting by killing Golzar.'

'And SIS will have fed you enough information and contacts that you can be Golzar's replacement.'

'Something like that,' Leila said.

'I assume Rees doesn't know you're here?'

Leila laughed. 'Rees doesn't know which way up his ass is on. He was so sure he held all the cards, had the game so stacked in his favour, he got sloppy. He wasn't hard to shake off, at least for a while.'

'And this is as close as you're going to get to a debrief,' Michael said. 'You're planning to disappear again? For good this time?'

'The Israeli's aren't looking for me for now, although I guess a holiday in Tel Aviv is off the menu for a while; Black Eagle will know that for now I'm out of reach; I've got no job except the one I've resisted for years as an international spook. As I said on Friday before all this messed things up, I need a break. And I really think I've earned one now, don't you?'

'No, Leila. I think you can bring down the corruption that led to a kill order being issued against a British agent without the slightest evidence that it was justified or warranted.'

'*You* can, Michael, not me. In fact, no. After this conversation, not even you. Don't you get it? I was their Jerusalem Blind. I was a puppet being pushed this way and that, but for what? Recruitment? Maybe, but even then… for what? Maybe it was so that I could infiltrate Black Eagle, or maybe bringing down CTC was their ultimate aim. Or both, or neither. And the game's not over for any of us.'

'And you don't intend to find out where it leads…?'

'It's not my job. Not any more. I just needed you to know the truth.'

Leila looked out of the window. A glimpse of red through the crack in the curtains told her it was time to move.

'I'll leave you to your crossword,' she said. 'Let me go without goodbyes. Hell, we wouldn't want the neighbours to see us together, now would we?'

'Be careful, Leila,' Michael said. 'And be back. Some time, be back.'

She kissed him and slipped out of the sitting room into the hall. The sun cast a mosaic of colours on the old flagstones through the skylight above the door. Something moved outside. She waited, hand on the door handle. Three…two…one…

'Good morning,' she said as she opened the door.

'Beautiful day,' the postman said. He handed her a small stack of envelopes. She gave him a few seconds to turn and walk back down the short path, then stepped out and closed the door behind her. In the porch she flicked through the mail, took one letter out of the stack and dropped the remainder through Michael's letterbox.

She then walked down the drive, turned left and away across the parched brown grass of Wimbledon Common.

* * *

Michael heard her greet the postman. He sat where she had sat, respecting her request not to say goodbye. He watched the last dregs of her coffee steaming in the mug, then stood and took it into the kitchen to be washed before the Lady of the House returned and started a line of enquiry he was too weary to get involved in...

While she had waited for the percolator, Leila had made herself at home and made one feeble attempt at yesterday's Quick Cryptic, which he himself had not even had time to look at. Four down, five letters, '*Of French and German county*'. She'd struck through the clue but not written the answer in, leaving the paper open by the coffee maker. Her need for coffee was greater, or maybe she had heard his key in the door. Or maybe she'd simply tired of solving puzzles.

As the post dropped through the letterbox he returned to the front room and watched her through the gap in the curtains as she crossed the road. On the edge of the park she stuffed a small envelope into the pocket of her skirt and glanced back towards the house.

And he wondered. Not where she would go or how she would evade capture – he knew she would find a safe place: she was resourceful, she would be OK.

But he had wondered from the moment he found her sitting in his front room why she had risked coming here. It wasn't just to see him – those days were behind them now. It wasn't for information – he had very little of any use to her, and she would have known that. It wasn't to tell her of her own plans, if she even had any yet – he had no right or need to know, and knowing could be dangerous for both of them. And he had been right on that score: she had told him almost nothing. She had said it was so that he knew the truth, but did he? And if he did, what could he do with it?

As he watched her walk away across the common, he knew why she had really come. She had risked everything when she was on the cusp of freedom to get that envelope. And the only way she could possibly have known it was about to be delivered was if she had sent it herself.

'What did you do, Leila?' he whispered. 'What the hell did you really do out there...?'

What had she been trying to tell him in that letter, but was now trying to hide? What admission or warning had been important enough to send – presumably from Israel several days ago – but was now too important to disclose? Or too risky – for him, for her, for all of them...?

Had she taken the tap on the shoulder, disappeared into that murky world of British Secret Intelligence?

Or had Thorne been right all along? Had Donald Aquila made her an offer she could no longer refuse...?